Dreams Writt... ~y

Joanne Keele

Chapter One
Bang to Rights

As Lorraine stood before the mirror, she couldn't help but be captivated by the vision staring back at her. Lorraine's olive toned complexion radiated a vibrant, healthy glow, accentuated by the soft, evening light filtering in. Lorraine's jet-black hair cascaded down in lustrous, silky waves, delicately framing her face and gently grazing her chest. Standing a tall at five feet nine inches and weighing a mere nine stone, Lorraine's figure was nothing short of a poetic masterpiece, a true embodiment of the timeless ideals of beauty and grace.

Lorraine didn't need to worry about problem areas like batwing or love handles, when one possessed a figure as magnificently curvaceous as her own, sculpted to absolute perfection. Lorraine's peachy, ample derriere practically begged to be caressed and admired. Lorraine's bust a sumptuous D-cup, was the epitome of perkiness and poise, never causing the slightest bit of trouble, Lorraine liked her melons, they was juicy. Lorraine couldn't help but sigh, utterly captivated by the exquisite vision that was her physical form.

The deal she had struck with the police came with one non-negotiable condition: seduce a high-ranking member of the mafia. Lorraine. As if her breathtaking good looks weren't enough to make him fall helplessly at her feet, now Lorraine was expected to engage them in conversation as well, the detective had high hopes, Lorraine wasn't sure she could for fill, Lorraine had never seduced anyone in her life.

Lorraine would maintain her freedom, and Lorraine's dear mother would avoid being locked away, so Lorraine had no choice but to rise to the occasion.

In a world where physical appeal can seemingly open any door, the Lorraine believes her beauty holds the key to navigating even the most challenging situations. With a deep breath, she prepares to put her master plan into motion a seductive strategy that she hopes will prove irresistible. As a knock interrupts her reverie, Lorraine recognises this as a pivotal moment, one that could potentially alter the course of her life. Lorraine's nerves flutter, embracing this as part of the act, smoothing her dress and sauntering confidently to the door.

Unaware of the twists that fate has in store, she assumes the figure waiting on the other side is no match for her alluring charms. Little does Lorraine know, however, that this evening's events are about to take an unexpected and potentially life changing turn, as fate's twisted sense of humour unfolds before her. The seduction plan, once believed to be a foolproof means of escaping any circumstance, is about to be put to the ultimate test.

Chapter One Part Two
The Low Down

When Lorraine answered the unexpected knock at her door, she was greeted by the unwelcome and imposing presence of Detective Jackson. Truthfully, she had been desperately hoping that the detective would not make an appearance, as his arrival typically signified some sort of troubling development or complication in a matter Lorraine had been fervently hoping to avoid. The sudden sight of his stern, determined expression filled me with a profound sense of dread, as Lorraine knew his presence on Lorraine's doorstep could only mean that the situation she had been desperately trying to evade had now come to a head. Despite her overwhelming reservations and trepidation, Lorraine steeled her nerves and resolved to face whatever reason had compelled the detective to seek me out. With a heavy heart, Lorraine prepared herself to confront the detective and whatever revelations or complications he had come to impart.

"Hi, Lorraine, can I come in?" asked Detective Jackson

"I guess." Lorraine Said begrudgingly

"Look, I know this isn't something you want to do, and you're backed into a corner. I get it, but you are my last hope at catching him."

"Just tell me who, where, and when."

"Lorraine, you do know this might take a while and not something that will happen overnight."

"Yeah, I guess."

"OK, Lorraine, tonight is the big opening of Dreams nightclub, and you are on the special list."

"OK, and who?"

"Mr. Steve McMatter's, he's the owner of the club. We suspect he has some dark dealings though, drugs, etc."

"OK."

"Don't be too quick or pushy. He's a ladies' man; he will come to you. You're his type."

"And how far do I go?"

"For now, tease him, get his attention, but don't follow through any further tonight."

"OK."

"Good luck, Lorraine."

After Detective Jackson departed, Lorraine closed the door behind him and paused for a moment, her heart racing with a profound sense of dread. The mere prospect of this impending encounter filled her with an overwhelming unease, as if she were treading upon a minefield, where one misstep could lead to disastrous consequences. Lorraine had closely followed the news reports chronicling this individual's alarming history, a litany of arrests for possession, murder, assault, and drug-related offenses.

Yet, somehow, he had managed to evade any lasting charges, a testament to his cunning and evasiveness. Faced with this precarious situation, she couldn't help but wonder if she might benefit from seeking guidance or advice to navigate the complexities that lay ahead. The stakes were high, and the potential risks were palpable, leaving her to ponder the wisest course of action to ensure her own safety and wellbeing.

The man Lorraine was preparing to meet cut an imposing and captivating figure. He possessed a striking, almost dreamlike stature, with a muscular build and a youthful, vibrant appearance in the picture Lorraine was shown. His mid brown hair was accentuated by subtle, flattering blonde highlights, adding depth and dimension to his striking features. Dressed impeccably in a tailored, high-quality suit, he exuded an air of refined sophistication that was both alluring and subtly intimidating. As Lorraine gazed upon her reflection in the mirror, she hardly recognised the woman staring back at her. Gone was her usual, more casual demeanour; in its place stood a woman transformed, clad in a figure-hugging black dress that elegantly accentuated her curves. Her hair had been artfully curled and styled, and her face adorned with elegant, expertly applied makeup.

The metamorphosis was startling, and Lorraine felt a palpable mix of nerves and determined resolve as she armed herself with the invitation and a small handbag, ready to embark on this risky, high-stake endeavour.

Detective Jackson had confidently assured Lorraine that this risky course of action was essential to gathering the necessary evidence to build a solid case against the elusive suspect, Steve McMatter's. Despite her initial apprehension and reluctance, Lorraine knew she had to see this through, her resolve steeled by the profound significance and high stakes of the task at hand.

With a deep, steadying breath to calm her nerves, Lorraine left the sanctuary and comfort of her house, her heart racing with a conflicting mixture of trepidation and unwavering purpose as she prepared to confront the unknown.

Chapter Two
Dreams

As Lorraine approached the exclusive club, the experienced and perceptive doorman immediately warmly welcomed Lorraine confirmed the privileged access to the coveted "special list." The moment Lorraine stepped over the threshold, she was enveloped by the pulsing energy and lively ambiance of the space, the thumping rhythms of the music setting an enticing tone for the evening's festivities. The music was helping to distract Lorraine from the bundle of nerves running through her body. Scanning the crowded dance floor and intimate seating areas, Lorraine carefully searched the throng of well-dressed patrons, her eyes scouring the room with purpose as she aimed to pursue the man she had been tasked to entice and persuade.

Unable to locate him immediately from the photo Lorraine was shown, Lorraine made her way confidently to the bar and placed her order, Lorraine's smooth and alluring. "A 'Sex on the Beach' cocktail, please," Lorraine requested, fully aware that the sensual sounding drink would help set the mood and put her in the right frame of mind to carry out the objective with poise and charm.

As Lorraine eagerly awaited the drink she had ordered, she took advantage of the opportunity to carefully survey the captivating ambiance that permeated the room. The space had been expertly styled in a visually striking and incredibly impressive manner, featuring a harmonious blend of diverse purple hues that were seamlessly interwoven with vibrant accents of deep, alluring blue. Strategically placed dashes of neon lighting and meticulously positioned sparkling elements worked in concert to cultivate an alluring and captivating atmosphere that was truly enchanting. The overall balance and design of the space were fantastic, showcasing the establishment's keen eye for aesthetic excellence and their unwavering commitment to creating an immersive and visually stunning environment for their patrons. To Lorraine she loved the environment that gad been created it gave way to a nice feeling she hadn't experienced for a long time.

Shifting her focus back to the bar, Lorraine was pleasantly surprised to discover that her drink had been thoughtfully placed before her. Curious about this unexpected gesture, Lorraine inquired about the cost, prompting the bartender to simply nod towards a gentleman situated at the far end of the bar, indicating that Lorraine's drink had been generously covered by this man in a wonderful suit, was this him if it was the photo did not do him any favours, he was seriously hot.

This unexpected act of kindness and hospitality left Lorraine feeling deeply grateful and intrigued, further enhancing the remarkable experience she was having within this visually stunning and warmly welcoming environment. The bartender's subtle gesture and the stranger's generous offer created a sense of intrigue and gratitude that elevated the overall atmosphere. Lorraine couldn't help but wonder about the motivations and circumstances that had led this individual to extend such a gracious gesture to an unfamiliar man. This unexpected display of hospitality added an element of mystery and delight to her experience, leaving her with a heightened appreciation for the thoughtfulness and generosity that can sometimes manifest in the most unexpected of moments, even among complete strangers.

The combination of the bar's captivating visual appeal and this heartwarming interaction contributed to a truly memorable and remarkable experience.

Lorraine turned and glanced in his direction, she couldn't help but be captivated by the striking, commanding presence of this good-looking man, it filled Lorraine with a flutter of flustered excitement as she took in his impeccable appearance up close. The suit he wore seemed to cling to his frame in a flawless, tailored fit, the shimmering quality of the fabric suggesting it was likely crafted from a luxurious, silver-grey satin material.

The way the light danced across the smooth, lustrous surface of his attire only served to enhance the overall elegance and refinement of his look. In that moment, Lorraine found herself unable to deny the undeniable truth this alluring man was simply impossible to ignore. His refined, polished aesthetic radiated an air of confidence and sophistication that was utterly mesmerising to behold. There was an undeniable magnetism and grace to his every movement, as if he carried himself with a regal, almost regal bearing. The mere sight of him was enough to capture one's full attention, drawing the eye and captivating the senses in a way that was truly spellbinding.

What was once a seemingly ordinary evening has now taken an unexpectedly delightful turn. At the centre of the gathering stands Mr X, commanding the attention of the assembled crowd of girls, a majority of whom are admiring and enthralled by his every captivating utterance.

Feeling emboldened by this charming spectacle, Lorraine raised her glass in a subtle gesture of acknowledgment, conveying her sincere appreciation for the truly delightful scene unfolding before her eyes. The atmosphere has become charged with an air of excitement and intrigue, making it clear that this evening may hold far more enjoyment and entertainment than Lorraine had initially anticipated. The presence of this man with his captivating charm and charismatic demeanour, has transformed the once ordinary gathering into a lively and engaging social event. The women in attendance, drawn to his magnetic personality, hang on his every word, their expressions reflecting a sense of enthrallment and admiration.

In this moment, the room seems to have come alive, buzzing with an energy that was previously absent. Sensing the shift in the atmosphere.

Lorraine observes the unfolding events; it became increasingly clear that this evening may hold far more in store than she had initially anticipated. The excitement and intrigue that now permeate the air suggest the potential for an evening filled with unexpected delights and engaging entertainment.

"Excuse me," Lorraine shouted to the barman, my voice projecting over the lively din of the establishment.

"Yes?" the barman responded, turning his attention towards Lorraine. Lorraine nodded discreetly towards the well-dressed individual at the centre of the crowd.

"Who is he?" Lorraine inquired; her curiosity piqued.

The barman let out a good-natured chuckle. "That's the owner, Mr. McMatters," he revealed, a hint of amusement in his tone.

Emboldened by the liquid courage coursing through her veins, Lorraine downed the last remnants of her drink, feeling a newfound sense of determination. The music had captured her and it was time to make her move, to break free from the gaggle of groupies vying for Mr. McMatters' affection and capture his undivided attention.

With a deep breath, Lorraine set her sights on the dance floor, ready to make her presence known and seize the opportunity that lay before her. Lorraine was determined to stand out from the crowd and catch Mr. McMatters' eye, fuelled by a mix of confidence and a touch of mischief. This was her chance to make an impression and potentially forge a connection with the esteemed establishment owner.

Lorraine positioned herself strategically within his line of sight, carefully avoiding any semblance of overt desperation or neediness. With a sensual, deliberate flick of her silky, glossy hair, she began to sway and groove sensuously to the pulsing rhythm, allowing the music to flow through her body and captivate his gaze. After a calculated interval, Lorraine seamlessly changed the direction of her dancing, ensuring our eyes would inevitably meet.

 And meet they did, she had successfully ensnared his rapt attention, and Lorraine fully intended to keep it.

Maintaining her confident, alluring movements, she continued to dance, secure in the knowledge that he was utterly transfixed by the captivating sight before him. Eventually, Lorraine sauntered over to the bar, her gaze lingering on him one last time, leaving him wanting more as she turned away. Lorraine ordered a refreshing drink, anticipation palpable. As she went to pass some money to the barman, he waved it away.

"Drinks are on the house all night. He must like you," the barman leaned in to confide.

Lorraine glanced back, but the mysterious benefactor had vanished. Lorraine sipped her drink through the straw, savouring the cool, crisp liquid as it passed her lips, the action deliberates and alluring. Time seemed to slip away as she indulged in an indulgent sixth drink, the pleasant effects of the alcohol gradually taking hold.

Sensing a slight unsteadiness, Lorraine made the responsible decision to call for a taxi, intent on ensuring a safe journey home.

However, just as she was about to place the call, Lorraine felt a gentle tap on her shoulder. Turning around, Lorraine was met with the captivating sight of Mr. Dreamy himself, his warm smile radiating a magnetic charm that instantly captured her attention.

"I've been watching you all night. Thought you would have had someone with you, but no one in sight. I've seen lots watching you, though," he remarked, his tone conveying a hint of intrigue. Lorraine introduced herself, and he offered her another drink, which Lorraine politely declined as she was preparing to head home.

"That's a shame. I was going to ask if you would like to join me in the VIP area," he said, his eyes sparkling with a hint of disappointment. Lorraine explained that she must go, but expressed her interest in taking him up on the offer another time. After our exchange, Lorraine glanced back as she reached the door to exit, and he was what could only describe as puzzled, stroking his chin. Lorraine could tell that she had managed to pique his curiosity and capture his attention.

Once Lorraine had returned to the comfort and familiarity of her own home, she eagerly kicked off her constricting shoes and shed the garments that had adorned her weary body, relishing the sensation of nestling into the welcoming embrace of her bed. Venturing out to bustling nightclubs had become an increasingly unfamiliar endeavour for her, one that Lorraine had clearly grown unaccustomed to over time. It wasn't the lively, pulsating atmosphere of the nightclub itself that posed a particular challenge, but rather the dreaded task of navigating the crowded dance floor in those towering, impractical heels that threatened to betray her every step. Before long, as her body sank into the plush mattress and Lorraine's mind began to unwind, she found herself drifting off into a deep, restorative slumber, her thoughts consumed by captivating dreams of the alluring and enigmatic Mr. Dreamy.

The allure of his magnetic presence and the tantalising possibilities he represented had taken hold of her imagination, lingering in her subconscious even as Lorraine succumbed to the blissful respite of sleep.

Chapter Two Part Two
Mr Dreamy

McMatters sat behind his desk, his mind consumed by the events that had unfolded earlier. He was taken aback by the sheer intensity of the pull he felt towards the vision that had graced his club. As a man accustomed to encounters with alluring women, this woman stood apart, different from all the others, possessing an indefinable quality that elevated her to a class of her own.

She exuded an aura of mystique that sent a palpable charge through him, as if his very hair had been electrified by her captivating presence. The enigmatic nature of this woman had left an indelible mark on McMatters, transcending the typical physical attraction he had experienced in the past.

There was an intangible essence to her, a certain je ne Sais quoi that had enraptured him, leaving Steve thoroughly intrigued and eager to unravel the mysteries that seemed to shroud her.

This reaction puzzled Steve, for he was a man accustomed to maintaining his composure in the face of alluring female company. Yet, this woman had managed to breach Steve's carefully constructed defences, awakening a sense of fascination and curiosity that he found himself unable to suppress. Her captivating presence had left an indelible impression, and McMatters was determined to uncover the secrets that lay beneath the surface of this enigmatic woman who had so thoroughly captivated him.

Although Steve had initially withdrawn from the situation to carefully study and analyse her, he was unexpectedly struck by a truly peculiar and perplexing mix of emotions. Despite his efforts to maintain an objective distance, he found himself increasingly captivated and intrigued by this enigmatic individual who seemed to have such a profound and unsettling effect on him.

There was an undeniable draw, a sense of fascination that compelled him to want to delve deeper and uncover more about this truly unique and fascinating creature before him. Her ability to evoke such a complex array of feelings within him, ranging from intrigue to bewilderment, only served to heighten his desire to better understand the source of this powerful influence that she seemed to wield over him.

Steve was determined to unravel the mystery surrounding this captivating person, driven by an irresistible curiosity to unveil the deeper layers of her captivating persona and the reasons behind her remarkable impact on his psyche.

His prudent and level-headed nature led him to exercise great caution, ensuring he avoided making any rash or impulsive decisions. Recognising the gravity of the situation, Steve promptly called out to Jarvis, his right-hand man and closest confidant, and recounted the entirety of the encounter. He knew he could rely on Jarvis's unwavering loyalty and trusted counsel. Jarvis immediately understood the significance of the events and recognised the need to be informed the moment she next stepped foot in the club. Without delay, Jarvis departed the office, intent on relaying the crucial details to the key members of the staff primarily the doorman and bartender, who are ever-vigilant and quick to notice even the slightest irregularities.

Confident that Jarvis would handle the necessary communication and coordination, Steve leaned back in his chair and took a sip from the drink that had remained untouched throughout the preceding events. With a plan of action now in place, a sense of reassurance washed over him, allowing his mind to wander back to the captivating encounter and the evening's unfolding developments.

Chapter Two Part Three
Operation Dreamy

Detective Jackson closely monitored the delicate operation unfolding at Club Dreams, observing his informant, Lorraine, as she skilfully worked to ensnare their elusive target, Mr. McMatters. Remaining discreetly in the background, Jackson coordinated a team of eight agents who had strategically blended into the crowd, maintaining a low profile as Lorraine maneuverer through the club. Jackson's agents were well-rehearsed and seamlessly swapped positions, operating in perfect sync to ensure Lorraine's safety as she carried out her pivotal role.

While Lorraine may be a thief, Jackson recognised that she faced a difficult and complex situation. He had been watching Lorraine and her mother for some time before setting this intricate trap, determined to leverage Lorraine's cooperation to finally apprehend McMatters, whom he had long been pursuing.

As he sipped his drink, Jackson witnessed the captivating, almost magical, erotic dance unfold before him, as Lorraine subtly made her presence known to McMatters, employing a masterful touch of subtlety in her execution.

McMatters, the unsuspecting target, had taken the bait that Lorraine had skilfully cast, now fully invested in her company. He covered the cost of her drinks and invited her to join him in the exclusive VIP area. However, just as McMatters believed he had secured Lorraine's attention, she unexpectedly departed, leaving him visibly perplexed. This unanticipated development piqued Detective Jackson's keen interest. Unlike previous attempts, where agents had directly requested access to the VIP area only to be promptly ejected, Lorraine's approach proved far more effective in capturing McMatters' undivided attention.

Detective Jackson suspects that Lorraine may have successfully ensnared her target during the captivating dance performance Jackson observed. Despite his best efforts, Jackson found himself transfixed by Lorraine's alluring movements on the dance floor, struggling to maintain his focus on the ongoing investigation. The seasoned investigator recognises that Lorraine's seductive tactics may hold the key to finally apprehending the elusive suspect, McMatters. In the early hours of the day, the determined detective plans to contact Lorraine to gather pertinent details and map out the way forward.

After previous attempts have fallen short, a measured, methodical approach may prove most effective in cracking this critical case. Jackson is resolute in his determination not to let this pivotal chance at bringing the suspect to justice slip through his fingers.

If Lorraine's prudent, deliberate tactics have indeed provided the breakthrough the investigation needs, then that is unquestionably the course of action the detective will diligently pursue, no matter how gradual or arduous the process may be. Jackson is willing to exercise patience and employ a steady, calculated strategy to ensure they capitalise on this promising lead and finally deliver justice.

Chapter Three
Miss Spencer

Lorraine lay luxuriously sprawled across her bed, savouring the silky, sensual caress of her satin sheets against her unclothed, delicate skin. The insistent, shrill ringing of the telephone pierced through the tranquil ambiance that had enveloped her, but in this blissful, indulgent moment, Lorraine found herself utterly disinclined to exert the physical effort required to reach over and answer the persistent call.

Her plush, inviting mattress had enveloped her in a state of pure, unadulterated comfort, making the prospect of leaving its cosy, welcoming embrace seem almost unbearably arduous. Lorraine sank deeper into the plush bedding, savouring the decadent sensations and the temptation to simply bask in the luxurious solitude, undisturbed by the outside world.

The sudden silence that followed the abrupt end of the phone call left her in a state of bewilderment, her mind racing to comprehend what had just occurred. Frustration welled up inside her as she rolled over and glanced at the clock, only to be met with the startling realisation that it was already ten o'clock in the morning. "Fuck!" Lorraine exclaimed, her brow furrowing in a mixture of confusion and annoyance.

The unexpected intrusion had rudely interrupted her much needed sleep, and Lorraine couldn't help but wonder what could have been so important to warrant such an early-morning disturbance. The sheer audacity of whoever had dared to call at such an ungodly hour left her perplexed and irritated, as she struggled to make sense of the situation. The deafening silence that now filled the room only served to amplify her bewilderment, leaving her unsettled and eager to uncover the reason behind this unwelcome disruption to her morning routine.

Squinting against the harsh, unforgiving glare of the morning sun, she slowly rose from the bed, Lorraine's body aching with the remnants of a restless night's sleep. Reaching instinctively for the familiar comfort and warmth of her plush robe, she wrapped it around herself, seeking solace in its familiar embrace.

As she made her way to the bathroom, she couldn't help but catch a glimpse of her reflection in the mirror a dishevelled, unkempt appearance that betrayed the turbulence of the previous night, her usually pristine visage now marred by the signs of a troubled slumber.

The shrill, persistent ringing of her phone suddenly pierced the air, shattering the relative silence. Quickly washing her hands, Lorraine hurried to answer the persistent caller, only to find that they had he tried to reach her four times that very morning. Clearly, Detective Jackson had little regard for the sanctity of sleep, his relentless attempts to contact her suggesting an unquenchable need for her immediate attention, a demand that seemed to disregard the basic human need for rest and recuperation.

"Hello, do you know what the time is?" Said Lorraine abruptly

"Morning Lorraine, I see you had a good night." Said Detective Jackson

"Well, I wouldn't go that far, it was OK, I did what you wanted."

"Lots more yet to do, Lorraine."

"Was last night not enough?"

"No, you know our deal, Lorraine. You need to trap him and feedback intel so we can arrest him. Only then is your job done."

"So, what's next?"

"As it's Saturday night, go to the club and see where it takes you. Let him lead, don't rush. He's too switched on, so go slow. We will be there."

"OK, OK, I get it."

"Good."

"But next time, how about you don't phone me so early? I was sleeping, you know."

"OK, not an early bird, got it."

"Bye."

At this juncture, the Lorraine had grown thoroughly exasperated, her patience worn thin, and she simply yearned to bring an abrupt end to the interminable phone conversation as quickly as humanly possible. The sheer, unadulterated frustration of having to grapple with this vexing situation, before Lorraine had even had the chance to Savour her first revitalising cup of coffee for the day was, in her estimation, completely unacceptable and utterly outrageous. In Lorraine's book it was nothing short of a criminal offense, a grievous injustice, to have to contend with such an aggravating, infuriating predicament at such an early, ungodly hour, when she had barely begun her daily routine. Her once-abundant reserves of equanimity had been pushed to the absolute limit, and she was now desperate, consumed by a fervent desire to escape the unpleasant interaction and move swiftly onward, reclaiming control of her day.

Realising she needed a moment of self-care, she decided to indulge in a bit of leisure time. This included some casual lounging, browsing the internet, and catching up on emails before hopping in the shower. Once out, Lorraine embarked on the meticulous task of styling her hair, a process akin to a military operation in its precision and attention to detail.

As Lorraine was amid carefully selecting a new nail polish colour, the shrill ring of the telephone suddenly interrupted her grooming ritual.

"Hi mum." Said Lorraine

"Morning Lorraine." At least her mum knew not to phone before 1pm.

"What's up, mum?"

"Oh, nothing. Just checking in to see if you're OK and that you're not messing up my life or throwing me in jail anytime soon."

"Thanks, mum. Great confidence you have in me."

"Oh, don't be dramatic. I don't mean it in a nasty way."

"Look, mum, I'm being forced to do things I don't want to do just to keep our asses out of jail. Don't worry yourself, though, aye?"

"I have been worried, you know."

"Ha! I'd like to see the day when you get worried about me."

"Now, don't be like that, Lorraine. You know I care."

"No, mum, all you care about is if you're going to jail. I'm the one who has to make sure it doesn't happen."

"Oh, Lorraine, don't think so poorly of me."

"I'm going, mum. I'm too busy saving our asses for this."

By this point, Lorraine had become thoroughly frustrated and dissatisfied with the situation. Her mother has a longstanding, deeply ingrained habit of making everything about her own desires and personal preferences, completely disregarding the legitimate needs, feelings, and perspectives of everyone else involved. This pervasive self-centred behaviour is a recurring, cyclical pattern that manifests in her interactions, leaving her feeling continually ignored, invalidated, and resentful.

It is immensely aggravating and disheartening to repeatedly have her own valid wants, concerns, and priorities brushed aside in Favour of whatever her mother unilaterally deems important now. Her mother's unwavering unwillingness to consider anyone's priorities but her own is a persistent source of great consternation, disappointment, and emotional turmoil for her. After meticulously painting her nails to a flawless finish, Lorraine hurried to the kitchen, her rumbling stomach signalling a ravenous hunger. The tedious process of carefully applying the nail polish had consumed valuable time, but now that the task was complete, her singular focus shifted to appeasing her growling appetite. With a heightened sense of urgency, she strode purposefully towards the kitchen, determined to find a suitable meal that would swiftly alleviate the persistent pangs of hunger that had been steadily intensifying.

Chapter Three Part Two
Dreams

Later that evening, Lorraine found herself grappling with a persistent dilemma the arduous task of selecting the perfect attire for the occasion. After diligently trying on two potential outfits, Lorraine held onto the hope that the third option would prove to be the charm. Delving into the depths of her wardrobe, she unearthed a dress that had been patiently awaiting its moment to shine, despite having resided there for over a year.

This vibrant red, form fitting dress had long captivated Lorraine's attention, yet Lorraine had never quite mustered the confidence to wear it, as the sheer vibrancy and curve-hugging silhouette often left her feeling vulnerable and acutely exposed. Slipping into the dress, however, Lorraine could not deny the alluring way it accentuated her figure, making her feel both elegant and powerful. The rich crimson hue exuded a sense of sophistication and commanding presence, yet the intimate fit also evoked a certain fragility and openness that Lorraine found both thrilling and unsettling.

Confronting her own self-consciousness, Lorraine knew that this dress had the potential to elevate her overall appearance and presence, if only she could embrace the vulnerability it inspired. An hour after finalising her preparations, Lorraine found herself en-route to the exclusive club, hailing a taxi to transport her to her destination. The anticipation of the evening's events filled her with a joyful excitement, as she eagerly looked forward to the opportunity to showcase her stunning ensemble and bask in the admiration of her peers.

The moment Lorraine arrived and stepped out of the taxi; Lorraine observed the vigilant doorman discreetly relay a message into his communication headset. This subtle yet attentive gesture demonstrated the club's commitment to maintaining a secure and well monitored environment for its distinguished members. The doorman then pivoted towards her, greeting her with a warm and welcoming smile, a testament to the club's exceptional attention to detail and VIP level service. Proceeding directly to the bar, Lorraine took note of the area's lively, bustling atmosphere, with the bartender visibly struggling to keep pace with the influx of people. Yet, despite the frenetic energy, he swiftly recognised Lorraine's presence and shifted his focus to attend to her needs.

"What can I get for you tonight?" The barman inquired, his professionalism shining through the hectic scene.

Lorraine responded confidently, "A Mary Jane, please," knowing this was the club's signature cocktail and trusting in the bartender's expertise to deliver an impeccable drink.

This time, Lorraine felt a sense of relief as she was able to easily pay for her drink, simply tapping her card at the bar. As Lorraine scanned the room, Lorraine couldn't help but take in the sophisticated atmosphere permeating the club. The aesthetics were visually striking, with a pleasantly refined ambiance that felt almost alluring, though she had to admit her perceptions may have been slightly skewed given her focus on Mr. McMatters.

The club's decor and atmosphere seemed designed to create an air of exclusivity and refinement, which Lorraine found both intriguing and a bit intimidating, not being entirely certain she belonged in such a high-end setting. The crowd itself was quite captivating, with a noticeable presence of young, attractive women.

On the far side of the dance floor, a group of them were moving energetically, their bodies swaying in sync with the pulsing, rhythmic music. Others stood around the tables, gently swaying to the beat, almost as if they were hesitant to fully commit to the dance floor, perhaps feeling a touch of self-consciousness. The overall scene exuded a certain air of exclusivity and refinement, drawing Lorraine in and heightening her senses.

It was as if Lorraine had been transported to a realm where the mundane concerns of the outside world melted away, replaced by an intoxicating atmosphere of indulgence and sophistication. Lorraine knew she had successfully captured the attention of a group of young lads, though their youthful age meant that any further engagement on her part would be considered highly inappropriate and unethical, bordering on predatory behaviour.

Acutely aware of the sensitive dynamic, Lorraine shifted her gaze around the room, where she noticed Mr. McMatters standing in the stairway, observing her with an almost amused expression as he witnessed the attention she was lavishing upon the room's occupants.

The tension in the air is so electric, Lorraine could practically feel it. It's incredible how the contrast between Lorraine's focus and Mr. McMatters' amusement created such an intense atmosphere, which sent shivers down her spine.

Lorraine's dance moves was mesmerising the way she moves with such grace and sensuality is captivating. She sways sensually to the music, gently caressing her arms, legs, and chest. Allowing her fingers to glide up to her neck and through her hair, Lorraine maintains the rhythm with fluid, graceful motions.

Lorraine knows owned the dance floor for multiple songs, she smoothly transitions back to the bar for another drink. This scene bursts with energy and excitement.

"Same again, please."

"Coming right up."

This time, as Lorraine held out her card to pay, the bartender turned and nodded in Mr. McMatters' direction. "He paid?"

"Indeed, you have made quite an impression on him. Though it's not just his attention you have captured tonight."

The bartender's words carried a knowing implication, suggesting that Lorraine's captivating performance on the dance floor had drawn the gaze of more than just Mr. McMatters.

Her alluring movements and sensual self-caresses had garnered the attention and admiration of the other males, who had undoubtedly been mesmerised by her confident and seductive display. The bartender's subtle remark hinted that she had successfully piqued the interest and desire of those around her, leaving a lasting impression that extended beyond just the one individual who had chosen to financially support her indulgence.

Lorraine turned towards Mr. McMatters, subtly raising her glass to him in acknowledgment. By this point, the three drinks she had consumed were noticeably affecting her, leaving me feeling pleasantly tipsy, she generally didn't drink much so the effects was hitting her much sooner than she had hoped. The lively music had Lorraine swaying lightly, the rhythm captivating her.

Suddenly, Lorraine felt a pair of hands slip around her waist, and as she turned, expecting to see Mr. McMatters, Lorraine was surprised to find it was one of the younger men, or should she say young boys, she had observed earlier. Feeling unimpressed, Lorraine firmly removed his hands, but the cheeky boy promptly replaced them, and moved closer. Lorraine forcefully took his hands off her once more, assertively declaring,

"Keep your hands to yourself, boys do not interest me!"

In the next moment, Lorraine witnessed the young man being abruptly pulled back with force, by his collar and Lorraine realised it was one of the bouncers. It seemed Mr. McMatters had not taken kindly to the unwanted advance.

"Here, this one's on the house," Mr. McMatters said, offering Lorraine another drink. "I think you might need it after that encounter."

"Thanks," Lorraine replied, gratefully accepting the drink.

"That cheeky little boy certainly needed to be put in his place."

As she approached the barman to settle her tab, Lorraine was taken aback when he unexpectedly shook his head, refusing to accept her payment. This unanticipated gesture left her puzzled and uncertain about his reasoning for denying Lorraine the attempt to compensate him for the drink. Sensing Lorraine's confusion, the barman leaned in and revealed the true motives.

"He only let you pay for the others so he could get your name." Suddenly, the penny dropped the barman's refusal to take Lorraine's money was a calculated move so McMatters could learn of Lorraine's identity.

"Oh, I see," Lorraine responded, now understanding the bartender's purpose. With a knowing smile, the barman simply said, "Enjoy." Lorraine turned to express her gratitude, asking, "What's your name?"

"Paulie," he replied."

"Well, thank you, Paulie," Lorraine said sincerely, appreciating his willingness to shed light on the McMatters unspoken intentions.

As Lorraine made her way across the room towards Mr. McMatters, she felt a growing sense of curiosity and anticipation, wondering what this unexpected encounter might lead to.

"Hello Lorraine," Mr. McMatters greeted her,

"Follow me."

Lorraine eagerly followed behind Mr. McMatters as he meticulously guided her up the dimly lit, winding staircase. Along the way, they passed a burly, intimidating bouncer stationed at the entrance, whose imposing presence acted as a formidable gatekeeper to the more exclusive realms that lay beyond.

As they ascended higher, the atmosphere grew increasingly refined and secluded, signalling their transition into a domain that was clearly reserved for only the most privileged and distinguished of guests. The anticipation built within Lorraine, as she could practically feel the air of exclusivity and sophistication enveloping them with each step they took. As they reached the top of the stairs, they found themselves immersed in a narrow, dimly lit corridor that emanated an alluring aura of exclusivity and privacy. To their left, a sturdy, uninterrupted wall created a tangible sense of seclusion, while to their right, the hallway was adorned with floor-to-ceiling glass panels that stretched its entire length.

These translucent panels offered tantalising glimpses of the vibrant, pulsating club scene unfolding below, heightening the anticipation and intrigue. Captivated by the intriguing atmosphere, the group proceeded down the corridor, their excitement building with every step. At the far end, a bold, neon sign glowed brightly, boldly proclaiming the area as the "VIP Area" a clear and enticing indication of its elevated, privileged nature, promising an exclusive and unforgettable experience.

In stark contrast to the lively and energetic atmosphere downstairs, this exclusive upper-level space conveyed a distinctly more intimate and sophisticated ambiance. The secluded lounge area was draped in a rich, moody colour palette of deeper, richer hues of purple, blue, and black, punctuated by strategically placed splashes of vibrant neon that cast a sultry, alluring glow throughout the space. Plush, low-slung velvet sofas and intimate, low-lying cocktail tables replaced the high-top tables and bar stools found on the main level, creating a cosy and inviting setting that beckoned guests to sink into the luxurious furnishings. This elegantly appointed and meticulously curated space offered a refined and exclusive retreat, catering to those seeking a more elevated and sophisticated nightlife experience.

"Who are you? " McMatters said with a harsh tone

A brief but palpable expression of frustration momentarily flashed across his countenance, disrupting his otherwise composed demeanour.

The sudden tension in his features and the subtle furrowing of his brow betrayed an underlying sense of irritation or displeasure that quickly surfaced before he regained his composure. This fleeting display of emotion stood in stark contrast to the generally calm and collected manner he had maintained, hinting at deeper currents of frustration or discomfort bubbling just beneath the surface. The outward display of this internal turmoil was a telling sign that something had struck a nerve, causing his carefully constructed façade to momentarily slip.

"Lorraine Spencer, would you like my middle name too?" the edge in her voice matching his tone.

Lorraine was now overwhelmed with a profound sense of confusion and unease, as if she had committed some grave transgression or misstep. The sheer weight of her actions, whatever they may have been, was bearing down on her heavily, leaving Lorraine wracked with a deep-seated feeling that she had strayed from the righteous path and made a grievous error. This all-consuming sensation of wrongdoing consumed her thoughts, casting a dark cloud over Lorraine's state of mind and filling Lorraine with a pervasive anxiety about the potentially severe consequences she might face as a result.

"Yes."

"Lorraine Hope Spencer."

"Okay, so who are you exactly?" he pressed, seeking more details about Lorraine's identity and background.

"I've just told you who I am. What is the meaning of this interrogation?" Lorraine responded; her tone tinged with a hint of defensiveness.

"What do you do for a living, Lorraine?" McMatters continued, probing further into the specifics of my professional life.

"Well, that's a story for another time, not now or here," Lorraine replied evasively, unwilling to divulge those personal details in the present moment.

"Did he hurt you?" McMatters asked, finally showing a modicum of concern. Oh, so now he deigns to express concern?

"No, but my mood has certainly been ruined," Lorraine retorted, the frustration evident in her voice.

As Lorraine's eyes were drawn to him, she was utterly spellbound by the miraculous softening of his facial features. It was as if a divine artist had gently brushed away the stern lines, revealing a breath-taking canvas of warmth and approachability.

Lorraine's heart raced with excitement as she glimpsed this awe-inspiring metamorphosis.

The contrast between his previous stoic demeanour and this newly revealed, multifaceted personality was so striking, it left her speechless. Unable to contain her wonderment, Lorraine felt an irresistible pull to engage with him directly.

It was like standing at the threshold of a wondrous, unexplored world, just waiting to be discovered. The anticipation was electric, sending shivers of excitement through her very being!

"Can I ask you something?" Lorraine sought answers; her curiosity piqued.

"Yes," he replied, his tone cautious yet attentive.

"Why were you hostile with me?" Lorraine pressed, determined to understand the motivations behind his guarded behaviour. He let out a sigh, a trace of resignation in his voice.

"I have to be careful these days. If it's not bimbos throwing themselves at me, it's cops trying to nick me. You could say it's made me cautious. Lorraine nodded, acknowledging the validity of his concerns.

"I understand."

"Do you, Lorraine?" he questioned, his brow furrowing slightly as he scrutinised her expression, seemingly seeking a deeper connection or empathy.

"More than you know," Lorraine responded, her own tone conveying a sense of empathy and shared experience, hinting at the possibility of a deeper understanding between us.

Lorraine, was handed a drink like a lifeline during this wild, swirling chaos. It's simply astonishing how the alcohol's fog lifted, revealing McMatters in crystal-clear focus.

The electricity between them, it's positively breath-taking for Lorraine she recognised the danger of giving in to temptation though and made the astounding decision to bow out for the night which even surprised herself.

"This has been a lovely evening, but I believe it's time for me to leave," Lorraine stated.

"Oh, you can certainly stay and enjoy the VIP area by all means. I hope I haven't scared you away in any way," McMatters replied, a hint of concern in his voice.

"No, no, you haven't," Lorraine reassured him. "I simply feel it's time for me to head home."

"If you insist, but please allow me to arrange a taxi for you. I wouldn't want that reckless individual to still be waiting for you outside," he offered, with a genuine tone of concern for her safety.

"Thank you, Mr. McMatters," Lorraine acknowledged.

"Please, call me Steve," he insisted.

"Well, thank you, Steve, and thank you again for the drinks," Lorraine said, expressing her gratitude as she prepared to depart.

Lorraine eagerly downed the last sip of her drink, and McMatters escorted Lorraine to the waiting taxi. As she climbed inside, he leaned in and gave her a soft, affectionate kiss on the cheek.

Lorraine could sense his pleasure at the intimate gesture, and it was clear he craved more physical contact. However, Lorraine knew she need to exercise caution and restraint for the time being. Lorraine was finding herself growing increasingly fond of Mr. McMatters, and she needed to extricate herself from the precarious situation the police have ensnared her in without inadvertently implicating him quickly as possible.

Lorraine was in conflict, she wanted him, needed him but should she, could she what was the rules?

Chapter Three Part Three
Confused

Steve McMatters paced restlessly around his office; his mind caught in a tumultuous maelstrom of conflicting emotions. This uncharted territory had him deeply unsettled, as he had never experienced such profound inner turmoil, especially not in the wake of an encounter with an alluring woman.

Undeniably, Lorraine possessed a captivating beauty, but it was the profound effect she had on him that truly had him twisted up inside. Lorraine emanated a mesmerising, aura-like presence that completely enraptured Steve's senses, as if she had an invisible, irresistible grip on his mind, body, and soul, rendering him powerless against her magnetic pull. Her sheer force of personality was so overpowering that it felt as though she could reach into the very depths of Steve's being and take control with just the power of her thoughts alone.

Utterly captivated, Steve found himself unable to break free from Lorraine's captivating allure.

Jarvis is conducting an exhaustive investigation, leaving no stone unturned as he delved deep into uncovering every detail about the mysterious woman. The more information Jarvis gathered the better, as the intel he had amassed painted an increasingly complex and puzzling picture of Lorraine Spencer. Despite feeling like he had accumulated a substantial amount of knowledge about her, Jarvis found himself no closer to fully comprehending the true nature of what was transpiring.

Recognising the significance of this, Jarvis was determined to leave no avenue unexplored, driven by a relentless pursuit of the facts. He suspected that if Detective Jackson and his team were indeed planning to use someone as bait to lure in the elusive McMatters, the vulnerable and enigmatic Lorraine

Spencer would make an all too convenient target. After all, while McMatters may possess a wealth of knowledge about Lorraine, Jarvis reckoned that the man was still grappling to fully grasp the intricate web of circumstances surrounding this enigmatic individual.

Although McMatters understood the need for prudence and vigilance, particularly given the apparent sway Lorraine seemed to hold over him, he couldn't shake the nagging sense that she was someone worthy of his trust.

Desperate to believe his instincts were sound this time, McMatters harboured the fervent hope that he wouldn't end up regretting his decision to let his guard down. After all, he had a well-documented history of impulsive and decisive actions that had occasionally backfired and worked to his own detriment.

Cognisant of this tendency, Steve remained cautiously optimistic that his trust in Lorraine would not prove to be another misstep, even as he steeled himself for the possibility that his faith in her could ultimately betray him. Steve couldn't help but feel a strong, instinctive sense that there was something truly extraordinary brewing between them.

His intuition told him that this connection they were forging had immense potential to develop into something profound and deeply meaningful. The way they seamlessly interacted and the effortless rapport they shared suggested the blossoming of a bond that could transcend the ordinary and blossom into something extraordinary. Steve found himself growing increasingly hopeful that his gut feelings were accurate, as he could palpably sense an undeniable, almost electric connection starting to take root. There was an undeniable chemistry and synergy between them that hinted at the prospect of a relationship of incredible depth and significance.

Steve couldn't help but feel a growing excitement and anticipation about the possibility of this bond deepening and flourishing into something truly special and extraordinary, this would be something Steve hadn't had on this level before, Steve felt nervous and excited.

Lorraine's actions had clearly deviated from the standard protocols and procedures typically followed by law enforcement agencies. This was an unconventional situation that required close observation and scrutiny to gain a more comprehensive understanding of the underlying circumstances.

There was an intriguing, almost magnetic quality about Lorraine that piqued the individual's interest and drew them in, unlike any previous experience they had encountered. This dichotomy left them feeling torn, pulled between a strong curiosity to delve deeper and the prudent need to approach the matter with a measured, cautious approach. Navigating this delicate balance would necessitate treading carefully as the events continued to unfold. Sinking into his chair at long last, a sense of weary relief washed over McMatters as he poured himself a drink. However, this time, he was deliberate in pouring a much smaller serving than his usual heavy-handed pour.

He knew he needed to maintain a clear, focused mind to stay sharp and vigilant there was no room for letting his guard down, not on this critical occasion. McMatters was determined not to make the same mistakes he had in the past, fully aware that any lapse in judgment or alertness could have dire consequences. With a deep, steadying breath, he steeled himself, resolving to meet the challenges ahead with unwavering attention and determination.

Chapter Four
Detective Jackson

Detective Jackson had convened his team for a crucial meeting, as he had been immersed in field work for most of the recent period. This gathering represented the first genuine opportunity for the entire group to come together and meticulously examine the specifics of their ongoing operation a step that was vital at this juncture. They had amassed a veritable wealth of material to sift through, including an abundance of photographs, video footage, and audio recordings gathered over the past several nights. It was imperative that they thoroughly reviewed all this information before Jackson could even begin to contemplate reaching out to their target, Lorraine.

Ensuring that the entire team was aligned and working from a shared understanding of the facts was an essential prerequisite for moving forward effectively. Since it was a Sunday, his team was working a mid-shift schedule, which meant they would all be arriving at the office shortly. He eagerly anticipated their arrival, hoping they would have some valuable information or insights to share from their work.

Around 11 o'clock, the team members began making their way over to his centrally located office. The office itself was designed precisely to his specifications, featuring a unique fifty-fifty split layout. The bottom half was constructed with solid wood panelling, while the top half was made of glass. This strategic configuration served two important purposes.

Firstly, it allowed Jackson to maintain constant visual oversight of the activities happening throughout his workspace, ensuring he could closely monitor his staff's productivity and engagement. Secondly, the transparent upper section made it considerably more difficult for employees to slack off without him quickly noticing. This meticulously crafted office environment reflected his commitment to cultivating a highly efficient and accountable workplace culture, where transparency and attentiveness were paramount.

Detective Jackson's team gathered to brief him, he was confident that this strategic office design would help drive optimal performance and accountability across the organisation.

"Morning everyone, has everyone got a coffee? Lots to discuss." As it seemed all had a drink the meeting started.

"Okay, so far, the operation codenamed 'Dreamy' is progressing according to plan. Lorraine has successfully contacted the target and has managed to lure him in, effectively reeling him closer. In hindsight, we may have wished we had employed this approach earlier, but nonetheless, we are where we are now.

Lorraine has managed to gain access to the VIP area without incident, which is a significant milestone. We can now feel cautiously optimistic that she might just pull this off. McMatters came to her aid, deploying the young recruit we had sent in, is a positive development.

The fact that the recruit was not injured is nothing short of a miracle, considering the inherent risks involved in this type of covert operation. This suggests that the planning and execution of this phase of the mission have been carried out with a high degree of precision and care, increasing the chances of a successful outcome."

"I've got some pictures, boss," said PC Winters.

"Hey, if you've got any photos, audio recordings, or chat logs that could be relevant, it would be great if you could share them. I'm trying to gather as much information as possible, so any documentation you have would be helpful. Just send them my way whenever you can."

"The barman is named Paulie. He's quite chatty. I've got pictures of the bouncers," said PC Jones.

"Boss, I've got pictures of McMatters with another guy who is currently unknown," said PC Maylan.

"Alright, let's move forward and get those photos printed up and the display board all set up. While we're at it, we should also make sure to obtain the names of the staff members who will be involved. However, we'll need to exercise an abundance of caution here.

We absolutely cannot risk even the slightest hint of this entire endeavour reaching the attention of McMatters. If he were to catch wind of it, there's no telling what he might do, and the last thing we need is for him to start poking around and asking questions about Lorraine.

So, let's tread very carefully and keep this whole operation under the radar, understood? We can't afford to slip up and jeopardise the success of this critical initiative."

As the others exited his office, leaving Jackson alone, he found himself drawn to the stack of photos before him. His gaze fixed intently on the image of Lorraine, captivated by Lorraine's radiant beauty in the vibrant red dress.

An unfamiliar feeling washed over him a sense of intrigue and fascination Jackson had never quite experienced before. He felt a stirring of arousal, a physical response that had been growing more frequent in her presence. Transfixed by the photograph, Jackson found himself unable to pull his eyes away, mesmerised by her alluring appearance. Recognising the intensity of these unexpected emotions, he took a deep breath, trying to regain his composure and make sense of the powerful feelings that had been stirred within him.

This was an unfamiliar territory, and Jackson knew he would need to collect himself and grapple with these newfound sensations that had been awakened. His phone suddenly sprang to life, emitting its familiar ring. Glancing at the screen, he recognised the internal extension it could only be one person calling. Sighing, he braced himself, fully expecting his boss to be putting the pressure on him again about that big arrest they had just made. The boss was always more concerned with the publicity and media attention than the actual police work, but he knew he needed to stand his ground and protect Lorraine, no matter what.

"Hello"

"Jackson it's Sargeant Cole"

"What can I do for you boss?"

"Just checking on the operation's progress, are you any closer to making an arrest?"

"It's going well, we are treading lightly after the last few failed attempts."

"That's great news, I'm really glad to hear it. Make sure you keep me in the loop on any updates or developments, and I'll do my best to run interference with the captain so they don't give you too much trouble or pressure you about it. You can count on me to have your back and help shield you from any unnecessary hassle from higher up. Just focus on handling your end of things, and leave the captain wrangling to me."

"Thanks boss, bye."

Jackson was fully cognisant that all the chatter surrounding pressure and expectations was merely superficial rhetoric, carrying little substantive weight. The true source of pressure stemmed solely from Sergeant Cole, but Jackson was determined not to let that weigh him down. He recognised that the stakes were exceptionally high for this operation, as its successful execution could make or break his career. If things were to go awry, he risked facing the very real prospect of losing his job. Despite the grandstanding and bravado, Jackson maintained a calm, level-headed composure, understanding that he needed to stay laser-focused and perform his duties flawlessly to guarantee the mission's triumph. He refused to allow the hyperbole and posturing to blind him to the genuine gravity of the situation at hand.

"Hello Lorraine, it's Detective Jackson"

"I knew it was you, at least it's a more convenient time"

"Yes, I remembered no early morning calls. Listen Lorraine, now you're getting on more familiar terms with McMatters, you need to make sure he can't see it's me who is calling. Store me as, as Andrew, it will be safer that way"

Ok I will Andy"

"So, Lorraine, how do you think it went last night?"

"Good, until some idiot tried putting his hands on me."

"That was one of us, Lorraine. I wanted to see what McMatters thought of you, it worked - the bouncer threw him out."

"Yes, they did, but it ruined my mood. I wasn't happy."

"McMatters wasn't exactly thrilled with the situation his demeanour towards me shifted noticeably, and he became quite suspicious for a period of time. It took me a bit of effort and patience to eventually win him back over and get him to warm up to me again."

"Okay, I won't test the waters, and I will let you lead."

"Good because it's me in there doing what you couldn't manage to accomplish."

"Since the club is closed on weekdays, why not take advantage of the downtime and do a little self-care? I'd be happy to send over some money to cover any expenses use it to go shopping and pick out some fabulous dresses for the upcoming weekend.

You deserve to feel confident and stunning, something that's sure to make him weak in the knees when he sees you all dolled up." Detective Jackson knew this was not just for Mr McMatters eyes, he couldn't wait to see how she looked.

"Thank you, I will do that. Bye, Andrew."

Lorraine's voice sent shivers over Jackson's body, as his name danced on Lorraine's lips, it was as if the universe itself held its breath. Each syllable, a tender caress that sent electric shivers cascading through his body, igniting every nerve ending with exquisite anticipation.

Her words, infused with such raw emotion, were like honey dripping from her lips, sweet and intoxicating. Jackson was helpless, utterly captivated by the melodic cadence of her speech. His heart, once steady, now pounded with a fierce intensity, threatening to burst from his chest. Lorraine's voice wrapped around him like a warm embrace, conveying a love so profound, so all encompassing, that it left him breathless and weak-kneed. The power of her words was undeniable, an invisible force that commanded his entire being.

Jackson's body betrayed him, responding with an urgency that was both thrilling and maddening. The pressure building within him was a testament to the irresistible pull of her vocal enchantment. Try as he might, Jackson could not maintain his composure. Her voice had shattered his defences, leaving him exposed and vulnerable.

He was putty in her hands, moulded by the passion in her tone, forever changed by the depth of emotion she conveyed. In that moment, Jackson knew with absolute certainty that he was hers, body and soul, captured completely by the spellbinding magic of her voice.

Chapter Four Part Two
Expenses

Despite getting a slightly later start to Lorraine's day, Lorraine was determined not to let the time crunch dampen her spirits. She knew this was her opportunity to treat herself, thanks to the unexpected financial windfall from Jackson. When Lorraine had checked her account and saw that he had transferred over five hundred pounds, she felt a surge of excitement at the prospect of indulging in a well-deserved shopping spree.

Lorraine was acutely aware that the nail salon she favoured had the tendency to close shop early on Mondays, so she felt a heightened sense of urgency to get there before they shuttered for the day. However, Lorraine refused to let this potential obstacle stand in her way. Lorraine was resolute in her determination to make the most of Jackson's generous gift and enjoy a pampering session at the salon, no matter what. With a positive and confident mindset, Lorraine knew she could navigate the time crunch and arrive at the nail salon before they closed.

Lorraine was eager to immerse herself in the relaxing experience and emerge feeling refreshed, rejuvenated, and ready to tackle the rest of her day with renewed Vigor. Lorraine was confident that she could turn this potential challenge into an opportunity to engage in some much-needed self-care and personal indulgence.

Two hours later, Lorraine had finally gotten herself together and was on her way to indulge in one of her favourite pastimes: shopping. For her, the act of browsing through stores and discovering new items was a cherished form of self-care, a way to treat herself and lift her spirits.

However, the presence of other shoppers often presented a challenge, as the alluring freebies and irresistible deals Lorraine encountered proved too tempting to resist, she was a thief after all. She could practically feel the giddy anticipation building up inside her, akin to a child being let loose in a candy store. Despite the distractions, Lorraine managed to stay focused and disciplined, successfully purchasing a dress that caught her eye.

As a bonus, Lorraine also acquired a free watch during her shopping excursion, the man didn't notice she had taken it. While the watch itself was a practical acquisition, it was the fact that she had obtained it at no additional cost that pleased her the most.

The thrill of scoring a valuable item without having to pay for it amplified Lorraine's sense of accomplishment and satisfaction with the day's shopping trip.

She was really starting to get the hang of this whole shopping thing, and by the time she reached the sixth store, Lorraine had already picked out two fabulous new dresses that perfectly complemented her personal style and figure. The first dress was a silky, deep purple number that hugged her curves in all the right places, accentuating her natural assets and creating a striking, sophisticated look. The other dress was a fun, mid-blue skater-style frock that was super flattering, offering a playful and youthful vibe.

And to top off Lorraine's stylish new wardrobe, she also snagged a sleek pair of black satin shoes that effortlessly tied the whole ensemble together, serving as the perfect finishing touch to her shopping haul.

In addition to her successful dress and shoe acquisitions, her day was truly made when Lorraine managed to snag a shiny gold watch, a sleek silver bracelet, and a dazzling white gold necklace adorned with glistening rubies and diamonds. With her new luxurious jewellery in tow, the only thing left for her to do was find the perfect bag to complete her stylish and polished ensemble, ensuring she looked and felt her absolute best. But first, she needed to address her growling stomach and satisfy her hunger pangs. Having skipped breakfast entirely, she was absolutely famished by the time the afternoon rolled around, with the clock nearing four o'clock. Given that the nail salon Lorraine had intended to visit was already closed for the day, she figured she might as well take a brief respite and grab a quick bite to refuel.

As Lorraine glanced across the street, the charming Italian cafe caught her eye the cosy outdoor seating area, adorned with delightful flower planters, looked like the ideal spot to pause, unwind for a few moments, and quell her rumbling stomach. The quaint, picturesque setting seemed to beckon her inside, promising a delightful and restorative dining experience.

"Hello, could I get a ham and cheese panini please, with a black coffee?"

"Of course, that will be nine pounds and ninety pence, please."

"Thank you"

"Take a seat, we'll bring it over, dear."

Scanning the charming and cosy Italian cafe, she couldn't help but take note of the lively, bustling atmosphere that permeated the space. The energy and liveliness of the establishment immediately enveloped her as Lorraine searched for an available seat. In the back corner of the eatery, her eyes landed on an empty spot with a pleasant view through the window, and she quickly made her way over, eager to claim the prime real estate. Once comfortably settled in, her order soon arrived, and Lorraine began to leisurely Savour each delectable bite, her senses delighted by the authentic flavours. As she ate, she found herself idly gazing out of the window, captivated by the constant flow of activity on the street outside, content to simply observe the world passing by while she indulged in her meal.

After scrutinising the crowd for approximately ten minutes, Lorraine thought she caught a glimpse of a familiar face. The person appeared vaguely recognisable, and the only location she could recall encountering them before was at the club she had visited recently. While Lorraine couldn't pinpoint the exact origin of her familiarity with this individual, the nagging sensation that they were someone she had met not long ago persisted at the back of her mind. This fleeting recognition, coupled with the inability to definitively place the person, left her slightly perplexed as she continued to observe the crowd, hoping to uncover the source of this lingering sense of familiarity.

Lorraine scoffed down the delectable meal, savouring every flavourful and tantalising bite. The combination of expertly seasoned ingredients and skilful preparation had created a truly delightful culinary experience, one that she relished with unbridled enthusiasm. Once she had cleaned her plate, leaving not a single morsel behind, Lorraine turned her attention to the steaming cup of coffee positioned before her. After allowing the brew to cool for a moment, she began sipping the rich, aromatic liquid, relishing the bold and complex taste that contained a subtle hint of decadent chocolate. The perfect balance of bitterness and sweetness danced across her palate, providing a thoroughly satisfying and indulgent sensory experience.

When Lorraine glanced up from her thoroughly enjoyed repast, she spotted Mr. McMatters' trusted lieutenant, the man who was perpetually by the boss's side, faithfully carrying out his duties.

She hesitated to call out to him, as she was unsure of the man's actual name, and she did not want to risk the awkwardness of shouting something akin to "Hey, you - the guy who's always with the boss!" Instead, she tried to catch his eye, hoping that he would notice her presence and approach, allowing her the opportunity to speak with him directly. However, the man remained oblivious to her subtle attempts at gaining his attention. Lorraine wrapped up her visit at the café and headed out, continuing her leisurely stroll up the main street.

As she approached the street corner, she spotted an intriguing accessory shop and, remembering she still needed to grab a new bag, decided to quickly pop in and take a closer look around. While casually browsing towards the back of the store, another customer strolled in and entered the shop. Eyeing a sleek, stylish black bag with a cushioned, satin exterior, she reached out to examine it more closely, admiring its sophisticated design and high-quality craftsmanship.

Suddenly, the other customer, a lady with vibrant, bright red hair and natural curls (the rest of her appearance was rather dull and unassuming), accidentally bumped right into Lorraine, causing the bag and a few other items to tumble and scatter across the floor.

Without hesitation, she bent down to quickly gather up the scattered belongings, determined to restore order and avoid any further disruption.

"Jackson said you're being watched," she said. "It's someone who works for McMatters, so act naturally."

"I'm so sorry."

"You will get a call later."

The woman had hastily departed the scene, but in her hurried exit, she had inadvertently left behind a bag. Intrigued by this fortuitous discovery, Lorraine decided to investigate the contents of the abandoned bag. Upon closer inspection, she found that the bag contained a price tag, indicating that the item had been on sale in the store.

Considering this a serendipitous find, Lorraine thought to herself, "Why not? This will complement my shoes perfectly." As Lorraine continued her shopping expedition, she stumbled upon a pair of sunglasses that immediately caught her eye. Without a moment's hesitation, Lorraine tried them on and was delighted to find that they fit her face impeccably. Seized by the thrill of her unexpected good fortune, Lorraine promptly added the sunglasses to the bag, along with her previous purchase, and proceeded to the checkout counter to complete her transaction. As it reached Teatime most shops in the area had already shuttered their doors or were in the final stages of closing for the day.

Recognising that Lorraine had reached her limit for the day, Lorraine decided it was time to call it quits. Her feet were absolutely aching, and all she could think about was getting home and relaxing, shedding the exhaustion of the day. Despite the fatigue weighing on her, Lorraine felt a strong sense of satisfaction with the items she had managed to acquire throughout the day's shopping excursion.

The unexpected freebies she had stumbled upon were the icing on the cake, further adding to her overall happiness and sense of accomplishment with the day's endeavours.

Chapter Five
Pressure

Jackson had his team maintain a constant, vigilant watch over Lorraine, with each member taking turns monitoring her activities around the clock. His relentless surveillance was driven by a fervent desire to amass as much incriminating evidence as possible against her. Jackson's heart raced as he found himself irresistibly drawn to Lorraine, a captivating enigma that consumed his every waking thought.

Lorraine's presence ignited a fire within him, an all-consuming passion that defied logic and reason. With each stolen glance, each fleeting moment in her company, Jackson felt himself falling deeper into an intoxicating whirlpool of desire.

The very thought of Lorraine sent shivers down his spine, her allure a siren's call he was powerless to resist. Jacksons mind reeled with the intensity of his feelings, a tempestuous storm of emotions that threatened to overwhelm him. Every fibre of his being yearned for her, an insatiable hunger that gnawed at his soul.

As he grappled with this overwhelming infatuation, Jackson's world narrowed to a singular focus: Lorraine. The fervour of his fixation both thrilled and terrified Jackson, pushing him to the brink of his self-control. He trembled with the force of his longing, his body aflame with a desire so potent it bordered on madness what was wrong with him?

In quiet moments of solitude, Jackson's thoughts inevitably drifted to Lorraine. His hands unconsciously sought relief, rubbing his groin, but it was too intense. Needing release, Jackson unzipped his trousers and rubbed, the intensity building as he imagined Lorraine's amazing body. Jackson couldn't stop, until he found release, gripping his manly part he moved his hand, faster and faster the intensity built up.

The intensity of his passion consumed him, leaving him breathless and yearning for more, forever changed by the depth of his feelings for this mesmerising woman. Jackson released the pressure as his body let go.

Detective Jackson's team would routinely provide him with detailed updates on Lorraine's activities while she was out and about, closely monitoring her movements and behaviours. He sat in his car that was parked down an alley way, intensely observing her every step and action, utterly amazed by the sheer dexterity and finesse she displayed.

Whispers had begun circulating within their circles that Lorraine had allegedly pilfered some valuable jewellery from an unsuspecting victim. Although he had maintained vigilant surveillance of her the entire time, Jackson had frustratingly failed to directly witness her commit the criminal act itself.

It was only through the incriminating CCTV footage that the evidence of her thievery had been irrefutably documented and substantiated. As the shopping expedition neared its conclusion, one of the team members reported a concerning observation - they had noticed a McMatters employee who appeared to be closely monitoring Lorraine's movements.

This discovery strongly suggested that McMatters was intensely scrutinising Lorraine's activities, a deeply worrying development.

The fact that such close surveillance was already underway, so early in the process, was particularly troubling. Jackson recognised that this could significantly complicate the situation, as even a minor misstep by him or his team had the potential to place Lorraine in a perilous and precarious position, jeopardising her safety and well-being.

The team now understood the gravity of the threat they were facing and the need to proceed with the utmost caution to protect Lorraine from the looming danger posed by McMatters' apparent determination to keep a watchful eye on her every move.

"Hey, PC Winters, could you do me a favour and casually bump into Lorraine? Make it seem like it's just an accident, but let her know that McMatters has been keeping an eye on her. You know, just kind of drop that little titbit in there, but make it seem natural, like it's no big deal. I'd really appreciate it if you could handle that for me discreetly."

"Will do, boss."

Jackson sat there, grimacing as he took a sip of his cold, bitter coffee that had gone stale and lost its once inviting aroma. Despite the unappetising and unappealing state of his drink, Jackson couldn't help but remain transfixed, watching the unfolding events before his eyes with rapt attention.

From his vantage point tucked away in the alley way, the entire scene appeared surprisingly convincing and lifelike, even if he wasn't exactly thrilled about being present to witness it firsthand. The compelling nature of the situation held his gaze, and Jackson rubbed his groin once more, he could feel himself losing his self-control as his erection was starting to show, once again.

What was happening to him? he knew he needed to get a grip, the question was what would he get a grip of? He had never felt this way before.

Chapter Six
Caution to the wind

Lorraine eagerly anticipated the call from Jackson, eagerly awaiting his communication and the opportunity to connect. However, her hopes were dashed when the anticipated call never materialised until the following day. Throughout the day, Lorraine had been compulsively checking her phone, constantly vigilant for any sign that Jackson would reach out. Yet, as the hours slowly ticked by, her initial anticipation gradually morphed into palpable disappointment as the wait for his call extended well into the next morning.

The protracted delay left Lorraine feeling increasingly frustrated, as she had been counting on hearing from Jackson at a more reasonable hour, only to be left hanging until the next day. The unfulfilled expectation and lack of timely communication from Jackson resulted in a sense of letdown and unmet desires for Lorraine.

"Hello Andrew"

"Hello, Lorraine! Did you enjoy your shopping spree?"

"Yes, thank you. I thought you were phoning yesterday?"

"I really wanted to take the time to develop a comprehensive plan to make sure we've got all our bases covered. You know, I didn't want to leave anything to chance or overlook any important details, so I put some serious thought into mapping out a detailed strategy to ensure everything is accounted for and addressed moving forward. That way, we can feel confident that we've thought through all the key considerations and have a solid plan in place."

"Oh, ok"

"No more in-person meetings. We will still be around in the background, but it's too risky to meet in person."

"Ok"

"Lorraine, do you know who was watching you?"

"Well, when I was at the club, I happened to spot this guy talking with McMatters. Then I see the same guy again while I was out shopping. It was kind of a weird coincidence to see him in two different places like that, don't you think? I'm not sure if it was just a random run-in or if there's more to the story, but it definitely caught Lorraine's attention."

"Do you know his name?"

"No. "

"Can you keep your ears open and see if you can find out?"

"Ok."

"I have to go now Lorraine, speak soon!"

Lorraine was undoubtedly intrigued by the peculiar circumstances unfolding before her, but she was careful not to let the situation overwhelm her. At the core of Lorraine's concerns lay a singular, overriding objective for this entire bewildering ordeal to reach its long-awaited conclusion. However, the path forward remained shrouded in uncertainty, leaving Lorraine to navigate the challenges ahead through a more improvised, seat of her pants approach.

Chapter Six Part Two
Jarvis

Jarvis embodied the very picture of physical fitness and mental acuity. He was a remarkably perceptive and exceptionally alert individual, one who closely observed everything and everyone within his purview. This heightened state of awareness was a matter of life and death for Jarvis, as he was required to maintain constant vigilance and attentiveness to his surroundings to ensure his own survival and wellbeing.

Jarvis's keen, piercing eyes and razor-sharp mind allowed him to take meticulous stock of his entire world, leaving no detail unnoticed. For in his line of work, or circumstances, overlooking even the smallest thing could have grave, potentially catastrophic consequences.

Jarvis's unwavering focus and profound situational awareness were essential tools that enabled him to navigate the perils and uncertainties that defined his existence, making him a formidable, resilient survivor in the face of any challenge. Jarvis had been discreetly observing Lorraine as she made her way into town, intent on indulging in a spot of shopping. It was impossible for Jarvis not to take note of Lorraine's impeccable sense of style and her remarkable eye for fashion. Catching glimpses of the items she had acquired, Jarvis couldn't help but feel certain that his employer, the esteemed Mr. McMatters, would be utterly enamoured by Lorraine's exquisite sartorial choices. There was no doubt that she possessed a remarkable talent for identifying pieces that were not only visually striking, but also brimming with a captivating allure.

As McMatters' most trusted and loyal confidant, Jarvis' primary role was to ensure the safety and well-being of his employer. It was easy to understand why McMatters found himself drawn to the captivating presence of Lorraine. With her undeniable charm and allure, she had a way of commanding the attention of all who crossed her path, leaving onlookers utterly mesmerised by her captivating aura.

Before submitting the report to his boss, which contained various visual elements like photos and video footage, Jarvis decided to give the video one last meticulous review.

As he watched it again, a subtle detail caught his eye, prompting him to rewind the footage and scrutinise it, frame by frame, in slow motion.

This extra level of diligence and attention to detail proved pivotal, as it allowed him to uncover something he likely would have missed otherwise, a brazen act of thievery committed by the Lorraine in the video. If his suspicions were correct, Lorraine had skilfully and surreptitiously pilfered a few items from unsuspecting fellow shoppers, demonstrating an impressive level of dexterity and evasiveness. Jarvis carefully gathered all the incriminating photographic evidence and placed it in the report envelope, ready to present to his boss.

However, Jarvis also retained a separate set of photos, which documented something even more significant he had managed to capture. The images were of Detective Jackson and members of Detective Jackson's team, whom he had spotted conducting surveillance on a certain individual: Lorraine.

This additional visual documentation, secured alongside the evidence of the theft, could prove invaluable in shedding light on a larger, more complex situation unfolding here. Jarvis' keen eye for detail and his willingness to thoroughly review the footage paid off, equipping Jarvis with a comprehensive report that could have far reaching implications for his organisation. The pressing question that has everyone on edge is the true nature of Lorraine's involvement in this matter. Is she covertly working for the opposing side, or is she actively collaborating with them? If neither of these scenarios is the case, then it appears that Detective Jackson may be attempting to manipulate Lorraine into assisting their efforts, even if it goes against her own interests.

Regardless of the specifics, this is undoubtedly a precarious situation that is bound to provoke a strong reaction from the boss, who will undoubtedly be closely monitoring the unfolding events with great intrigue. This entire scenario has the potential to devolve into a complex, high stakes game as one photo of Detective Jackson gives way to something else, this would cause significant risks and consequences. The boss will undoubtedly be keeping a watchful eye, fully aware that the outcome could have far reaching implications.

Chapter Six Part Three
McMatters and Javis

"Hey, boss," says Jarvis quite upbeat.

"Hello Jarvis, how's the mission going?"

"It's been interesting, that's for sure."

"Oh?"

"I followed Lorraine on a shopping trip. She spent a pretty penny but got some amazing outfits."

"Intel on the mission Jarvis please?"

"Yeah, no problem at all. Here are the pics you wanted, and I also put together a super detailed report on Lorraine. Went all-out on this one, really dug deep to uncover as much as I could.

And get this, while Lorraine was out shopping, I noticed she was being tailed by some of Detective Jackson's team. There are a few shots of them in the second envelope."

"What was she doing that got their attention?"

"While observing her, I didn't pick up on anything out of the ordinary at first. However, after replaying the video a few times and scrutinising it frame-by-frame in slow motion, I started to notice her slick, impressive moves. It's clear she's an incredibly skilled and talented woman, with lightning-fast reflexes and impeccable technique that's simply fantastic to behold, she has light fingers"

"Do you think that's what got their attention?"

"Hmm, I've got a bad feeling about this. It seems like she's heading down a path that's just going to lead her straight into a deep, dark hole that she's not going to be able to climb back out of. She's really setting herself up to be completely trapped, and it's only a matter of time before that happens. I just hope she realises what she's getting herself into before it's too late."

"And what's your advice, Jarvis?"

"Well one other photo is included. It sheds another angle I thought you might be interested in"

"Oh?"

"We'll need to keep a close eye on both Jackson and Lorraine for the time being. The detective seems to know Lorraine is getting friendly with you, but it seems he's having thoughts of his own too! So, we'll want to monitor the situation closely and make sure nothing sketchy is going on. Can't be too careful, you know?"

"OK, Jarvis. Get your men to watch both, and thank you. You have done well."

Chapter Six Part Four
The Report

As Jarvis prepares to divide his crew into teams to monitor both Jackson and Lorraine, McMatters approaches the club staff to provide them with photographs of the detective and some of his team members. This strategic move ensures the staff can remain vigilant and alert the team if the targets are spotted on the premises.

McMatters cannot help but be awed by Jarvis's remarkable organisational prowess as he observes the unfolding scene. Twelve men, including Jarvis himself, make their way out to the staff parking area, demonstrating Jarvis's exceptional ability to coordinate and direct his team with remarkable efficiency.

Shortly after, Jarvis returns and McMatters watches as his right-hand man heads back upstairs to the office, likely to attend to further business and continue overseeing the day-to-day operations with the same level of proficiency and competence that has earned McMatters' admiration.

With the necessary report, photos, and video materials carefully gathered by Jarvis, McMatters diligently makes his way back home, feeling a growing sense of confidence and anticipation. Jarvis had clearly invested substantial time and effort into compiling this comprehensive information, and now that McMatters can review it in the comfort of his own space, he is eager to take a close and thorough look. Carrying Jarvis' meticulous work product, McMatters is optimistic that he will be able to efficiently conclude this project, leveraging the detailed insights and documentation that Jarvis has provided.

The moment McMatters stepped through his front door, he made a direct and purposeful beeline towards his private study.

Without delay, he proceeded to pour himself a substantial serving of his preferred alcoholic beverage. McMatters had a strong intuition that he might require the bolstering effects of this libation, given the immense volume and intricate nature of the report he was about to meticulously review. With a deep breath, he steeled himself and began carefully perusing the document, knowing full well the challenges that lay ahead.

Steve started with the report gathered on Lorraine. At a mere Six years of age, Lorraine first came to the attention of the local social services department, when she was temporarily removed from her home and placed in protective care. The catalyst for this intervention was her mother's ongoing and severe alcohol abuse issues, which had created an unstable and potentially dangerous living environment for the young child.

While the mother's drinking problem was the immediate and most visible concern that prompted the authorities to act, they suspected there were likely deeper, more complex underlying factors contributing to the troubling home situation. The issue was eventually brought to the attention of social services after a concerned neighbour reported hearing persistent crying and distressed, anguished screaming emanating from the home. This indicated a highly disturbing and volatile domestic environment, which required urgent investigation and action to safeguard the well-being of the young girl.

When the Police arrived at the property, they were confronted with a deeply disturbing scene. There, they found a young six-year-old child, Lorraine, completely unclothed and lacking access to even the most necessities, such as food and water.

The authorities immediately recognised the severe neglect and unsafe living conditions the child had been forced to endure, and they promptly took Lorraine into protective custody. Regaining custody of her daughter proved to be a lengthy and arduous process for Lorraine's mother, taking nearly ten months.

This was only made possible after the mother was able to convincingly demonstrate that she had overcome her previous issues. Through her determination and hard work, she had become sober and significantly improved her overall lifestyle and living situation, creating a safe and nurturing environment for Lorraine's return.

When Lorraine was just Eight years old, the Police found her out on the streets late at night, a highly concerning and inappropriate situation for a child. Upon further investigation, the authorities discovered that Lorraine had been caught stealing food from a local shop, likely driven by desperation due to her dire home circumstances. Tragically, it was revealed that Lorraine's mother had been arrested that same evening for breaking into a place and stealing several items. This precarious situation placed a significant burden on the young Lorraine, who was left without a parent to care for her. Lorraine's mother faced serious legal consequences, receiving a one-year prison sentence.

However, the process of regaining custody of her daughter Lorraine extended for an additional year, resulting in a total separation of two years between mother and child. This prolonged period away from her primary caregiver undoubtedly had a profound and disruptive impact on the young Lorraine, as she navigated the complexities of the legal system and anxiously awaited her mother's return.

Despite the immense hardship, Lorraine's mother was eventually able to reunite with her daughter after the extended separation, providing much-needed stability and support.

When Lorraine reached the pivotal age of Twelve, her life took an abrupt and unfortunate turn for the worse. This dramatic shift was catalysed by a series of deeply troubling events. Firstly, Lorraine's mother was arrested and charged with the serious crime of burglary.

This was followed by a violent altercation with the Police, in which the mother was accused of assaulting an officer with a weapon. As a result of these distressing circumstances, Lorraine found herself thrust back into the foster care system, a situation she had hoped to have escaped. To make matters even more devastating, Lorraine's mother was ultimately sentenced to a lengthy Four-year prison term, with no possibility of early release.

This meant that Lorraine would be deprived of her maternal figure for an extended period, compounding the trauma she had already endured. Tragically, Lorraine's placement with a new foster family proved to be another source of unimaginable hardship. The foster parents subjected the young girl to a relentless campaign of both physical and emotional abuse, essentially treating her as an unpaid servant within their home.

This cruel and exploitative environment only served to further erode Lorraine's sense of safety, security, and self-worth.

At the tender age of Fifteen, Lorraine made the bold and daring decision to run away from her home, disappearing entirely for several years and completely dropping off the radar until she reached the legal age of Eighteen. Regrettably, her troubles did not end there, as she was later apprehended by the Police for shoplifting from the very same store she had targeted in her younger years.

However, rather than pursuing legal charges, the shop owners devised a unique and compassionate punishment for Lorraine.

Instead of sending her to jail, they required her to work at the store as part of her sentence. The couple who owned the shop were cognisant of the difficulties Lorraine faced in her home life with her mother, and they made the compassionate decision to offer her a place to stay and a roof over her head. By taking Lorraine in and providing her with a safe and stable environment during this tumultuous period of her life, the shop owners demonstrated a remarkable level of understanding and empathy.

They recognised the importance of offering support and guidance to those in need, rather than simply doling out harsh punishments.

After meticulously managing her finances and diligently saving a portion of her earnings over an extended period, Lorraine was eventually able to accumulate enough money to fulfil her long-held aspiration of purchasing a flat of her own. This achievement represented a profound and highly meaningful milestone in her life, as she now possessed a place that she could genuinely call home. A personal space that belonged to her alone. A tangible reward for her years of unwavering hard work and steadfast financial discipline.

The flat served as a source of immense pride and personal fulfilment, a testament to her perseverance and the fruits of her labour. This newfound sense of homeownership imbued her with a profound feeling of security, stability, and a deep-rooted connection to the place she could rightfully claim as her own.

The elderly couple's untimely passing left Lorraine as the sole beneficiary of their entire estate, including all their personal effects and material possessions. Recognising the unique opportunity presented by this unexpected inheritance, Lorraine made the strategic decision to liquidate both the family's small retail business as well as her own modest living space. Through these calculated sales, Lorraine was able to generate a substantial financial windfall. Leveraging this sizable sum of money, Lorraine was then able to acquire a significantly larger, more comfortable Three-bedroom house, complete with its own private outdoor garden area.

This enabled Lorraine to dramatically upgrade her living situation, transitioning from her previous modest accommodations to a more spacious and well-appointed residential property. This provided her with enhanced amenities and a higher quality of life.

Lorraine's mother, after an extended absence lasting several years, ultimately returned home. However, the dynamic between mother and daughter had undergone a profound transformation during the intervening period. Too much time had elapsed, and the pain and estrangement they endured had exacted a heavy emotional toll.

While they continue to communicate, their interactions were often tense and confrontational, as the years spent apart had left an indelible mark on their relationship. The vast chasm of time and unresolved hurt had made it immensely challenging for them to fully reconnect and recapture the deep bond they had once shared.

The scars of the past continued to linger, creating a barrier that impeded their ability to fully reconcile and rebuild the strong familial ties they once enjoyed.

Lorraine's mother harboured a profound and lifelong obsession with diamonds and other precious, glimmering gems an infatuation that she instilled in her daughter from a remarkably young age.

Lorraine, it appears, not only inherited her mother's penchant for all things sparkly and lustrous, but had also emerged as an even more skilled and accomplished thief than the maternal figure who first ignited this captivation within her.

While Lorraine's mother may have been the one to initially introduce her to the irresistible allure of diamonds and other valuable trinkets, Lorraine has undoubtedly surpassed her progenitor's prowess when it comes to the art of stealing these highly coveted, shiny objects. Lorraine's natural talent, honed skills, and unwavering determination have allowed her to excel far beyond her mother's capabilities in this illicit, yet lucrative, pursuit. McMatters didn't know if it the attraction to shiny diamonds the thrill or was Lorraine trying to find a thrill big enough to satisfy her needs.

McMatters absentmindedly realised his glass was completely empty, unable to recall drinking its contents. Shrugging, he poured himself another round and leaned back, deeply contemplating everything he had just read.

It was abundantly clear that Lorraine had managed to capture Detective Jackson's undivided attention and his fixation on Lorraine was troubling. The poor woman had already endured far more than her fair share of hardship.

Now McMatters found himself grappling with a difficult choice. Should he reach out and offer Lorraine his aid, or maintain a prudent distance for her own protection? Assisting her could very well benefit him as well, but it was nonetheless a weighty decision fraught with complexities.

There was an undeniable allure to Lorraine that only served to complicate the situation further. What was it precisely that drew Steve to this enigmatic woman, and should he heed that magnetic pull?

McMatters sat staring at the photo Jarvis had included that he managed to capture and it did not please McMatters at all, Detective Jackson could be a major problem.

Chapter Seven
Maxine

Maxine couldn't help but feel utterly dejected and down on her luck. Once again, she had made the unfortunate mistake of choosing the wrong romantic partner, and the consequences had come back to haunt her in the most devastating way. As Maxine gazed into the mirror, a sense of dread and self-loathing overcame her at the sight of her battered and bruised appearance.

Maxine's nose was swollen and broken, her eyes were blackened and discoloured, and a nasty gash across her cheek was sure to leave a permanent, unsightly scar. But the physical injuries were just the tip of the iceberg. Her upper arms were covered in dark, ugly bruises, and her wrist was encased in a rigid cast.

The tears rolling down Maxine's cheeks only served to intensify the sting of her wounds, both physical and emotional. It was a stark and painful reminder that she had truly messed up this time, making choices that had led her down a path of suffering and despair.

Maxine had found solace and respite at the Women's Refuge Centre, a facility singularly dedicated to supporting and empowering women who had endured the harrowing experience of domestic abuse. Although the centre's physical appearance may have appeared a bit worn and its furnishings second-hand, these superficial qualities were of little consequence to Maxine. In her current state, all that truly mattered was that she had finally secured a roof over her head and access to nourishment, necessities that provided the safety, security, and stability she so desperately craved after the immense trauma Maxine had suffered. In that pivotal moment, the material condition of the centre paled in comparison to the profound sense of refuge and respite it offered, allowing Maxine to begin the critical process of healing and rebuilding her life on firmer foundations.

Maxine had found herself trapped in a profoundly difficult and harrowing situation. After a concerned neighbour contacted the authorities regarding the disturbance at her residence, the police arrived on the scene to discover Maxine unconscious at the base of the staircase.

The individual responsible, Dan Smithson, had already fled the premises before the officers could apprehend him. Maxine was promptly transported to the hospital, where medical professionals conducted a comprehensive examination and battery of tests to assess Maxine's condition.

Following the hospital visit, the police escorted Maxine to the station so she could provide a formal statement detailing the events that had transpired. Utterly drained both physically and emotionally, Maxine was relieved when the officers recognised the women's refuge centre as the optimal location for her to seek refuge and recover during this profoundly troubling ordeal. The authorities understood this specialised facility was uniquely equipped to offer Maxine the comprehensive support and protection she desperately needed in the wake of this devastating incident.

Maxine grappled with the daunting task of confiding in Lorraine about the recent events that had unfolded. She was fully committed to sharing this information, but each time the chance arose, Maxine found herself faltering, unable to muster the requisite courage or formulate the appropriate words.

This hesitation was further exacerbated by Maxine's own realisation that she had not always fulfilled her role as Lorraine's mother in the manner she should have, a sobering truth that filled Maxine with a profound sense of shame and remorse. Maxine recognised that she had profoundly let her daughter Lorraine down over the years, and she could understand the hostility Lorraine might harbour towards her as a result.

However, Maxine did not hold any ill will or resentment towards her daughter. She knew that the fault lay entirely with herself, not Lorraine. As the parent, Maxine was the one who had utterly failed in her responsibilities, dropping the ball and neglecting to properly care for and safeguard her child. Maxine's own tumultuous lifestyle, marked by repeated stints in jail and abusive relationships, had created an unstable and unsuitable environment for raising a child.

Maxine deeply regretted these failures and wished she had been a more nurturing, protective, and dependable mother for Lorraine. Maxine grimaces in discomfort as she heavily plops down on the ratty, grime covered sofa, wincing from both the throbbing pain of her recent physical assault and the grimy, unkempt state of the tattered furniture.

Maxine now finds herself in a difficult dilemma, torn between her desire to reach out to her estranged daughter Lorraine for help despite the overwhelming feelings of embarrassment and shame, or to remain at the Women's Refuge Centre where she currently resides. Maxine's current circumstances are bleak.

Maxine is completely destitute, with no possessions or stable place to call home. She wonders anxiously whether Lorraine would even be willing to let her stay, given that Maxine has never been invited to her daughter's residence. An unnerving concern also weighs on her mind. What if Lorraine still harbours resentment over Maxine's past shortcomings as a parent? The prospect of being turned away by her own child only amplifies Maxine's sense of desperation and vulnerability in this trying moment.

It was already eleven o'clock in the morning, so Maxine knew her daughter Lorraine would be up and active by now. Calling Lorraine always made Maxine feel a bit anxious, and in this moment, she could really use a stiff drink to calm her frayed nerves.

However, Maxine understood if Lorraine caught wind of her drinking, she would likely react by promptly kicking Maxine out.

Recognising this, Maxine decided that the time had come to make a genuine, lasting change. From this point forward, Maxine was done with all the nonsense. No more tolerating unpleasant men, no more engaging in theft, and no more indulging in alcohol.

Maxine was determined to get her life back on the right track once and for all, with Lorraine's wellbeing taking precedence.

Chapter Seven Part Two
The Call

Lorraine was blissfully immersed in her singing, revelling in the moment as she belted out her favourite tunes while enjoying the refreshing comfort of her shower. However, as it so often happens, the shrill ringing of the phone suddenly interrupted her melodic reverie.

Yet, Lorraine was determined not to let this unexpected disturbance ruin her cherished singing session. She steadfastly resolved to let the caller wait until she had finished savouring the pleasures of her invigorating shower, knowing full well that a relaxing bubble bath would have been her true preference over a mere quick rinse. After towelling off and getting dressed, Lorraine carefully wrapped her damp hair before turning her attention to the unanswered call. The unfamiliar number displayed on the caller ID piqued her curiosity, and she decided to return the call, eager to discover what the person on the other end had wanted. Lorraine's unwavering commitment to completing her singing ritual, despite the interruption, exemplifies her ability to maintain focus and derive joy from the simple pleasures in life, even when faced with unexpected distractions.

"Hello, Women's Refuge Centre. How can I help you?"

"Oh, hello. I have just missed a call from this number, but I don't know anyone at the Women's Refuge Centre."

"If I could have your name, I'll see if I can find that information for you."

"Yes, of course. My name is Lorraine Spencer."

"Hold for a minute please."

Please hold.

Please hold.

Please hold.

"Oh, thank you for holding, Lorraine. I found that it was Maxine Spencer who called you."

"My mum is at the centre?"

"Yes, she is."

"I'm on my way. Thank you for letting me know."

"You're welcome."

Lorraine sat on the edge of the bed, her emotions in a state of flux, feeling unsettled and uncertain about the events that had just transpired. Without taking the time to properly dry her damp hair, Lorraine quickly ran a brush through it, hoping the hasty grooming wouldn't result in a frizzy mess later.

Slipping on her shoes, Lorraine headed straight for the women's refuge centre, determined to seek answers and gain a deeper understanding of her family's past. Over the years, Lorraine's relationship with her mother, Maxine, had not been the closest, but Lorraine realised she didn't have the full picture of her childhood. She couldn't bring herself to harshly judge or be too hard on Maxine, as she didn't know the reasons behind why her upbringing hadn't been what it ideally should have been.

Perhaps by visiting the refuge centre, Lorraine would uncover the truth and gain the insight she so desperately sought. Driven by a mixture of emotions, Lorraine knew she needed to confront the past to move forward. The uncertainty that lingered from the recent events had left her unsettled, but she was resolute in her pursuit of answers. With a sense of purpose, Lorraine made her way to the refuge centre, hoping to finally piece together the missing elements of her family's history.

Chapter Seven Part Three
A Watchful Eye

Jarvis couldn't help but notice Lorraine hastily exiting her home, her still damp hair and concerned expression immediately catching his eye. Intrigued by her hurried departure, Jarvis decided to discreetly follow her, his curiosity piqued by the unusual sight. Jarvis maintained a safe distance, keenly observing Lorraine as she navigated the streets with a sense of urgency. Her demeanour suggesting a pressing matter that required her immediate attention. Lorraine was behind the wheel of her trusty old green Mini, and she handled the car with remarkable agility it reminded Jarvis of a dodgem as Lorraine threw it around with speed, weaving in and out of traffic as she made her way to the Women's Refuge Centre. The fact that she was willing to risk breaking traffic rules to reach her destination only further fuelled Jarvis' curiosity. Who did Lorraine know that was staying at the Refuge Centre? What could be so important that she would go to such lengths to get there? Jarvis was intrigued to uncover the reason behind Lorraine's hurried and seemingly concerned departure from her home.

After patiently waiting for approximately ten minutes, Jarvis was startled when a police car suddenly pulled up and parked in the lot adjacent to the Women's Refuge Centre.

This unexpected law enforcement presence immediately piqued his curiosity and raised a multitude of questions. Was the police visit related to Lorraine, or the individual she had come to the centre to see? Were the officers there to speak with someone else entirely different, perhaps regarding a separate incident or investigation? The sudden arrival of the police vehicle had transformed what had been a relatively mundane situation into one shrouded in intrigue, leaving Jarvis to ponder a host of possibilities about the nature and purpose of the officers' presence at the refuge centre. The unexpected turn of events had undoubtedly captured his attention and sparked his imagination, as he found himself eager to uncover the underlying reasons behind the police's sudden appearance.

Twenty minutes after arriving at the women's refuge centre, Lorraine emerged, carefully escorting another woman whose face was badly swollen and bruised, obscuring her identity.

The woman's injuries were a clear and distressing indication of the violence and abuse she had endured. Right behind them, two police officers came out of the building, suggesting the involvement of law enforcement in facilitating the woman. The officers handed the woman a card, likely containing important information or resources, before promptly departing in their patrol car, leaving the refuge's parking lot. Meanwhile, Lorraine, with a gentle and compassionate demeanour, was diligently helping the injured woman into the backseat of her well-worn, compact green Mini, ensuring she was settled in safely and securely.

This scene painted a vivid picture of the refuge's critical role in providing a haven for victims of domestic violence, with Lorraine's attentive care and the police's intervention highlighting the collaborative efforts to support and protect vulnerable individuals. Jarvis trailed cautiously behind Lorraine's compact vehicle as it navigated the winding roads back to her residence. Knowing the importance of his investigation, he immediately instructed a couple of his most trusted associates to discreetly monitor the situation and report any relevant developments while he departed to get the photographs promptly developed. Jarvis was acutely aware that McMatters would want to be updated about this perplexing turn of events. He was determined to uncover the identity of the mysterious woman as quickly as possible to provide his boss with the comprehensive analysis that was demanded.

Chapter Seven Part Four
Jackson

Jackson had taken proactive measures to ensure he remained closely informed of any developments related to Lorraine and her mother Maxine. He had previously configured a system flag that would automatically notify him whenever either of their names was entered into the database. This allowed him to maintain a vigilant awareness of any issues or situations that arose, enabling him to address them swiftly and decisively as they occurred.

Jackson had dispatched two members of his team to investigate the matter further and provide him with timely updates, ensuring he could take immediate action to resolve any concerns that surfaced.

Jackson carefully reviewed the detailed report documenting the specifics of Maxine's assault, which included a comprehensive list of her injuries as well as her written statement. Although he did not yet have any photographic evidence, the officers assured him they would reach out to the hospital to obtain a copy of the medical records. Just as Jackson was concluding his examination of the report, PCs Jones and Benson arrived on the scene, coinciding with Lorraine's arrival to pick up her mother. To maintain an air of normalcy and legitimacy, the officers made a concerted effort to appear casual and unassuming during the encounter, mindful of the possibility that the perpetrator, McMatters, might have someone keeping a watchful eye on the situation. To that end, the officers discreetly provided Maxine with a business card before departing, ensuring the interaction appeared routine and above board.

While the officers were interviewing Maxine at the Refuge Centre, they were able to convince her to provide a signed statement regarding a man named Dan Smithson. During this time, the officers also took additional photographs of Maxine to document the situation. Furthermore, the officers informed both Maxine and Lorraine that Detective Jackson was the lead investigator on the case and that they had already submitted a warrant request for Smithson's arrest. This concerted effort by the police suggests they were determined to make substantial headway in resolving this pressing matter in an expedient manner.

What Lorraine and her mother Maxine failed to comprehend was that Jackson had every intention of filing charges against Dan Smithson, regardless of whether Maxine decided to take any further action or not. Jackson had amassed an overwhelming amount of evidence to support his case. The neighbour living adjacent to the scene had already provided the police with a comprehensive written statement earlier that same day.

Chapter Eight
Lorraine's Place

Since Lorraine picked her mother, Maxine, up from the Women's Refugee Centre, Maxine had been uncharacteristically silent, a telling sign that something was weighing heavily on her mind. Maxine simply did not know how to articulate her thoughts and feelings in that moment, as she was grappling with a profound sense of shame and embarrassment. The emotional turmoil had also left her physically pained, making it difficult to engage in conversation. Maxine's anxiety was further compounded by the fact that she had never been invited to see Lorraine's home.

This was not due to a lack of desire on her part; quite the contrary, Maxine had long yearned for the opportunity to visit her daughter's place of residence. However, the invitation had never materialised, leaving Maxine feeling excluded and disconnected from this important aspect of Lorraine's life. The current situation presented a rare and potentially significant chance for Maxine to gain deeper insight into her daughter's world, and she was understandably apprehensive about how this encounter might unfold.

Lorraine unexpectedly pulled the car over and parked in front of the house, even though she had a perfectly functional driveway available. This puzzled Maxine, but she opted to remain silent and refrain from voicing her curiosity.

The house they had arrived at was notably larger and more impressive than any of the modest dwellings Maxine had inhabited in the past, a clear testament to Lorraine's professional and financial success. While Maxine felt a twinge of envy at the sight of her daughter's prosperous circumstances, she was ultimately proud that Lorraine had managed to achieve such an enviable level of comfort and security.

However, Maxine found herself uncertain about the architectural style or historical era represented by the grand residence, unable to place its design within a specific time.

"Lorraine, what is the era is this house? Georgian or Victorian?"

"Neither, Mum. It's Edwardian."

Maxine shrugged her shoulders, indicating a lack of knowledge about the details of the property. The home had undergone significant updates, with the windows replaced by new, modern PVC units in a warm, wood-like brown tone. The front door seamlessly matched this updated aesthetic. Stepping outside, a spacious porch greeted visitors, featuring a bench on each side beneath the porch roof. Hanging from the posts below the porch were two beautifully maintained hanging baskets.

On the left side, the basket overflowed with a vibrant mix of Blues, Whites, and Yellows, while the right-side basket showcased a harmonious blend of Pinks, Purples, and Blues that complemented the well-tended front garden. The garden itself, though not expansive, was meticulously cared for, with a small, neatly trimmed lawn surrounded by an array of colourful, flowering bushes. Maxine, though unfamiliar with the specific types of flowers, could not help but admire the overall well-kept and visually appealing nature of the front landscaping, Maxine didn't know her daughter had these skills, she knew she didn't get it from herself.

"Are you coming?" Lorraine asked smiling

Maxine made her way to the hallway, but as she reached the entryway, she was immediately struck by the captivating decor that lay before her. Completely taken aback, she found herself utterly gobsmacked by the impeccable style and refined taste her daughter had showcased in this space. The room exuded a modern, sleek, and undeniably stylish aesthetic that was simply eye-catching.

What truly captured Maxine's attention was the unexpected use of black woodwork, a bold choice that stood in stark contrast to the more common white or cream tones typically seen.

Yet, the striking effect of the dark hues against the room's other elements was remarkably captivating, lending an air of sophisticated elegance. The walls featured a stunning marble-like finish, while the floor was covered in pristine white tiles that provided a sturdy, non-slip surface.

The carefully selected fixtures, including a ringed, layered LED light fixture suspended from the ceiling, as well as a matching silver-toned lamp positioned on a sleek black side table in the corner, all seamlessly came together to create a cohesive, visually striking ambiance. Maxine couldn't help but be thoroughly impressed by her daughter's impeccable design sensibilities, which had transformed this once ordinary space into a truly captivating and stylish environment.

Maxine had likely been standing and surveying her surroundings for some time, as when her gaze finally lowered, she noticed Lorraine observing her with an amused expression.

"I don't use most of the rooms in the house," commented Lorraine.

"Why not?"

"It's too big for just myself, so I tend to stick to just a few."

Maxine's puzzlement only grew as she wondered if the rest of the home's decor was not adequately embellished to truly captivate. However, Lorraine's next move quickly dispelled any lingering doubts, as she opened a door on the right side of the hallway, revealing a sight that left Maxine utterly awestruck. The dining room's decor was nothing short of mesmerising, featuring rich, dark wood tones - perhaps walnut, Maxine was clueless on most things she now knew. The wood had been expertly varnished to a gleaming finish.

At the centre of this elegantly appointed space stood the table, a true work of art. Its design was reminiscent of a cracked open tree trunk, with the rough, inner portion of the wood turned inward to create a captivating contrast. Joining the two halves of the wooden slab was a tranquil blue hue, slightly darker along the edges where the rugged inner bark had once been. Maxine was completely enthralled, unable to discern the exact nature of this unique and breathtaking feature, but utterly captivated by the sheer beauty of the colours and craftsmanship. Lorraine then approached the table and touched a hidden control, causing the inner area to illuminate, sending ripples of vibrant colour radiating throughout the room. Maxine could scarcely contain her amazement, her jaw dropping open in sheer wonderment at the stunning display unfolding before her eyes.

Maxine's eyes swept across the room, immediately drawn to the impressive drinks cabinet that stretched along the side wall, occupying a prominent recess. Lorraine approached the cabinet and interacted with something on its surface, causing it to illuminate and perfectly complement the elegant dining table nearby. Adjacent to the cabinet stood the room's centrepiece a magnificent fireplace, its walnut surround contrasting beautifully with the crisp white tiles that framed the old fashioned, open flame hearth.

Topping the fireplace's mantelpiece was an array of modern, stylish ornaments, further enhancing the room's sophisticated, yet welcoming ambiance.

Maxine was utterly at a loss for words as she surveyed the breathtaking room before her. The floor was composed of genuine, richly hued walnut, its surface meticulously varnished to a smooth, lustrous finish.

The walls, painted a pristine white, served to amplify the serene, calming blue tones of the contemporary furniture that adorned the space. Dominating the centre of the room was a long, elegant table, above which hung a striking light fixture. This light, unlike the one in the entryway, bent and twisted gracefully along the full length of the table, casting a warm, inviting glow over the entire scene.

The harmonious blend of luxurious materials, soothing colours, and artful lighting created an atmosphere of unparalleled tranquillity that left Maxine momentarily speechless.

Lorraine strode back through the entryway, turning right down the hallway and pushing open a door that unveiled the pristine kitchen. Maxine was once again taken aback by the immaculate state of Lorraine's home. The kitchen floor was covered in lustrous marble tiles that perfectly complemented the equally elegant marble countertops and breakfast table. The high gloss black cabinetry and doors shimmered under the light, creating an air of sophistication. An intriguing glittering material adorned the sink, captivating Maxine's attention.

The walls had been painted a striking teal hue, and tiny concealed lights underneath the cabinets and table cast a mesmerising glow, illuminating the entire space and reflecting off the floor beneath the central island.

Maxine marvelled at Lorraine's impeccable design sense and meticulous attention to detail in maintaining such an impeccably clean and visually striking kitchen. Maxine's body ached with a sharp, throbbing pain from the beating she had endured, the medication had worn off, the pain mow unbearable. The physical trauma, coupled with the overwhelming emotions she was experiencing, left her feeling drained and desperate for a moment of respite.

Needing to collect herself before facing the rest of the house, Maxine carefully pulled out one of the stools that sat beneath the island counter in the kitchen, slowly lowering herself onto the sturdy seat. The familiar weight of the stool provided a small sense of stability and comfort as she took a few deep, steadying breaths, preparing herself to confront the challenges that lay ahead.

Maxine found she had tears rolling slowly down her face which she tried hard to hide wiping them away with her sleeve.

Chapter Eight Part Two
Mixed Emotions

Lorraine's heart was heavy with a complex mix of emotions as she arrived to pick up her mother, Maxine, from the Women's Refuge Centre (WRC). The past had been profoundly painful for Lorraine, leaving her with a myriad of unanswered questions that had long weighed on her mind. Why had she been forced to fend for herself from such a young age? Why had she been so neglected? Was it that Maxine never wanted a child, or did she resent Lorraine for hampering her own life? These where the pressing questions Lorraine had yearned to address for years, and now, as she reunited with her mother, she found herself hesitant, unsure if this was the right moment to finally seek the answers she had craved. Lorraine's feelings were a turbulent blend of apprehension, vulnerability, and a deep longing for understanding.

The trauma and neglect of her childhood had undoubtedly shaped her in profound ways, and she was acutely aware that this reunion with Maxine had the potential to either provide the closure she so desperately needed or reopen old wounds. As she guided her mother to the car, Lorraine steeled herself, knowing that this encounter could prove to be a pivotal moment in her life, one that could finally shed light on the mysteries of her past and pave the way for a more harmonious future.

As soon as Lorraine laid eyes on the badly beaten mum Maxine, she was immediately overcome with a profound sense of empathy and compassion. Despite the strained relationship with her mother and Maxine's apparent lack of care, Lorraine made the conscious decision to rise above the past and be the better person by extending a helping hand. This pivotal moment allowed Lorraine to see her mother's vulnerability in a new light, shedding fresh perspective on their complex dynamic. Lorraine had previously been reluctant to let her mother see where she lived, knowing full well the contrast between her own comfortable living situation and her mother's more precarious circumstances.

Lorraine recognised that, much like herself, her mother had also resorted to thievery when faced with difficult times, underscoring the empathy and understanding Lorraine now felt. This realisation marked a significant shift in Lorraine's perspective, as she began to view her mother not just as a parental figure, but as a fellow human being struggling with the challenges of life.

When Lorraine arrived at her house, the expression on her mother Maxine's face was one of palpable bewilderment and astonishment. Maxine had never encountered a living environment quite like this. Her previous residences had been starkly different either the homes of Lorraine's various boyfriends or halfway houses that were invariably unkempt and in a state of disrepair.

The sheer contrast between Lorraine's comfortable, well-maintained abode and Maxine's accustomed living situations evoked a potent mixture of confusion, intrigue, and even a sense of admiration within Maxine. This was clearly a far cry from the modest, sometimes even squalid, accommodations Maxine had grown accustomed to calling "home" over the years.

Lorraine gently assisted her mother, Maxine, as she carefully exited the old, battered Mini that they had been traveling in. Maxine visibly winced in discomfort, demonstrating the physical strain and difficulty she experienced in squeezing out of the cramped vehicle.

As they approached the house, Lorraine couldn't help but notice the well-tended front garden that her mum was enjoying, a sight that seemed to captivate Maxine's attention, causing her to take her time admiring the meticulously maintained landscape before entering the home. Once they finally made it inside, Lorraine was struck by the powerful emotions that played across her mother's face, an open book of raw feeling that anyone observing could easily read.

The shift in Maxine's expression, from the earlier discomfort to this newfound intensity, was palpable and deeply moving, hinting at the complex emotions and memories that this homecoming had evoked within her. Lorraine enthusiastically guided her mother through their family home, eagerly showcasing the various design elements that she had meticulously curated to create the stunning interior. Lorraine took great pride in the thoughtful selection of furnishings, artwork, and decor that transformed the space into a harmonious and visually captivating environment.

She delighted in sharing the inspiration and vision behind each carefully chosen piece, hoping to elicit a sense of awe and appreciation from her mother.

However, as the tour reached the kitchen, Lorraine's mother suddenly appeared overwhelmed by the experience. The sheer beauty and sophistication of the decor seemed to have an unexpectedly profound impact, triggering an emotional response that Lorraine had not anticipated.

Sensing her mother's discomfort, Lorraine quickly sprang into action, putting the kettle on to prepare a soothing cup of tea, recognising that a moment of calm and respite might help to alleviate the situation. As Lorraine's mother tried to settle onto one of the stools, Lorraine's heart ached to see her beloved mum struggling.

With tender concern, she noticed her mother discreetly wiping away tears, the pain clearly becoming overwhelming. Lorraine's chest tightened with empathy, understanding how challenging this moment must be for her mother.

In that poignant instant, Lorraine saw her mother in a new light not just as the strong, nurturing figure she'd always known, but as a vulnerable human being facing the challenges of aging. This realisation stirred a deep well of compassion within Lorraine, filling her with a renewed sense of love and a gentle urge to support and protect her mother.

Lorraine's perspective shifted, her heart opening to a more profound appreciation for her mother's journey and well-being.

She silently vowed to be there for her mother, offering the unconditional love and care that had should have been given to her

Chapter Nine
Update for McMatters

Jarvis was confident that his dedicated team had done an exceptional job in gathering all the pertinent information requested for these two distinct cases. With the relevant files neatly organised in hand, Jarvis now turned his attention to anticipating how his superior, the discerning and demanding McMatters would react to the detailed reports he was about to present.

Jarvis knew McMatters expected nothing less than excellence, and he was determined to deliver a comprehensive, well-substantiated assessment that would withstand the scrutiny of the seasoned department head. The success of these investigations rested squarely on Jarvis's ability to effectively communicate the team's diligent efforts and the compelling evidence they had amassed.

"Jarvis, good afternoon. How's the intel coming?" asked McMatter's

"It's coming along fine, boss. I've two files for you to read. Can I get you a drink?" asked Jarvis.

"A coffee would be great. Grab yourself one and come sit with me."

Jarvis quickly departs to prepare the requested pair of Americano coffees, eager to rejoin his boss in the office. Jarvis takes great pride and enjoyment in the office environment, as the meticulously curated decor aligns perfectly with his refined aesthetic sensibilities. The rich, warm hues of the red mahogany furnishings create a sophisticated and cohesive ambiance throughout the spacious room.

The minimalist design of the two desks positioned within the office exude an air of elegant simplicity, devoid of any unnecessary clutter or disorganisation. The pristine cleanliness of the office is such that one could comfortably dine directly off any available surface, testament to Jarvis' fastidious attention to detail and dedication to maintaining an impeccably professional workspace.

When Jarvis returns to the office, he sees McMatters is reading the report on Lorraine and the Women's Refuge Centre, he flicks through the photos and returns to the report. Jarvis knew he had questions because he had questions too.

"So, Jarvis, you think this is a relative of Lorraine's?"

"Yes, I think it's her mum. I'm waiting on confirmation of this."

"It would be surprising if it is, considering what her mum put her through growing up."

"It would depend on loyalty from my viewpoint. Although she hasn't had a great experience growing up, if it is her mum, the only reason to me would be that Lorraine has an understanding which has made her loyal to her mum, and that's if it is her mum."

"I see."

Jarvis, an inquisitive and determined individual, understands that simply sitting idle will not lead him to the answers he seeks. Rather than passively waiting for the solutions to come to him, Jarvis recognises that he must take a proactive approach to find the information he requires.

With this realisation, Jarvis decides to get up from his seated position and leave in pursuit of the answers he needs. This proactive mindset and willingness to act demonstrates Jarvis's conviction that he must be the one to drive his own discovery and learning process, rather than expecting the answers to simply materialise while he remains stationary.

"I will let you know when I find something boss." Jarvis gets back to work.

Chapter Nine Part Two
McMatters

McMatters observed as Jarvis departed the room, then poured himself a glass of his preferred beverage. With a sense of anticipation, he turned his attention to the second file that Jarvis had entrusted him with, containing information about Detective Jackson. McMatters was determined to thoroughly review the contents.

As he began reading, McMatters felt a growing conviction that this additional documentation would provide valuable insights and potentially critical evidence that could help steer McMatters in the right direction. Jarvis's team has conducted meticulous surveillance of Detective Jackson, yielding compelling evidence that suggests an unhealthy fixation on Lorraine especially with the photo Jarvis managed to take, McMatters now knows what a dirty little man Detective Jackson really is.

The data indicates that Detective Jackson has been personally monitoring Lorraine's movements and activities almost constantly, almost stalker-like behaviour, going beyond the scope of a professional investigation. Rather than merely taking photographs, Detective Jackson has been using high-powered, long-lens binoculars to closely scrutinise Lorraine's actions and behaviour from a distance.

This level of direct scrutiny, and his hands-on himself approach with the observation points to a deeper, more troubling psychological preoccupation with Lorraine. Furthermore, when Detective Jackson is not directly observing Lorraine, he has assigned members of his team to maintain a vigilant watch over her, ensuring that she is under near-constant supervision. This obsessive, almost stalker-like behaviour hints at a disturbing personal fixation that extends far beyond the bounds of a typical law enforcement inquiry. Jarvis firmly believes that Detective Jackson's unhealthy fixation on Lorraine may pose a significant risk to her well-being, potentially leading to a concerning, sinister situation in the future.

The meticulous surveillance data gathered by Jarvis's team provides a compelling case for a deeper investigation into Detective Jackson's motivations and actions.

McMatters downs the drink he has in hand, feeling a deep sense of disgust towards the creep Detective Jackson and his stalker-like behaviour. He firmly believes that no one should ever have to explicitly say "no" or "back off" when it comes to unwanted advances and to watch someone and play with yourself. Detective Jackson should know better.

Instead, any romantic or sexual overtures should be made with the clear, affirmative consent and respect of the other person, rather than simply taking such liberties without permission. McMatters is adamant that this kind of entitled, predatory mindset has no place in civilized society and must be condemned in the strongest possible terms.

McMatters poured himself a refreshing beverage, the cool liquid providing a brief respite as he immersed himself back into the case file.

The evidence suggested that Detective Jackson had been closely monitoring the women's refuge centre long before Lorraine or the local authorities had even become involved. This revelation raised concerning questions about the detective's motivations and potential conflicts of interest.

As he continued reading, a growing sense of unease settled over him, the implications of Jackson's clandestine surveillance casting an ominous shadow over the entire investigation. Detective Jackson was observed making a call, and shortly thereafter, a police vehicle promptly arrived on the scene. An officer was then seen handing a card to the visibly battered woman.

This sequence of events suggests that Detective Jackson may have been actively intervening to assist the woman, potentially with the aim of facilitating her connection to Lorraine. The critical question that now arises is whether McMatters, will take any action in response to this development. Given the sensitive nature of the situation and the potential implications for the ongoing investigation, it will be crucial for McMatters to carefully consider the appropriate next steps to address this new information and ensure a thorough and effective resolution.

Chapter Ten
Friday Night

Lorraine's mother was in a distressing physical condition, with her body covered in unsettling bruises and discoloration. The various shades of purple, blue, and yellow on her skin are a clear indication of the severity of her injuries, which include broken ribs, a broken nose, a broken wrist, and a fractured jaw.

The visible trauma she has endured is undoubtedly causing her immense pain and suffering. Sadly, Lorraine has also observed her mother's emotional withdrawal and detachment during this difficult time. The extent of the physical abuse she has experienced has clearly taken a significant toll on her mental and psychological well-being, leading her to retreat and isolate herself.

Recognising the urgency of the situation, Lorraine has offered her mother, Maxine, the opportunity to stay with her for the time being. However, Lorraine has established a clear set of rules to ensure a safe and stable living environment. No men, no drinking, no stealing, and no parties.

While Lorraine may have struggled to maintain a serious demeanour when conveying these guidelines, the underlying concern and care for her mother's well-being is evident, and it was only while she got herself back on track, you could say to safeguard Maxine, and her recovery. Lorraine is determined to provide a secure and supportive space for her mother to heal, both physically and emotionally, during this difficult phase.

Lorraine was conflicted about her impending outing to Dreams Nightclub, which was part of an unwanted arrangement. Yet, despite her reservations, she couldn't deny the underlying excitement and nervousness she felt.

Lorraine was undeniably attracted to McMatters, and she could sense the palpable chemistry between them whenever they were in the same room. The allure was almost electric, stirring a powerful craving within her. However, Lorraine was unsure of how far she should take this budding attraction.

Detective Jackson had not provided clear instructions on whether she should pursue a physical relationship or a more prolonged connection with McMatters. It was an ambiguous situation, one that Lorraine found increasingly difficult to navigate, given the intensity of her desires. The feelings she was experiencing were unlike anything she had felt before.

She had this overwhelming urge to be intimate with McMatters, to the point where she found herself fantasising about ripping off his clothes without a care for who might be watching. Lorraine had never encountered such a potent and immediate sense of arousal after just meeting someone.

Lorraine had just stepped out of the refreshing shower, her mind focused on preparing for her anticipated encounter with McMatters later that evening. With a keen eye for fashion, she had carefully selected the perfect ensemble to accentuate her natural beauty. The velvet purple dress she had chosen was not an overpowering hue, but rather a captivating, silky plum tone that would elegantly complement her complexion. The dress's luxurious fabric and flattering cut would elegantly drape over her figure, highlighting her feminine curves in a sophisticated and alluring manner.

To complete the look, she paired the dress with her new black satin purse and matching satin shoes, creating a cohesive and sophisticated style that seamlessly blended the different elements. As Lorraine stood in front of the mirror, she meticulously considered the finishing touch, the colour of her lipstick. After testing a few shades, she settled on a delectable chocolate plum, a harmonious blend of two complementary tones that would effortlessly tie the entire ensemble together. The rich, velvety hue would add a touch of sensuality to her lips, perfectly complementing the elegance of the dress.

With her sleek, super shiny hair styled and her makeup applied to perfection, Lorraine felt confident and ready to embark on her anticipated encounter with McMatters, knowing she looked stunning and ready to captivate her intended audience.

Chapter Ten Part Two
The Club

Lorraine arrived at Dream's exclusive nightclub building around 10pm, her presence immediately recognised by the attentive doorman on duty. As soon as the seasoned security professional caught sight of Lorraine approaching, a welcoming smile spread across his face, and he discreetly leaned into his communication headset to alert the staff inside. Lorraine paused momentarily next to the doorman, who greeted her warmly, no doubt aware of her privileged status as a frequent and welcome visitor to the luxurious establishment.

"Hello"

"Hello Miss Spencer"

"Call me Lorraine and what might I call you?"

"Mike, hope you have a nice night Lorraine"

"You too Mike."

Lorraine found great fulfilment and excitement in the act of entering the realm of Dreams. The vivid, kaleidoscopic colours that painted the dreamscape never failed to captivate her senses, evoking a sense of wonder and enchantment.

Moreover, the charged, electrifying atmosphere that permeated the dream world had a mesmerising quality, making it feel as if the very air was alive and pulsating with energy. But perhaps most alluring of all was the captivating, melodic music that seemed to emanate from the very fabric of the dream, gently luring her deeper into its immersive, hypnotic embrace.

For Lorraine, the experience of traversing these fantastical, dream like landscapes was a truly captivating and rewarding one that she relished every time.

Lorraine should be truly grateful to Detective Jackson for intervening and enabling her to experience enjoyment and leisure in ways she had long been deprived of. The nightclub setting was highly uncharacteristic and unfamiliar territory for Lorraine, as it was not the type of environment she had ever found pleasure or comfort in prior to this occasion.

Detective Jackson's thoughtful intervention and guidance allowed Lorraine to step outside her typical comfort zone and engage in an activity that, while initially foreign to her, ultimately provided a refreshing and rewarding change of pace that she had been lacking for an extended period.

Lorraine owes a debt of gratitude to Detective Jackson for orchestrating this meaningful opportunity for her to rediscover a sense of joy and fulfilment that had eluded her for years.

Detective Jackson had taken Lorraine hostage due to her compulsive obsession with shiny, valuable objects that belonged to others. The reason Lorraine was present at the nightclub in the first place was that she had been apprehended while unlawfully entering and burglarizing private residences. Her insatiable desire for coveted possessions had driven her to commit these criminal acts, leading to the confrontation with the detective who now held her captive. Lorraine's fixation on acquiring gleaming, prized items, regardless of their rightful ownership, was the fundamental motivation behind her presence at the nightclub and the subsequent hostage situation. Lorraine was abruptly jolted out of her pensive reverie when an inconsiderate individual carelessly bumped into her, disrupting her train of thought. Shaken from her moment of introspection, Lorraine decided to make her way over to the nearby bar.

"Good evening, Lorraine and what will you be fancying tonight?"

"Hi Paulie, I think I will have a Blue Ocean tonight… easy on the ice though!"

"Coming right up"

Lorraine was absolutely captivated by the throbbing rhythm of the music pulsing through the lively atmosphere tonight. As she waited for her drink order, she couldn't help but sway and shimmy to the infectious beat, her body moving in sync with the dynamic melody. When Paulie finally delivered her refreshing beverage, Lorraine eagerly reached out to effortlessly tap her payment card, eager to indulge in the flavourful concoction.

Taking an initial sip, Lorraine's eyes widened in delighted surprise this might just be the finest Blue Ocean cocktail she had savoured in recent memory, the expertly blended flavours dancing across her palate in an exquisite symphony. Lorraine was thoroughly enchanted by the sublime taste and invigorating ambiance, completely immersed in the vibrant, energetic ambiance of the evening.

When Lorraine glanced upward, she couldn't help but notice that both Paulie and McMatters had been intently observing her, their expressions clearly amused by something.

Unfazed, Lorraine signalled to Paulie that she was ready for another drink, and without hesitation, he moved to fulfil her request. Lorraine's unwavering demeanour and her ability to maintain composure in the face of their obvious amusement suggested a certain level of confidence and poise, qualities that likely contributed to her ability to command the situation with a mere gesture.

The music pulsed through Lorraine's veins, igniting a fire within her very soul! Her body, a vessel of pure emotion, swayed with unbridled passion as the intoxicating beat consumed the crowded club.

The second cocktail coursing through her veins was like liquid lightning, unleashing a torrent of exhilaration and fearless confidence! Driven by an irresistible force, Lorraine surrendered herself to the siren call of the dance floor.

Her heart raced with anticipation, yearning to immerse herself in the electrifying atmosphere and lose all inhibitions to the music's seductive embrace! Every movement of Lorraine's body was a testament to raw, unbridled sensuality.

Her dance steps, perfectly attuned to the mesmerising rhythms, were an expression of her innermost desires and passions. The DJ, a true maestro of emotion, wove a tapestry of sound that elevated Lorraine's performance to breath-taking heights! On that pulsating dance floor, Lorraine became a living, breathing work of art her every gesture a brushstroke of pure, unadulterated passion.

The music, the atmosphere, and Lorraine's hypnotic movements fused into an unforgettable symphony of desire and uninhibited joy!

Lorraine was acutely aware of the prying eyes upon her, a sensation that only served to further fuel her confident, alluring movements on the dance floor. In that moment, the presence of Detective Jackson had all but slipped from her mind, eclipsed by her singular focus and determination to captivate her audience.

Lorraine's world had narrowed to the rhythmic sway of her body and the singular objective of securing the attention and affection of her target, McMatters. All other concerns had been pushed aside, leaving her singularly driven and laser-focused on achieving her goal. Lorraine, feeling parched, made her way over to the bar, her footsteps quickening with a growing thirst.

Observant Paulie, the bartender, had been anticipating her arrival and had already begun preparing her usual beverage.

As Lorraine approached the counter, Paulie discreetly shielded the card reader, preventing her from making a payment, and instead passed the drink directly into her waiting hands, accompanied by a mysterious note.

You look great tonight

-S-

XX

Lorraine smiled blushing a little and looked around to see if she could see him

"Look up," said Paulie

Paulie couldn't help but smirk as he observed the unfolding situation, fully aware of the underlying dynamics at play. From his vantage point in the hallway leading to the VIP section, he spotted Lorraine approaching. With one hand resting on the glass partition, he discreetly motioned with his finger, beckoning her to come closer.

Lorraine momentarily hesitated, unsure if the gesture was indeed intended for her, so she quickly scanned the area to see if anyone else was heading in the same direction towards the exclusive McMatters lounge. Lorraine's delicate fingers embracing that mesmerising azure elixir, exuded an aura of sheer magnificence as she glided towards the VIP sanctuary. Her every move was a symphony of elegance and confidence, captivating all who witnessed her approach.

The formidable guardian of this exclusive realm, a mountain of muscle and authority, bestowed upon her the honour of entry with a single, powerful gesture. Each movement was a masterpiece of grace and intention, her very essence pulsating with an electrifying sense of purpose. As she swept down that hallway, her gaze locked on her goal, the air crackled with anticipation. And there, at the pinnacle of this thrilling journey, stood McMatters a figure of immense influence, his face alight with unbridled joy and eager expectation.

The mere sight of Lorraine's approach set his heart aflame with excitement, for he knew that her presence would ignite the very atmosphere with passion and intrigue!

Chapter Ten Part Three

VIP Room

McMatters' heart raced as his eyes locked onto Lorraine, her every movement a mesmerising dance that set his soul ablaze. Each step she took down the hallway was like being drawn in with an irresistible force. Waves of electric energy radiated from her, crashing over him with an intensity that left him breathless and weak-kneed.

He was utterly spellbound, his gaze unbreakable, as if Lorraine had cast an enchanting spell upon him. Her presence ignited a fire within McMatters, a burning desire that consumed his every thought and sensation. With each graceful stride, the flames of his passion roared higher, an all-consuming inferno of attraction that threatened to engulf him entirely.

McMatters felt powerless against the raw, primal magnetism that pulled him towards her, his entire being crying out for her touch, her smile, her very essence. Lorraine was a vision of pure, intoxicating beauty, her allure so potent that McMatters felt dizzy with longing. She commanded his attention completely, effortlessly captivating him body and soul. Tonight, she was beyond stunning, a radiant goddess who outshone the stars themselves.

Overwhelmed by his fervent emotions, McMatters rushed to the VIP area door, his hands trembling with anticipation as he held it open. His heart pounded furiously as Lorraine approached, every fibre of his being electrified by her proximity.

As she glided past him, the intoxicating scent of her perfume nearly bringing him to his knees, McMatters knew he would forever be under her spell, hopelessly and passionately devoted to the enchanting Lorraine.

"You look amazing in that dress Lorraine."

"Thank you! I'm glad you approve."

McMatters approached a circular table that was partially encircled by a plush, velvet upholstered sofa. On the opposite side of the table, there were two stools positioned to provide additional seating. The soft, luxurious texture of the sofa's fabric invited comfort and relaxation, while the stools offered a more formal, functional option for those seeking a place to sit and engage.

This arrangement of furnishings created a versatile and inviting space, allowing for both casual lounging and more structured interactions around the central table. McMatters, feeling the weight of the situation bearing down on him, swiftly picked up his glass and downed the contents in a single, determined motion. He knew that the robust, potent nature of the drink was precisely what he needed in that moment to steady his nerves and fortify his resolve. The familiar burn of the alcohol as it travelled down his throat provided a fleeting sense of fortification, allowing him to steel his emotions and focus on the task at hand.

McMatters' heart raced when Lorraine approached him every fibre of his being alive with anticipation. With a burning desire, he orchestrated their encounter, his soul yearning for Lorraine's touch. As he took her drink, his fingers tingled with the promise of connection.

McMatters hand, trembling with passion, caressed her face, feeling the silken strands of her hair. Time stood still as he leaned in, his lips meeting hers in a kiss that set his world ablaze. It was tender yet fierce, a declaration of unspoken longing and fiery desire. How McMatters ached for more! His entire being cried out for Lorraine, craving a deeper, more intimate embrace. But alas, the cruel constraints of their surroundings held them back.

With a heart heavy with unfulfilled passion, he tore himself away from their heated exchange. Yet even as he moved to the far side of the sumptuous velvet sofa, his eyes never left Lorraine. Every stolen glance, every subtle gesture was charged with unspoken desire.

In this dance of restrained passion, McMatters' heart pounded with the thrill of pursuit, his soul aflame with the promise of future encounters, free from the prying eyes of the VIP lounge.

"So, Lorraine, tell me about yourself," asked McMatters trying to control himself.

"As an only child, I didn't have the benefit of growing up with siblings, which led to some challenges in my upbringing. I made my fair share of mistakes and encountered numerous wrong turns along the way.

However, a turning point came a few years later when I experienced the profound pain of heartbreak. This difficult emotional journey ultimately helped shape my character and perspective.

Determined to move forward, I took the leap of purchasing a property, which I later sold, allowing me to acquire the home where I now reside," Lorraine explained.

"Interesting summary. I'd like to hear more sometime," McMatters remarked, his curiosity piqued. He was eager to learn more about Lorraine's background and experiences. Shifting the conversation, he inquired, "But what about work? What do you do for a living?" McMatters was genuinely interested in understanding Lorraine's professional pursuits and how they might factor into the discussion.

McMatters sensed there was more to uncover, and he was determined to delve deeper and gain a more comprehensive understanding of Lorraine's life and perspectives.

"Well, as it is, I don't need to work as such. I keep my income topped up by occasionally dabbling in various endeavours, which has admittedly landed me in a situation." Lorraine admitted quietly. "However, those past mishaps are a story best saved for another occasion," she added with a wry smile, her tone conveying a sense of both resignation and a hint of mischief underlying her words.

Lorraine's financial situation afforded her a certain degree of flexibility, allowing her to selectively engage in supplemental activities to maintain her desired standard of living, although this approach had not always been without its fair share of complications and challenges.

McMatters observed Lorraine closely and detected a subtle vulnerability in her demeanour as she alluded to a concerning issue that had recently landed her in a precarious situation. He could sense this was a deeply unwelcome development for her, and his intuition led him to wonder whether it was directly connected to Detective Jackson's involvement or if it stemmed from some other source of trouble.

McMatters was determined to uncover the root of Lorraine's distress, recognising that she was likely experiencing a significant degree of unease and apprehension over the unfolding circumstances.

"So, what about you Steve? Tell me about yourself."

McMatters gathered himself and wondered how much to tell or how vague to be.

"Well, you know I'm quite a private individual, Lorraine, but if I had to summarise myself in a few words: I was raised as an only child. Unfortunately, both of my parents have passed away. This exclusive club has been a lifelong dream of mine that I've worked tirelessly to bring to fruition. Despite my inherently guarded nature, I'm immensely proud of what I've accomplished here, and I am eager to share this magnificent space with others who appreciate the finer things in life."

"So, last time we met you mentioned you had a few run ins with the police?"

"Yes, I have run into issues with law enforcement in the past, but I have managed to avoid any serious legal consequences so far. It seems to be due to the persistent efforts of one police officer who is determined to find a way to incriminate me. This officer appears to hold a preconceived notion that all club owners are the same and are engaged in illicit activities.

Despite his best attempts to set some kind of trap for me, I have thus far been able to evade his efforts to have me arrested or imprisoned. It is clear that this officer has a vendetta against me and is going to great lengths to try to find a way to take me off the streets, but I remain vigilant and will continue to defend myself against any unfounded allegations or attempts at entrapment."

"I wish I could escape it." Lorraine whispered

McMatters had undoubtedly heard Lorraine's previous statement, but he strategically chose to feign ignorance. Perceptive and attentive, McMatters had picked up on the subtle cues that suggested Lorraine was in a difficult situation and in need of assistance. Rather than directly acknowledging her struggle, he adopted a more discreet approach, recognising that Lorraine might be hesitant or uncomfortable about openly expressing her need for help. By maintaining an outward appearance of obliviousness, McMatters demonstrated a thoughtful and considerate approach, allowing Lorraine the opportunity to open and seek the support she required on her own terms.

McMatters had determined that they had engaged in a lengthy and substantive discussion, and now it was time to shift gears and return to more immediate concerns.

Recognising that Lorraine required a distraction to redirect her focus, McMatters positioned himself as the ideal individual to provide that necessary diversion, With a keen understanding of the situation. McMatters strategically changed the conversation in a new direction, prepared to offer Lorraine the distraction she sought during this pivotal moment. As Lorraine found herself seated next to McMatters, it felt almost as if fate had orchestrated their encounter. Shortly after, McMatters discreetly signalled to the bartender upstairs, ordering two drinks. Once the beverages had been delivered, McMatters couldn't help but notice that they were the only ones occupying the VIP section at that moment.

The exclusivity of their setting, combined with Lorraine's proximity, created an undeniable sense of intimacy and opportunity that seemed to hang palpably in the air around them.

McMatters' heart raced as he delicately traced his finger along the rim of his glass, the cool liquid a stark contrast to the fire burning within him. With unbridled desire, he reached for Lorraine, his touch electric against her silken skin. The air crackled with tension as his fingers danced beneath her dress, discovering her tantalising secret of no underwear. McMatters breath caught in his throat, desire coursing through his veins like liquid fire.

Lorraine's body responded to his expert touch, he dipped his finger into Lorraine's drink and slid his fingers under Lorraine's dress teasing the edge of her most delicate of areas, before gently sliding into Lorraine, her passion rising to match his own. Their eyes locked, conveying a thousand unspoken promises. The intensity of their connection was palpable, threatening to consume them both.

McMatters drained his glass, the action a silent signal that set their hearts ablaze with anticipation. Unable to contain himself any longer, McMatters rose, his body betraying his intense arousal under his trousers, McMatters grasped Lorraine's hand, their fingers intertwining with urgent need. They rushed into the cool night air out of the upstairs rear exit, the contrast only heightening their burning desire.

The sleek black car awaited them, its beige leather seats promising a sanctuary for their passion. McMatters guided Lorraine towards the car, his touch both gentle and insistent, their bodies humming with the promise of the night to come.

They drove in near silence, exchanging only a few brief words, with a few teasing touches keeping him wanting Lorraine throughout the journey. As they approached their destination, the electric gates swung open automatically, detecting the approaching car. Pulling into the designated parking space, McMatters promptly exited the car and gallantly opened the door for Lorraine, demonstrating his courteous and attentive demeanour. McMatters could sense the questions and palpable sense of wonder that Lorraine was experiencing, but now they both recognised the profound need they had for one another.

The electric intensity of their connection had grown to a fever pitch, and it yearned to be released and expressed. McMatters knew they could no longer resist or deny the powerful pull between them it had become an undeniable force that demanded to be reckoned with.

The time had come for them to surrender to the inexorable magnetism drawing them together, to finally give in to the consuming passion that had been building steadily. Neither could continue holding back; the tension had reached a breaking point and required resolution through their mutual embrace.

"Follow me, Lorraine."

Chapter Ten Part Four
McMatters Home

Lorraine was completely captivated and enthralled the moment McMatters' touch graced her skin. She knew, without a doubt, that he had claimed her, but more significantly, she had claimed him in return.

The unmistakable bulge in his trousers did not escape her notice, and the sight of it only served to heighten her growing excitement and arousal. His caress was like silk against her flesh, leaving Lorraine utterly spellbound. Never had she experienced such a tender, delicate touch, one that rendered her momentarily speechless with its gentle, sensual power. As Lorraine sat in the car with McMatters, her mind was flooded with a whirlwind of conflicting thoughts and emotions. One part of her was telling her that she had made a foolish decision by getting into a Car with someone she barely knew. The rational side of her brain warned her of the potential risks and dangers associated with such reckless behaviour.

However, the other half of her psyche simply didn't care about the consequences. Lorraine's entire being pulsed with an insatiable hunger for touch, her body now alive with the memory of that electrifying connection. The raw, untamed excitement of this new intimacy had ignited a fierce, primal desire within her, unlike anything she'd ever experienced before. She yearned desperately for more, much more of this intoxicating sensation, this forbidden ecstasy that threatened to engulf her completely. Her mind raced, a tempest of conflicting emotions.

The voice of reason whispered caution, but it was drowned out by the deafening roar of passion, urging her to throw herself headlong into reckless abandon. Lorraine found herself utterly powerless. Her better judgment lay shattered at her feet as the irresistible temptation before her beckoned, promising unimaginable pleasures. She trembled on the precipice of surrender, every fibre of her being crying out for the exquisite touch that would set her free.

As Lorraine approached the property, guided by Steve McMatters, she was utterly spellbound by its breath-taking grandeur. The sheer scale and exquisite design of the house left Lorraine absolutely mesmerised, her expectations completely shattered by the unparalleled splendour before her eyes.

Every inch of the property, from its imposing size to its meticulously crafted architecture and immaculately groomed grounds, was a testament to unrivalled beauty and sophistication.

As McMatters swung open the door, Lorraine's senses were overwhelmed by an interior so magnificent, so utterly beyond comprehension, that she was transported to a realm of pure amazement!

It was a symphony of luxury that played upon every sense, far surpassing even the wildest dreams of splendour! Each painstakingly crafted detail, from the most delicate architectural embellishments to the sumptuous furnishings, contributed to an atmosphere of such overwhelming magnificence that it defied description.

Lorraine found herself completely and utterly captivated, lost in a world of unparalleled beauty and elegance that mirrored the awe her mother must have felt when beholding the impressive scale and refinement of Lorraine's own abode. It was a moment of pure, transcendent wonder, etched forever in the annals of her memory!

McMatters abrupt dismissal of the house tour caught her off guard. With a heart-pounding intensity, he seized her hand, their fingers intertwining as they raced up the majestic staircase, their footsteps echoing with the rhythm of their beating hearts.

Breathless, they burst into his private sanctuary, a room so magnificent it stole the very air from her lungs. The bed, a colossal masterpiece, dominated the space like a throne fit for royalty, its ornate frame reaching towards the heavens.

And there, sprawled across its vast expanse, was a vision that set her soul ablaze hundreds upon hundreds of delicate petals, their soft pinks and pure whites creating a symphony of colour that sang to her very core. Lorraine's eyes drank in the sight, her heart racing with unbridled excitement.

The cloud-like mattress beckoned her, promising to envelop her in its luxurious embrace, while the petals whispered tales of passion and romance. This wasn't just a room; it was a dreamscape, a fantasy brought to vivid, pulsating life.

Every fibre of her being tingled with anticipation, her senses overwhelmed by the intoxicating blend of grandeur and intimacy. Surrounded by such breath-taking beauty, Lorraine felt alive, truly alive. Her spirit soaring with the promise of the unforgettable experiences that surely awaited her in this enchanted realm of desire.

McMatters swept Lorraine into his arms, their bodies melding together in a fiery embrace. His lips crashed onto hers with unbridled hunger, igniting a spark that blazed through their veins. Consumed by desire, he trailed searing kisses down the elegant slope of her neck, each touch sending electric shivers across her skin. McMatters' passionate caresses were a symphony of sensation, expertly orchestrated to fan the flames of Lorraine's longing. His ardent devotion left her gasping, her heart racing as she burned with an insatiable need for his fervent touch.

Every movement… every breath… was charged with raw, unrestrained passion, their bodies moving in perfect, sensual harmony. McMatters' hands traced the alluring curves of Lorraine's body, his touch electric as he gently turned her.

Steve's lips found her neck, each kiss a spark igniting their passion. With exquisite care, his fingers danced up her spine, seeking the zipper that held her dress in place. Slowly, deliberately, he unveiled her, his desire palpable in every movement. Lorraine's choice of attire was a masterpiece of seduction.

The amethyst velvet fell away to reveal a stunning purple satin corset, hugging her curves in all the right places. McMatters' breath caught as he recalled their earlier encounter, knowing the tantalising secret that lay beneath nothing but Lorraine's bare, silky skin. The air crackled with anticipation; their bodies alive with desire. Every touch, every breath was charged with an intoxicating mix of lust and tenderness.

They were lost in a world of their own making, where passion reigned supreme and inhibitions melted away like morning mist.

Lorraine's dress fell gracefully to the floor, pooling around her feet as she turned to face him, her gaze locked with his.

Driven by desire, she reached out and began to caress him, her fingers tracing a tantalising path from the top of his body. With nimble movements, she deftly removed his tie, the silky fabric slipping through her fingers. Continuing her exploration, Lorraine shrugged off his jacket, the well-tailored garment finding its way to a nearby chair.

Then, as their lips met in a passionate kiss, her nimble fingers made quick work of the buttons on his shirt, slowly revealing the toned physique hidden beneath.

Lorraine's hands roamed sensually across her McMatters chest, caressing his bare skin with a delicate, teasing touch. She lightly traced the contours of Steve's muscular torso, pausing to gently tease and flick his hardened nipples between her fingertips.

Lorraine then lowered her head, her soft lips enveloping one nipple in a slow, sensual sucking motion, her tongue swirling and flicking against the sensitive flesh. As Lorraine ministered to his chest, her nimble fingers simultaneously worked to deftly undo the buttons on Steve's trousers, gradually exposing more of his body to her hungry gaze and wandering caresses.

At this juncture, McMatters was eagerly anticipating Lorraine's arrival, his arousal clearly visible through the thin fabric of his boxers.

It had been quite some time since Steve had felt this level of anticipation and excitement. Steve found himself consumed by a ravenous desire for Lorraine's company and affection.

McMatters ardently embraced Lorraine, his heart pounding as she entwined her legs around him. Their bodies melded together in a passionate fusion, the heat between them electric and intoxicating. Steve revelled in the exquisite sensation of Lorraine's soft, warm skin against his, their intimate connection igniting a fire that consumed them both.

Every touch, every breath was charged with an intense, almost overwhelming desire that threatened to engulf them entirely. Gently, Steve laid Lorraine down on the bed and parted her legs, exposing her to his hungry gaze.

Steve then leaned in and captured her lips in a passionate, sensual kiss, his hands caressing her curves. Slowly, Steve trailed a path of feather-light kisses down the length of her captivating form, pausing to lavish attention on her most sensitive bundle of nerves.

As his skilled tongue began teasing and caressing her passionate body, Lorraine's breath quickened and she let out a deep, pleasured moan, Lorraine's body surrendering to the delicious sensations. McMatters could sense Lorraine's eagerness and willingness to engage in this intimacy. With a delicate and considerate approach, Steve gradually and tenderly entered her, establishing a slow, rhythmic cadence that elicited excited, pleasured cries from Lorraine. Their bodies moved in perfect synchronization, the shared sensations of their passionate encounter evoking joyful, gratified moans of ecstasy from them both.

Both Steve and Lorraine experienced a powerful, simultaneous climax, which vividly illustrated the profound intensity and intimacy of their passionate connection. In that electrifying moment, their bodies intertwined in a breath-taking dance of passion! Every touch, every breath, every heartbeat pulsed with an intensity that defied description. As they reached the pinnacle of ecstasy together, it was as if the universe itself paused to witness their profound connection.

This wasn't just physical pleasure; it was a transcendent experience that spoke volumes about the incredible bond they shared. Their synchronised release was like a supernova of emotion, radiating the depth of their understanding and the strength of their unity. In that instant, they weren't just two individuals, they were one heart, one soul, united in a love so powerful it could move mountains!

Chapter Ten Part Five
Jackson

Detective Jackson was visibly agitated and unsettled as he kept a watchful eye on Lorraine's current location the lavish, palatial residence of the affluent McMatters family. This opulent home, a stark contrast to Jackson's own modest abode, served as a constant reminder of the socioeconomic divide that separated him from Lorraine's world. Determined to get a better vantage point for his surveillance, Jackson carefully scanned his surroundings, ensuring no one was in the immediate vicinity.

Seizing the opportunity, he swiftly exited his car and dashed across to the property, taking cover behind the thick shrubbery lining the boundary wall. Crouching low, he raised his binoculars and peered intently over the imposing wall, his gaze fixed on the luxurious residence and the activities unfolding within, Jackson didn't think of himself as a peeping tom.

Detective Jackson observed intently as Lorraine approached and entered the McMatters' residence, with McMatters himself hastily ushering Lorraine inside. Carefully scanning the building, Jackson located the specific bedroom room where the two individuals had convened.

Jackson had never instructed Lorraine to get so intimately close to McMatters, and he now deeply regretted orchestrating their encounter. Jackson's heart raced with an uncontrollable passion for Lorraine, a fire burning deep within his soul. Every fibre of his being ached to hold her, to experience the exquisite sensation of her lips meeting his in a fervent embrace. The detective's mind swirled with vivid fantasies, imagining the intoxicating pleasure of exploring every inch of her body. This all-consuming desire had taken root in Jackson's very core, leaving him breathless with longing. Jackson's heart raced with an all-consuming desire for Lorraine, his every thought and breath devoted to the dream of their passionate union. Jackson yearned to merge their very essences in a fiery embrace that would ignite the cosmos with its intensity.

From his vantage point, Detective Jackson's eyes were riveted to the window, taking in every detail of Lorraine's form. As McMatters slowly revealed her beauty body, piece by tantalising piece, Jackson felt a primal surge of longing course through his body. Each discarded garment fanned the flames of his desire,

Jackson's body responding with unbridled enthusiasm.

The sight of Lorraine's bare skin sent shockwaves of arousal through him, his erection straining urgently against his trousers, a physical manifestation of the burning passion that consumed him.

Overcome by his growing arousal, Detective Jackson hastily unzipped his pants, not out of a desire for comfort, but rather to indulge in the sensations coursing through his body, he had to release.

Lorraine's attire has triggered an intense and potentially dangerous situation. Jackson's thoughts are completely overtaken by inappropriate desires. The detective caressed his arousal with increasing fervour, his movements driven by an insatiable craving for Lorraine. At this point, he had become completely engrossed in his own escalating desires, Jackson didn't notice he was being watched, he was unable to resist the temptation that Lorraine's presence has provoked.

Chapter Ten Part Six
The Watcher Becomes the Watched

Jarvis was taken aback and deeply troubled by Detective Jackson's alarming shift in behaviour. It appeared that the seasoned investigator had abandoned his professional protocols and ethical standards, veering dangerously off course. Rather than directing his team to conduct the standard surveillance operations, Jackson had seemingly gone rogue, adopting the tactics of an obsessive stalker.

This sudden and concerning change in his conduct raised serious questions about his motivations and the potential consequences of his actions. Jarvis knew he would need to intervene quickly to understand the situation and prevent further unethical or illegal activities from occurring under Jackson's direction. Jarvis closely documented the rapidly unfolding events by capturing a series of detailed photographs.

He recognised the highly concerning and sensitive nature of this situation, and knew that his supervisor, McMatters, would need this critical information as soon as possible. Jarvis was taken aback by the aggressive actions being taken by Detective Jackson, who appeared to be pursuing the matter with an unusually intense and determined approach, even though he did not seem to be officially on duty now. The gravity of the circumstances and Jackson's seemingly excessive involvement sparked Jarvis's curiosity and concern, leaving him to wonder just how serious and potentially dangerous this situation had become.

Jarvis understood that he might have to step in and interact with Detective Jackson at some point, though he sincerely hoped such an eventuality would never come to pass. However, Jarvis was fully prepared to take all necessary actions, no matter how challenging or unconventional, if the situation ultimately demanded his intervention.

He was steadfastly committed to doing whatever it took to address the matter at hand, even if it meant putting himself in a difficult or uncomfortable position. Jarvis knew the stakes were high, and he was unwavering in his determination to be ready to act decisively if called upon to do so.

Chapter Eleven
Unwanted Attention

Jarvis waits patiently in the Club's office, anticipating the arrival of his boss, McMatters. As he passes the time, Jarvis pours himself a drink from the decanter of Rum situated on his side of the room. McMatter's area is distinguished by a desk, drawers, filing cabinet, and the fine whisky, which is reserved for the executive. McMatters, being a man of refined tastes, has no favourite when it comes to single malt; he simply appreciates the quality and complexity of this sophisticated spirit. In contrast, Jarvis's side of the office is marked by his own desk, a comfortable sofa, and a decanter containing his preferred rum selections.

Unlike McMatters, Jarvis has developed a discerning palate, favouring specific brands such as Rum bullion, Captains Tiki Rum, and even the more unconventional Deadman's Fingers, which had become popular lately . This subtle difference in their drink preferences serves as one of the few distinguishing factors between the two of them, highlighting their individual tastes and preferences. McMatters arrives at the club around 7pm.

"Evening Jarvis."

"Hi boss"

"How's the mission going?"

"I'm worried. I believe Lorraine has a problem, and now we have a problem."

"Go on…"

"When you and Lorraine went to your place, Detective Jackson followed, clearly intent on covertly observing your activities. At first, he remained in his car, maintaining a watchful presence. Soon after, he emerged from his car and moved towards the nearby bushes, leading you to assume he had stepped away to attend to a personal need.

Yet, this was not the case. Unbeknownst to the detective, I was watching him. From my vantage point, I witnessed Jackson peering through his binoculars while engaging in inappropriate and unethical conduct. Recognising the opportunity to capture this compromising moment of him having his release! I quickly sprang into action, meticulously documenting the scene with a series of incriminating photographs."

"I see…"

Jarvis watched his boss, Mr. McMatters, pace back and forth across the office, clearly agitated. The tense situation was palpable as Jarvis observed McMatters pour himself a stiff drink, likely to calm his nerves. The boss's restless movements and the sound of the glass clinking against the decanter suggested a level of stress and unease that had taken hold of the room.

"Boss, I have a proposal. This behaviour Detective Jackson is pursuing violates police policy and could be misconduct. We should compile evidence, including any incriminating photos, and forward it to his superior. This will allow us to hold Detective Jackson accountable. Taking this stand sends a clear message that it won't be tolerated."

"Who's his boss?"

"Sergeant Cole, from what I've gathered. He is known to be a strict adherent to rules and procedures within the department. Based on the intelligence I've obtained; he is widely regarded as someone who rigidly enforces protocol and insists on absolute compliance with established guidelines and policies. Sergeant Cole is renowned for his unwavering commitment to upholding the letter of the law and ensuring that all operations strictly follow the predetermined processes and regulations. His reputation precedes him as an officer who places a premium on order, discipline, and meticulous attention to detail above all else."

"OK, let's try this first but if this doesn't work, and he doesn't back off, he will need a different kind of lesson".

Jarvis, the diligent right-hand man, promptly acknowledges the request with a nod. He then proceeds to take a sip from his beverage, allowing the refreshing liquid to revitalise him, before turning his full attention to the task at hand. With a focused demeanour, Jarvis sets about meticulously sorting through the relevant files, determined to organise the necessary documentation for Sergeant Cole in a thorough and efficient manner.

Chapter Eleven Part Two
Sergeant Cole

Sergeant Cole hurriedly made his way into the office, having rushed through his morning routine without stopping to have breakfast. The pressing demands of his schedule had left him little time to properly tend to his basic needs before the start of the workday. As a result, Sergeant Cole found himself arriving at his desk feeling slightly frazzled and uncomfortably hungry, a combination that was sure to make the tasks ahead more challenging than they needed to be. Nevertheless, he quickly set about addressing the pressing matters at hand, determined to power through the morning despite his growling stomach and harried state of mind.

"Wendy, could you be a doll and grab me some breakfast? One of those amazing toasties would be super!"

"Of course I will, what would you like on your toastie?"

"Door stopper bread, double egg, sausage, cheese and Bacon please Wendy."

"Coming right up!"

Robert (Sergeant Cole) was absolutely captivated by his beloved toasties, which he typically indulged in as a special Friday treat. Even though he had already enjoyed one just the day before, he knew his appetite simply wouldn't hold out until dinnertime without something more to sustain him.

The temptation of those warm, crispy, and delightfully Savoury toasted sandwiches was simply too strong for him to resist, as they had become a cherished ritual that he eagerly anticipated each week. Despite having just recently satisfied his craving, the allure of those toasties was simply too powerful, and Robert knew he would have to succumb to the temptation once again.

The parcel sitting on Sergeant Coles desk immediately caught his attention, as it was wrapped in an unusual black paper rather than the more typical white or brown packaging. This stark contrast against the normal packaging colours made the parcel stand out and piqued his curiosity.

Parcels wrapped in this atypical black paper were out of the ordinary, sparking his interest and prompting him to investigate further. The distinctive wrapping material was enough to divert his focus from his other tasks, as it represented a noticeable deviation from the standard packaging he was accustomed to encountering on his desk. Robert knew it had gone through security checks.

Robert poured his freshly made coffee and opened the parcel. Inside the parcel was a file with a ribbon wrapped around it. Attached was a note.

For the attention of
Sergeant Cole
Private & Confidential

Robert had a bad feeling about this and wondered where it had come from. The absence of postage marks on the wrapping suggested it was hand-delivered to the police station. Wendy arrived with his toastie, so he put the file aside and positioned a napkin, tucking it into his collar. After he had eaten his toastie, he felt ready to examine the file and discover why it had been hand-delivered to him.

FAO Sergeant Cole

I am writing to bring to your attention the highly concerning and unacceptable behaviour exhibited by one of your detectives, Detective Jackson. Based on the substantial evidence we have gathered, Detective Jackson has been engaged in a pattern of egregious misconduct, including public indecent exposure, peeping with sexual intent, stalking, and performing sexual acts in public view.

Specifically, we have obtained photographic evidence documenting two separate incidents, at different locations and on distinct dates where Detective Jackson was clearly seen committing these deplorable acts. The visual evidence is irrefutable and leaves no doubt as to his guilt.

Given the severity and criminal nature of these transgressions, I strongly urge you to take immediate disciplinary action. Detective Jackson's actions represent a profound betrayal of the public trust and are completely antithetical to the standards of conduct expected from a member of law enforcement.

Allowing such behaviour to go unchecked would be a grave disservice to the community you serve and would tarnish the reputation of your department. I trust you will view this matter with the utmost seriousness it deserves and take swift, appropriate measures to address Detective Jackson's egregious misconduct. The well-being and safety of the public must be the top priority.

A prompt and thorough investigation followed by just disciplinary action is of the utmost importance. There are deep concerns regarding Detective Jackson's psychological well-being that stem directly from the nature of the public offenses he has committed.

Given the severity and sensitive nature of these incidents, I felt it would be prudent to bring this matter to your attention before the situation potentially escalates further.

As the supervising authority, you are in the best position to address Detective Jackson's problematic behaviour and underlying psychological issues in a timely and appropriate manner. Proactive intervention is crucial to ensure these public offenses

do not continue or worsen, which could have
significant consequences both for the individual
officer and the department.

I wanted to provide you with this opportunity to
assess the situation and determine the most effective
course of action to effectively manage Detective
Jackson's conduct and safeguard the public trust.
Early intervention and access to necessary resources
or support may be instrumental in preventing further
incidents and mitigating any broader impacts.

Sergeant Cole leaned back in his chair; his brow furrowed with a growing sense of concern as he scrutinised the incriminating photographic evidence before him. There was no denying the clarity of the images they clearly showed Detective Jackson at the scene, leaving no room for ambiguity or doubt. Cole knew this revelation would have serious implications, both for the investigation and for the reputation of his colleague. Cole realised that he could no longer ignore the damning visual proof.

"Wendy!" Sergeant Cole shouts.

Wendy enters the office and shuts the door.

"Find Detective Jackson, and tell him he's to go to the boardroom and wait for me to arrive."

Wendy left to track Detective Jackson down, meanwhile Sergeant Cole knows what must be done and doesn't like it one bit, he picks the phone up.

"Internal affairs, please."

Chapter Twelve
Lorraine

Lorraine sauntered home at 10am, her outfit still consisting of the same dress she had worn the previous evening. Her typically well-groomed appearance was slightly dishevelled, with her hair displaying a subtle disarray that suggested she had not had the opportunity to properly attend to her look that morning.

The rumpled state of her attire and tousled hairstyle conveyed the impression that Lorraine had likely arrived directly from a late night out.

"And what time do you call this?"

"I'm an adult, Mum, and it's my house."

"Even so, you could have called. I was worried."

"Sorry, I'm not used to anyone being here."

Lorraine hurriedly made her way upstairs, her mind racing as she turned on the shower. Sitting down on the bed, she began methodically undressing, her movements betraying a sense of distraction. Her thoughts kept drifting back to the previous night, when she had shared an intimate encounter with McMatters.

Lorraine was still reeling from the sheer intensity and electrifying sensations that had overwhelmed her during their passionate tryst experiences she had never encountered before, leaving her in a state of profound shock and disbelief. The remarkable abilities of the individual known as McMatters were truly awe inspiring. His prowess was so exceptional that it defied description, leaving the observer struggling to fully comprehend the sheer magnitude of his accomplishments. The number of profound and deeply satisfying experiences they both had was simply staggering, leaving them utterly overwhelmed and unable to keep track of the sheer intensity and frequency of the ecstatic sensations they elicited. The feats of McMatters were nothing short of magnificent, transcending the bounds of ordinary human capacity and elevating the realm of physical intimacy to unprecedented heights, Lorraine wondered why she hadn't had this experience before in any relationship.

Lorraine stepped into the shower, deliberately taking her time to ensure a thorough cleansing. She meticulously lathered her skin, working the fragrant soap into a rich, creamy lather that left her feeling refreshed and silky soft to the touch. Allowing the warm water to cascade over her body, Lorraine lingered, savouring the soothing sensation as she methodically cleaned every inch, determined to emerge from the shower feeling rejuvenated and completely refreshed.

After stepping out of the shower, Lorraine meticulously dried her hair, running the towel through the strands to absorb the moisture. She then proceeded to straighten her hair, skilfully gliding the heated styling tool from root to tip. As Lorraine's shiny, sleek tresses caught the warm glow of the sunlight streaming in through the window, they seemed to shimmer and reflect the ambient illumination, lending an irresistible lustre and vitality to her appearance.

Lorraine sat at her vanity mirror, absentmindedly running a brush through her hair as she became lost in thought, replaying the events of the night repeatedly in her mind.

Unbeknownst to her, her mother stood quietly in the doorway, observing Lorraine's pensive state with a subtle look of amusement. Lorraine was so deeply immersed in her daydream that she failed to notice her mother's presence, her focus entirely consumed by the vivid recollections playing out in her imagination.

"Who is he?"

Lorraine's daydream was suddenly shattered as she became acutely aware of her mother's presence in the doorway. Snapping back to reality, Lorraine felt a sense of confusion wash over her, unsure of how long her mother had been standing there observing her. Adding to her bewilderment, Lorraine realised that her mother had spoken, but she had completely missed the words, her mind having been lost in the reverie just moments before.

Struggling to regain her focus, Lorraine now found herself in the awkward position of needing to acknowledge her mother's statement, despite having no recollection of what had been said, Lorraine must have had a blank expression on her face.

"Who is he?"

"I'm not sure what you are on about…"

"I've been standing here twenty minutes. Not only could you not see me, but you didn't hear me either, so who is he?"

Lorraine found herself in a state of uncertainty, unsure whether her recent intimate encounter with McMatters was merely a fleeting one-night stand or held the potential for something more meaningful. Deep down, Lorraine yearned for a deeper connection, though she acknowledged the likelihood that their relationship may not extend beyond that single passionate night.

Amidst this internal conflict, Lorraine's thoughts also turned to Detective Jackson, a figure of concern in her mind. The lack of a call from him, which was highly unusual, left Lorraine wondering about his intentions and the implications of her planned visit to the club later that evening. She hoped that perhaps he would reach out the following day, shedding light on the situation and offering clarity on the path forward or better yet, Lorraine hoped Detective Jackson would let her go and leave her alone.

Lorraine carefully selected her attire for the evening, meticulously planning each element to create a stylish and alluring ensemble. She had chosen a mid-blue satin skater dress, which would elegantly accentuate her figure and drape gracefully over her curves.

To complement the dress, she paired it with a set of chic black satin high heels that would elongate her legs and add a touch of sophistication to her look. Completing the outfit, Lorraine added a matching black satin handbag, ensuring a cohesive and polished aesthetic. Lorraine's careful curation of this outfit was driven by her desire to impress her companion, McMatters.

Lorraine hoped that not only would he appreciate the refined and fashionable exterior she had crafted, but that he would also be captivated by what lay beneath the carefully selected garments. Lorraine's attention to detail and strategic styling choices were all part of her calculated effort to allure and captivate McMatters, leaving a lasting impression that would heighten the anticipation and excitement of their evening together.

Chapter Thirteen
The Board Room

The boardroom was strategically located at the far end of the Police Station on the fourth floor, ensuring maximum privacy and confidentiality. The use of soundproof glass panels around the room guaranteed that any sensitive information discussed within would be completely shielded from prying ears, making this space an ideal setting for the high-level discussions that required complete discretion.

The centrepiece of the boardroom was a large, oval shaped table, crafted from sturdy pine, providing ample space for the key people to gather and deliberate. Apart from the chairs surrounding the table, the room was intentionally devoid of any other furniture, creating a minimalist and focused environment that would allow the participants to concentrate solely on the matters at hand without distractions or unnecessary clutter.

Detective Jackson was the first to arrive at the boardroom, feeling puzzled as to why he had been summoned there. As he waited, a growing sense of apprehension began to set in. Fifteen minutes ticked by, and still no one else had joined him. Finally, after a full twenty minutes had elapsed, Sergeant Cole arrived, adding to Jackson's mounting unease about the reason for this unexpected meeting.

"Why am I here Sarg?"

"All will be revealed shortly Jackson."

"Who are we waiting for?"

"Don't worry, not much longer…"

Ten minutes after Sergeant Cole had arrived, Detective Jackson noticed three individuals approaching the boardroom, none of whom he had encountered previously. Carefully observing their movements and behaviour, the seasoned detective maintained a vigilant eye, prepared to assess the situation and determine if these unexpected visitors posed any potential threat, or held relevant information pertaining to the ongoing investigation.

With years of experience honing his investigative skills, Jackson remained alert, ready to engage the newcomers and gather any clues or insights that could aid in unravelling the mystery at hand.

"Welcome! Please take a seat." said Sergeant Cole

"And you must be Sergeant Cole?" shaking the Sergeant's hand,

"Detective Jackson nice to meet you" Detective Jackson offered a hand to the mysterious visitor

The other two were quiet, establishing that the one talking was the one in charge

"I am Alison Stevens. With me, I have Claire James-Jameson and Neil Glover. We are from Internal Affairs. This meeting will be recorded while we lay out the situation and the complaint made. At this stage, I won't be asking any questions. After lunch, we will start the questioning process. Detective Jackson, you are free to bring a representative with you if you feel one is required when the questioning starts. Do you understand, Detective Jackson?"

"Yes!"

"Okay, so it has been brought to our attention that on two occasions, which we are currently aware of, acts have been performed in public: one in a car and the other in a bush. The acts in question fall under public indecency, sexual acts in a public place, and exposure. Are you following so far, Detective Jackson?"

As Jackson listened, he could feel the blood draining from his face, his heart pounding in his chest. How could anyone possibly know what he had done? He had been so careful, so meticulous in covering his tracks. Surely, they couldn't be talking about him ... it had to be someone else they were referring to, someone else who had committed the heinous acts he was desperately trying to conceal.

Jackson's mind raced, searching for any possible explanation that didn't incriminate him, but the growing sense of dread and panic threatened to consume him. Jackson had to remain calm, collected, and convincing, lest his guilty conscience betray him.

"A file was sent to Sergeant Cole this morning. The file, from an unknown sender, contained a letter and two envelopes. Each envelope held the date of the offense and evidential photos"

Jackson looked at Sergeant Cole and noticed he had a dismayed look on his face. Cole refused to look at Jackson. "They are talking about me! Jackson thought, they know."

"We're going to stop for lunch now. I advise you to bring a representative with you when we return, Detective Jackson."

"End of first stage interview. Adjourned for lunch. Reconvening at 2pm"

Sergeant Cole, Detective Jackson, and the three individuals all rose from their seats and proceeded to exit the boardroom in silence. Sergeant Cole glanced over at Detective Jackson, but found himself at a loss for words, the gravity of the situation weighing heavily upon him.

As Sergeant Cole and the other three departed the room, Detective Jackson was left alone, his head buried in his hands as Jackson wrestled with the difficult decision of determining who he could trust to represent his interests in this delicate matter.

The air was thick with tension and uncertainty, as Detective Jackson grappled with the complexities of the unfolding events and contemplated his next course of action.

Chapter Thirteen Part Two
Sergeant Cole

Sergeant Cole was absolutely infuriated that Detective Jackson's actions had made him appear incompetent and foolish. The gravity of the situation demanded that he take immediate and decisive action. As the first step, Sergeant Cole knew he had to bring in Internal Affairs as an impartial, external entity to thoroughly investigate the matter. This would ensure a fair and unbiased assessment of what had transpired. Additionally, Sergeant Cole recognised the necessity of involving the Human Resources department to attend the subsequent meeting with him.

This would safeguard the proper protocols and interests of both the police force and Detective Jackson, providing a balanced and professional approach to addressing the sensitive issues at hand. Sergeant Cole took the initiative and made the necessary call to the HR department, ensuring that an appropriate representative would be present at the upcoming meeting. With this administrative task handled, he then turned his attention to drafting a series of critical letters that would need to be addressed. The first letter was an official suspension notice for Detective Jackson.

This suspension would remain in effect for the duration of the ongoing investigation, allowing for a thorough and impartial review of the situation. Recognising the gravity of the circumstances, Sergeant Cole also prepared a contingency letter detailing the potential for a revocation of Detective

Jackson's title and termination of his employment contract.

This document was placed in a secure file, to be utilised only if the worst-case scenario materialised. Finally, Sergeant Cole composed a public statement regarding Detective Jackson's contract status. This communique would be reviewed by the HR team before being released, ensuring that the information shared was accurate and appropriately handled. Throughout this process, Sergeant Cole maintained his steadfast commitment to handling the matter directly, without delegating these critical tasks to others.

His unwavering dedication to addressing the situation personally underscored his sense of responsibility and his determination to see the matter through with the utmost care and diligence.

Wendy, concerned for her friend's wellbeing, thoughtfully brought in a warm coffee and a nourishing chicken and bacon sub roll, hoping the sustenance would provide some comfort. However, despite the kind gesture, Sergeant Cole found himself struggling to overcome the gnawing sense of worry and unease that had taken hold.

Though his body craved the sustenance, his stomach churned with anxiety, making it difficult for him to fully enjoy the meal Wendy had so considerately provided. The detective's mind was consumed by the pressing issues at hand, leaving him unable to fully

Savour the small kindness extended his way during this time of distress.

Chapter Fourteen
The Pub

Jarvis, the seasoned commander, had meticulously orchestrated the deployment of his teams to ensure comprehensive coverage and surveillance of the various criminal elements operating within the city. With a keen eye for strategy and an unwavering commitment to his mission, Jarvis had divided his forces into specialised units, each tasked with monitoring and gathering intelligence on the different factions vying for power.

Team Alpha was assigned to the day shift Lorraine watch, while Team Bravo took on the evening shift, providing around the clock vigilance over this critical location. Team Charlie, known for their investigative prowess, had been dispatched to monitor the activities of Detective Jackson during the day, with Team Delta taking over the evening shift to maintain a continuous presence.

Recognising the emergence of a new crime family, the Santos, Jarvis had deployed Team Echo to closely observe their movements and activities, determined to stay one step ahead of their burgeoning operations. Meanwhile, Team Foxtrot had been entrusted with the evening shift, ensuring that no suspicious behaviour went unnoticed.

The Bennetts, a long-established crime family known for their ruthless approach, were not overlooked by Jarvis. Teams Gastro and Hailstorm had been assigned to monitor their activities, providing Jarvis with a comprehensive understanding of the shifting power dynamics within the criminal underworld. Jarvis's meticulous planning and strategic deployment of his teams demonstrated his exceptional leadership skills, and his unwavering commitment to maintaining control over the complex web of criminal activities that threatened the city's stability.

With a keen eye for detail and a deep understanding of the players involved, Jarvis was determined to stay ahead of the game. Foxtrot, a key team, reported in early this morning with updates on the rapidly escalating situation involving the Santos crime family. Although Foxtrot's team was not the direct target of the incident, one of Jarvis's associates was severely injured in the altercation.

It appears the Bennetts, a rival criminal organisation, carried out the attack after the Santos group encroached on their territory and interests. The Bennetts are primarily involved in the trafficking of cocaine and cannabis, while the Santos family specialises in the arms trade and the distribution of high-end luxury vehicles.

When the Santos decided to expand their operations into the cannabis market, the Bennetts perceived this as a direct threat to their established criminal enterprises and retaliated swiftly and violently.

The resulting clash was a chaotic and turbulent scene, underscoring the intense rivalries and tensions that exist between these powerful crime families as they vie for dominance and control over lucrative illicit markets.

The Bennetts, a notorious local family, stormed into The Birch, is the main pub of the Santos territory, launching a vicious assault on anyone and everyone in their path.

Blood splattered the pub walls, pooled on the floor and sprayed the ceiling. In response, the rival Santos clan immediately opened fire, unleashing a hail of bullets that turned the establishment into a chaotic scene of bloodshed and chaos, pools of blood and bodies lay all around the pub floor and chairs.

The escalating violence soon attracted the attention of the authorities, much to the anger and frustration of Jarvis, the powerful underworld figure who secretly controls both families.

Jarvis, infuriated by the fact that one of his trusted associates had been seriously injured in the melee, now finds himself in a precarious position, as the delicate balance of power he has carefully maintained has been shattered by this latest outbreak of open hostility between the warring families.

Jarvis is a shadowy, elusive figure who operates in the criminal underworld, maintaining a low profile and avoiding direct involvement in the affairs of his organisation.

Jarvis' meetings with the leaders of various crime families are conducted in absolute secrecy, and his punishments for transgressions are swift and decisive. This air of mystery and unpredictability is precisely why none of the major crime families dare to cross Jarvis or his crew.

Now, however, Jarvis finds himself enraged after one of his trusted associates was injured due to the actions of both the Bennetts and a Santos the crime families.

The Bennetts will undoubtedly come to regret the day they set foot in that fateful pub, without his permission, for Jarvis is a formidable adversary who does not take kindly to such affronts against his organisation and his people.

Chapter Fifteen
Internal Affairs

Karen from Human Resources, along with Sergeant Cole and Internal Affairs division team, had held a private, closed-door meeting to thoroughly discuss and deliberate the status and fate of Detective Jackson. This high level, confidential gathering represented a critical juncture in the investigation and decision-making process surrounding the detective's conduct and standing within the department.

The presence of both HR and Internal Affairs personnel underscored the gravity of the situation and the need for a comprehensive, impartial review. As key stakeholders, they would carefully examine all relevant evidence and information to determine the appropriate course of action regarding Detective Jackson's future role and standing within the police force.

This private meeting provided a forum for the key decision-makers to engage in candid, uninterrupted discussions. This allowed them to meticulously analyse the details of the case, consider potential mitigating or aggravating factors, and ultimately reach a well-informed, justified conclusion.

The outcome of this meeting would undoubtedly have significant implications for Detective Jackson's career trajectory and the overall integrity of the department.

"Sergeant Cole, what are your thoughts on the events with regards to Detective Jackson?"

"I find it truly unbelievable that Detective Jackson, who has served as a detective for the past seven years without any prior complaints or issues coming to light, would engage in such egregious behaviour. However, the fact that he has openly admitted to his actions leaves little room for doubt. Given the severity of the situation, I firmly believe that he should be immediately suspended from duty without pay until a full investigation can be conducted.

The evidence against him appears to be quite damning, and if these allegations were levelled against anyone else, they would have almost certainly faced arrest and prosecution by this point. The double standard at play here is deeply troubling and undermines the principles of justice and accountability that our law enforcement system is meant to uphold.

This case highlights the critical need for rigorous oversight, transparency, and consistent application of the law, regardless of an individual's position or tenure within the department. Anything less would be a grave injustice and a betrayal of the public's trust. I strongly urge the relevant authorities to take swift and decisive action to address this matter in a fair and impartial manner."

"Karen, as Human Resources, what are your views?"

"He has taken responsibility for his actions and has acknowledged his wrongdoing. However, he is struggling to control his impulses, particularly when it comes to the situation involving Lorraine. To address this concerning behaviour effectively, I would strongly recommend that he undergo an extensive course of intensive therapy for a period of at least six months. During this time, I believe it would be prudent for him to receive half of his regular pay while the investigation into the matter remains ongoing.

This approach would provide him with the professional support and resources needed to work through the underlying issues driving his actions, while also ensuring that he is held accountable and can make the necessary changes to his conduct. Only through a comprehensive therapeutic intervention can we be confident that he will develop the self-control and behavioural modifications required to prevent similar incidents from occurring in the future."

All three from the Internal Affairs division huddled together, speaking in hushed, conspiratorial tones as they engaged in a private discussion. The low volume of their voices and furtive body language suggested they were sharing sensitive information or coordinating a covert operation, intentionally keeping their conversation out of earshot.

The secretive nature of their exchange hinted at the discreet and delicate nature of the matters they were addressing within the internal investigative unit.

Finally, the Internal Affairs division separated and began to outline their decision.

"Based on the circumstances presented, we firmly believe that a comprehensive one-year therapy program, accompanied by a period of reduced pay during the ongoing investigation, would be the most appropriate course of action. Furthermore, we recommend that Detective Jackson be demoted from his Detective rank and reassigned to the position of a Police Constable on light duties until he has successfully completed the entirety of the recommended therapy. This multifaceted approach will not only address the underlying issues but also ensure a structured path for the officer to regain their full professional capabilities. Do we all concur that this is the best way forward?"

The meeting attendees unanimously agreed to the proposal, with a resounding chorus of affirmative responses echoing throughout the room. With consensus achieved, the chairperson then declared the meeting adjourned, signalling the successful conclusion of the day's discussions and the collective decision-making process.

Chapter Sixteen
Sweep

McMatters waited silently, the exclusive VIP section of the club, remains closed for a few more hours. However, Jarvis, accompanied by four of his trusted associates, was working their way through the club. McMatters, being familiar with Jarvis and his men, recognises their presence as a clear indication that they are here to conduct a thorough sweep of the premises.

The strategic positioning of this VIP enclave, separate from the main club, suggests that the primary venue must be free of any unwanted surveillance devices or listening equipment, ensuring the privacy and security of their operations. As Jarvis's men meticulously sweep the premises, Jarvis takes the opportunity to pour himself and McMatters a stiff drink.

However, Jarvis is determined to maintain complete discretion on this sensitive matter until the entire club has been thoroughly cleaned and secured.

"Shall we move to the office?"

"Indeed!"

Jarvis' security team is conducting a thorough sweep of the premises. This swift and coordinated operation ensures the workplace remains secure and free from any potential threats or disruptions. Given the efficiency and urgency with which Jarvis' men are carrying out this security protocol, the situation requires immediate attention and compliance from all personnel. McMatters maintains a discreet silence, fully cognisant of Jarvis' established routine and possessing a deep understanding of his counterpart's ways. Rather than questioning Jarvis's actions or motives, McMatters adopts a patient stance, content to wait until the necessary sweep is completed. This unwavering patience and deference serve to safeguard both McMatters and Jarvis, as it allows them to navigate their shared circumstances with the utmost care and caution.

McMatters recognises that by respecting Jarvis's procedures and methods, they can ensure the continued protection and security of their respective interests, a prudent approach that has been honed through their longstanding familiarity with one another.

"All clear!"

"Thank you, can you make sure all exits to the building are secure?" asked Jarvis

"Will do, boss!"

"Afternoon McMatters! We have important information to talk about. It's regarding events that unfolded last night. It's not good at all."

"How bad?"

"I have a guy in the hospital with serious injuries. He's survived two surgeries so far and is holding on. I've sent care packages to him and his family while he's out of action. Now, as for the cause: The Bennetts decided the Santos were stepping on their toes, as the Santos started dabbling in one of the Bennetts' areas: cannabis. The Bennetts acted without consulting me. They stormed the local pub the Birch, Bennetts decided to hack as many as they could to bits.

The Santos defended themselves and shot the place up. My guy was in the wrong place at the wrong time. He got a bit of both... slashed and shot."

"Well, that certainly sounds like an eventful night indeed. Alright, let's set up a meeting. The Bennetts clearly need to be taught a lesson, and the Santos require a firm discussion. However, it's also important that the Santos understand you've already addressed the problem at hand. From this point forward, we need to ensure there is no further action is taken by either family."

"That's my plan. I'm thinking of bringing both families together, and the Bennetts are going to get a valuable lesson in front of the Santos. After the Santos receive a stern warning and a clear reminder that any changes to our operations must come through me, this meeting will serve as a powerful demonstration of my authority and the consequences for defying it. By uniting the two families and asserting my leadership, I can ensure that my directives are followed without question, solidifying my position and the Santos' subservience to my oversight. This strategic move will leave no doubt in anyone's mind about who is truly in charge here."

"it's crucial to ensure you have a full team of free crew members accompanying you. They need to witness the force being applied, as this will lend credibility to your actions. Additionally, you'll need a location that is off the grid. A few years ago, you managed to seize an old factory through force. Though it's now just a shell, the building is sizeable and isolated from the grid, making it an ideal hideout. Be sure to have all the necessary vehicles positioned just inside the entrance. Finally, activate the signal jammer before proceeding, as this will prevent any unwanted communication or interference."

"Will do, boss!"

"Let me know once it's done."

Chapter Seventeen
Sergeant Cole

Internal Affairs left the police station and Sergeant Cole and Karen from HR drafted up the paperwork regarding Detective Jackson.

FAO: Detective Jackson

Given the sensitive and ongoing nature of the investigation, a Temporary Suspension of duty will be implemented, effective as of today, May 6th, 2024. This suspension will remain in place for the duration of the investigation, which will be subject to regular three-monthly updates and comprehensive reviews. This measured approach ensures that the investigation can be conducted thoroughly and objectively, while maintaining appropriate oversight and transparency throughout the process.

A temporary suspension of duty is a necessary and prudent step to facilitate a comprehensive and impartial investigation, with the goal of upholding the integrity of the organisation and ensuring a fair and just outcome.

Due to your prominent public profile and role as a recognisable figure, the decision has been made to temporarily revoke your rank of Detective. When you return to active duties, you will be reinstated at the lower rank of Police Constable and assigned to light duties. This administrative change is necessary to maintain the impartiality and integrity of law enforcement operations. This ensures that your public persona does not unduly influence or undermine the public's trust in the investigative process.

While this may be a challenging transition, it is an essential measure to preserve the credibility and fairness of the department's activities. Your expertise and experience will continue to be valued, but in a capacity that minimises potential conflicts of interest or perceptions of bias. This adjustment in your status is a prudent and judicious step to uphold the principles of ethical policing that the community expects and deserves.

A mandatory one-year therapy program will also be implemented. You will be required to complete the full series of therapy sessions before your eligibility for higher-ranking duties can be reconsidered. This comprehensive approach ensures that individuals have access to the necessary professional support and guidance to address any personal or mental health concerns that may be impacting their work performance or career advancement.

This will also cover issues brought up by the investigation. By making therapy a mandatory component, the police force can demonstrate a strong commitment to the overall well-being and professional development of its workforce, recognising the vital role that mental health plays in achieving sustained success and productivity.

Yours Faithfully

Sergeant Cole and
Karen Nugent from (HR)

Sergeant Cole takes a deep, steadying breath, steeling himself for the confrontation ahead. With a sense of resolve, he buzzes Wendy and firmly requests that she allow Detective Jackson access to his office. This direct approach conveys Sergeant Cole's determination to cooperate fully with the ongoing investigation, despite the sensitive nature of the situation. By maintaining a calm, authoritative demeanour, he aims to project an image of transparency and willingness to assist the detective in uncovering the truth.

Detective Jackson enters the office, his shoulders slumped and his head hung low, bracing himself to learn of his impending fate. The weight of uncertainty and apprehension is palpable as he slowly makes his way to the desk, preparing to face whatever consequences or decisions lie in store. With a sense of trepidation, he anticipates the news that will determine the next steps in his career, knowing that the outcome could drastically impact his professional future.

"Sit down, Jackson!" Sergeant Cole demanded.
"Would you like a drink?" asks Karen trying to lighten the mood

"No thanks. I'd like to just get this over with."
Remarked Jackson

"Ok. So, Jackson I know this has been a hard day for you. I'm hoping you can understand and keep up with this." says Sergeant Cole

"We have drafted this letter up for you. It explains what will happen, and what we require, and the view of the police force." Karen gently explains

"Don't worry! we have tried to cover everything. We will complete the investigation as soon as possible!"

"Ok…"

Jackson gathers the letter and departs Sergeant Cole's office, his steps heavy with resignation. He proceeds to his own workspace, collecting his personal belongings as he prepares to exit the premises. However, as he makes his way out, he notices that he is being accompanied by PC Winters, an escort assigned to ensure his departure.

The eerie silence that permeates the rest of the office is palpable. Jackson is acutely aware that his colleagues are privy to the events that have transpired, heightening his sense of humiliation and discomfort.

Chapter Eighteen
Santos

The head of the Santos family has just concluded a tense phone conversation with Jarvis, leaving him feeling deeply unsettled. Jarvis is known to have a formidable reputation, one that no prudent individual would ever dare to defy. What truly concerns Santos, however, is the realisation that Jarvis answers to an even more intimidating superior.

A revelation that amplifies the gravity of the situation exponentially. The mere thought of crossing paths with Jarvis' enigmatic boss fills the Santos patriarch with a profound sense of dread and apprehension, as he fully comprehends the perilous consequences that could arise from such an ill-advised confrontation. Navigating this delicate predicament will require the utmost caution and strategic manoeuvring on Santos' part, lest he risk incurring the wrath of forces far beyond his control.

Jarvis has informed Santos that one of his associates was present at the scene when the incident occurred at the local pub, and as a result, this individual now requires extensive hospitalisation lasting several months.

To make amends and rectify the situation, Santos is prepared to pay a substantial sum of one hundred thousand pounds to the injured party. Santos recognises the critical importance of maintaining Jarvis' support and backing, as losing Jarvis's endorsement would be devastating to their operations, leaving them floundering and vulnerable in the competitive landscape.

Santos is willing to take any necessary steps to make things right with Jarvis, understanding that preserving this crucial alliance is vital to their continued success and their survival in the industry. The situation has taken an ominous turn, as Santos now owes a favour to the formidable crime boss Jarvis.

This is a deeply concerning development, as Jarvis is not the type of individual one wants to be indebted to. As a powerful and ruthless figure in the criminal underworld, Jarvis will undoubtedly leverage this debt to extract whatever he desires from Santos, be it an illegal activity or something even more nefarious.

While the thought of Santos being compelled to carry out Jarvis' bidding is a bitter pill to swallow, it is arguably preferable to the alternative outcomes that could have arisen, had Santos not acquiesced to this demand.

The looming spectre of Jarvis' influence and the uncertainty of what he may request poses a significant threat, one that Santos will need to navigate with great caution and calculation.

Jarvis has told him to go to the old factory on the edge of town at eight o'clock tonight.

Chapter Eighteen Part Two
Bennetts

The head of the notorious Bennett crime family has just hung up the phone after a deeply unsettling call with the notorious Jarvis. While he is aware of Jarvis' fearsome reputation within the criminal underworld, the Bennett patriarch is equally confident in his own family's formidable standing and influence. As the largest importers of cocaine and cannabis in the region, the Bennetts wield immense power and control over the illicit drug trade. The Bennett leader was confident if the time ever came he could over power Jarvis and make a power play for full control of all families.

Without their vast network and resources, the local market would be left in a state of devastating drought, with supplies drying up to the point of complete desolation. Bennett been warned numerous times by other influential crime bosses not to cross the formidable Jarvis, but he had dismissed their dire warnings, convinced that Jarvis was not as powerful or intimidating as they claimed.

The Santos crew had clearly overstepped their bounds by attempting to sell drugs on Bennetts turf without his explicit approval, and they ultimately paid a steep price for their foolish transgressions. Maybe Jarvis would teach Santos a lesson as they caused it after all.

Jarvis, the influential figure in the organisation, had explicitly instructed Bennett to attend a meeting with Santos at the dilapidated, abandoned factory on the outskirts of the city.

However, if Jarvis assumes that Bennett would show up without his trusted tools and equipment, he would be sorely mistaken. Bennett had no intention of going to this critical meeting unprepared. He was determined to bring his essential gear, as he knew that being equipped and ready for any situation was paramount in this line of work.

Bennett was not about to be caught off guard or appear anything less than fully capable in front of Jarvis and Santos. He would ensure he had everything he needed to handle whatever might arise during the meeting, regardless of Jarvis's expectations.

Chapter Nineteen
Lorraine

It was a typical Saturday night, yet Lorraine's old self would have found herself unusually thrilled at the prospect of staying in rather than going out. Lorraine is absolutely over the moon, and it's all because of McMatters. They had the most incredible, out-of-this-world intimate encounter that just blew Lorraine's mind!

Now, she can't stop thinking about McMatters - it's like he is living rent-free in her head 24/7! Lorraine was not quite sure how to handle these intense feelings. It's totally new territory for her, and she's both thrilled and a little nervous about it all.

Her previous long-term relationship had lasted for a year before her partner's true nature was ultimately revealed, leaving Lorraine jaded and guarded. However, this new connection with McMatters felt fundamentally different. Lorraine was determined to keep her eyes wide open, fully aware and attentive, determined not to repeat the mistakes of the past. Lorraine had a clear objective in mind when she ventured out to find the perfect dress for a special occasion that evening.

Her shopping trip proved fruitful, as she ended up selecting several options. But Lorraine's journey of self-expression through fashion is a testament to the power of confidence and self-love. Her choice of a sophisticated, sleek black dress wasn't just about clothing; it was a bold statement of embracing her unique beauty. The curve hugging silhouette celebrated her form, reminding us all that true elegance comes from within. With each carefully chosen accessory from the dazzling crystal adorned heels to the sleek satin tights. Lorraine crafted a look that was uniquely hers. Her high ponytail wasn't just a hairstyle; it was a crown of self-assurance.

As she gazed into the mirror, she saw more than her reflection; she saw the embodiment of her inner strength and allure. Lorraine's confidence was inspiring. As Lorraine prepared for her night out, applying her makeup and calling her taxi, she wasn't just getting ready, she was setting the stage for a magical evening of celebration, hopefully with Mr McMatters.

"Oh, it will be a good night tonight" she thought.

Maxine shouted up that her taxi was here, so she grabbed her bag and headed for the door. Lorraine jumped in the taxi, and she was off. Half way to the club the taxi veers off course into a secluded area down a side street, Lorraine couldn't shake an unsettling feeling that had crept up on her. The driver's casual explanation of him needing a pee may seem innocent, but one must question the wisdom of stopping in such an isolated location.

Lorraine spotted another car stop at the top of the street, at this precise moment only serves to heighten her suspicion. Lorraine was suddenly vigilant and trusting her instincts, was trying to tell her something.

Lorraine's growing unease was a warning sign that should not be ignored.

Chapter Nineteen Part Two
Team Alpha

Team Alpha was a specialised security detail tasked with closely monitoring and protecting Lorraine, a high-profile individual, who had recently caught the attention of the influential and powerful boss, McMatters. Given Lorraine's rising prominence and the boss's personal interest in her wellbeing, Team Alpha's mission was of the utmost importance, as they were responsible for always ensuring Lorraine's safety and security.

The team, composed of two skilled and vigilant members, was expected to maintain a constant and discreet surveillance over Lorraine, anticipating and swiftly addressing any potential threats or risks that may arise.

They had carefully tailed the taxi that had picked Lorraine up, keeping a discreet distance to avoid arousing suspicion.

However, their concern grew as they noticed the driver abruptly veer off the expected route, diverging from the road that led to the club where they had anticipated Lorraine was headed. This unexpected deviation immediately triggered a sense of unease, as it became increasingly clear that something was amiss.

The sudden change in direction and the driver's evasive manoeuvres raised red flags, leaving them with a strong intuition that the situation was not unfolding as it should. Alpha Team arrived in a sleek, silver BMW at the end of the street and observed the taxi driver exit his vehicle and walk towards a nearby bush. This behaviour suggests the taxi driver may have needed to urgently relieve himself, potentially due to a pressing personal necessity.

While the situation appears unusual, there is no clear indication that anything untoward or concerning is transpiring. Without further context, it would be unwise to make any definitive judgments, as the taxi driver's actions could simply reflect a common, innocuous occurrence.

Chapter Nineteen Part Three
Jackson

Jackson was utterly dejected, his spirit crushed by a profound sense of defeat and overwhelming depression. The humiliation Jackson had experienced at the police station had been truly unbearable, leaving him feeling completely demoralised. In the wake of this deeply traumatic incident, Jackson found himself succumbing to intense emotional turmoil, breaking down and crying uncontrollably as he struggled to cope with the weight of his anguish and shame. But when all the tears had dried up and nothing remained but a lingering sense of shame and betrayal, Jackson's emotions shifted from sorrow to a deep, simmering anger. Jackson was not angry with himself for his transgression itself, Lorraine had been worth that momentary indulgence.

No, Jackson's fury was directed inward, at his own carelessness and lack of foresight. It puzzled him, who was it that had captured those intimate, private moments on camera, breaching his trust and exposing his vulnerability? Jackson's mind raced as he grappled with this violation, the realisation that someone had betrayed his confidence and thrust his personal life into the harsh glare of scrutiny. This breach of privacy only served to further inflame Jackson's sense of outrage, as he struggled to come to terms with the profound breach of trust and the ramifications it would have on his life going forward. Anger and resentment began to build within him because of the sequence of events and the fact he got caught.

First, he felt a strong sense of animosity towards his boss for bringing in Internal Affairs, which he perceived as an intrusive and unnecessary measure. This initial anger then extended to his colleague Karen, as he interpreted her behaviour as patronising and dismissive. Finally, the culmination of these negative emotions led to him feeling deeply frustrated and upset at having to be escorted from the police station by PC Winters. The compounding nature of these angry feelings, from his boss to his co-worker then to the police officer, created an overwhelming sense of indignation and resentment that Jackson struggled to contain. When he arrived home, Jackson immediately turned to drinking cheap whisky in a desperate attempt to dull his emotional turmoil.

After polishing off three quarters of a bottle, his inebriation had reached a point where Jackson had completely trashed his house, leaving it in a state of disarray from top to bottom. However, rather than reflecting on his own actions, Jackson now found himself irrationally angry at Lorraine. In his addled state, he irrationally blamed her for 'teasing him,' leading him on, and looking so devastatingly attractive.

As if she were somehow responsible for his destructive, self-destructive behaviour. The man's inability to take accountability for his own choices and actions had led Jackson down a dark, self-pitying path fuelled by alcohol and misplaced resentment.

Jackson had a plan forming in his intoxicated mind, someone had to pay so he watched Lorraine's house and as soon as an opportunity arrived Jackson acted upon it. Jackson seen the taxi arrive outside Lorraine's house, so he sprang into action. Approaching the driver, Jackson requested assistance in placing his bag in the cars trunk. Unsuspecting, the taxi driver complied, exiting the car and walking to the rear.

In a sudden, calculated move, Jackson struck the driver over the head, rendering him unconscious. The driver was then gagged, bound, and unceremoniously shoved into the trunk of the car as quickly as possible, leaving him helpless and trapped.

Chapter Twenty
Jarvis

Jarvis arrived at the designated location well before the other rival crime families were expected, allowing him ample time to meticulously prepare the scene for the impending lesson. Jarvis began by thoroughly testing the signal jamming device, ensuring it was functioning flawlessly and would effectively disrupt any attempts at communication or summoning assistance.

With the technical aspects secured, Jarvis then strategically positioned two tables on either side of the entryway, strategically placed to still permit the flow of traffic through the area.

The team has meticulously scoped out potential sniper vantage points within the target building and is now in the process of setting up concealed sniper positions. As a precautionary measure, the team has also strategically stashed firearms at various strategic locations throughout the premises, in case the situation at the upcoming meeting takes an unfavourable turn.

In the span of just fifteen minutes, the Santos family, a sizable group of around fifteen individuals including their leader, arrived at the location. Upon their entrance, they were promptly subjected to a thorough security check, during which they were instructed to place any weapons they were carrying on a table to the left. They all sat down and waited silently and patiently.

Shortly after, within the next ten minutes, the opposing Bennetts group also made their appearance. This faction was notably more confrontational in demeanour. Twenty turned up from the Bennetts family, they too were directed to deposit all their weapons on a separate table, this one situated to the right.

The arrangement ensured that both parties would have their respective arms returned to them at the conclusion of the meeting, allowing the proceedings to unfold in a controlled and secure environment. This precautionary measure was likely implemented to mitigate the risk of any violent escalation during the high-stakes negotiations that were about to take place between the two families. As predicted, the confrontation between the rival factions, the Santos and the Bennetts, was marked by a stark contrast in their chosen armaments.

The Santos arrived on the scene wielding an array of formidable firearms, including guns and grenades, while the Bennetts opted for more traditional melee weapons, such as swords and jungle knives of various designs.

This juxtaposition of modern, high-powered firearms and time-honoured bladed instruments created a visually striking and somewhat ironic scene, which undoubtedly piqued the interest and amusement of the observer and boss, Jarvis. The stark differences in the weaponry employed by the two groups underscored the depth of the longstanding feud and the willingness of both sides to resort to potentially deadly force to assert their dominance.

The Santos' reliance on ranged, explosive ordnance suggested a more aggressive, overwhelming approach, while the Bennetts' preference for close-quarters blades hinted at a more personal, visceral style of combat. This clash of combat philosophies and technological disparities added an intriguing layer of complexity to the confrontation, making it a compelling spectacle for the onlooker, Jarvis.

Jarvis addresses both families as he starts the meeting.

"Okay, so after recent events, we are now here in a meeting. Who can explain what happened?"

"I can verify my nephew went away and came back with some marijuana for personal use. He shared it at a party. Word got back to the Bennetts that he was dealing, but he wasn't." Said Santos.

"Bennetts care to comment on this?" Asked Jarvis.

"It's bollocks, Jarvis! He was dealing!" shouted the Bennetts

"Santos… what are my rules?"

"All changes go through you, Jarvis."

Jarvis strides purposefully to the sword display, his eyes locking onto a formidable blade. "This weapon is exceptional, Bennett," he declares, seizing the hilt and raising the sword with unmistakable authority. Jarvis played around swinging it in the air and fixing his grip, slowly Jarvis was moving into the middle of the two families, Jarvis was still facing the Bennetts.

Now within striking distance of the Bennett family patriarch, Jarvis unleashes the blade's deadly potential without hesitation.

In one decisive sweep, Jarvis decapitates the family's leader! The head of the Bennetts leader drops and rolls across the floor, showing a grim reminder of Jarvis' power.

The room falls deathly quiet as the witnesses grasp the gravity of their situation, their lives were now entirely in Jarvis' hands, and he will not tolerate any foolish moves.

"Do we understand the rules? Or do I need to demonstrate again?"

While the team's sudden understanding of Jarvis' authority and decision-making abilities is noteworthy, it's crucial to recognise the potential dangers that lie ahead. The revelation of an even more ruthless figure above Jarvis should serve as a stark warning to all families involved. The power dynamics at play were complex and potentially volatile. The families are now mindful that challenging or defying directives could lead to severe consequences, given the formidable nature of those in charge.

However, what truly unnerved them even further was the realisation that Jarvis' own superior was a far more ruthless and formidable figure. This unsettling awareness of the power dynamics at play left the group feeling uneasy and apprehensive about the potential consequences of defiance.

"Bennetts, you must take immediate action to clean up this mess. (Jarvis gestures the severed head on the floor.) Furthermore, one of my men was injured because of your actions, and the Santos have had to compensate his family.

However, Bennetts, you will be held accountable and are required to pay one hundred and fifty thousand to the injured man's family by the end of the day. Is that perfectly clear? "The tone conveys a sense of authority and demands compliance from the Bennetts.

The language is direct and leaves no room for ambiguity, emphasising the seriousness of the situation and the consequences the Bennetts will face if they fail to meet the stated requirements by the given deadline.

"Yes." Said one of the Bennetts

"It looks like we have a new Bennett leader" said Jarvis Pointing to the only one who had balls to answer Jarvis.

"To avoid attracting attention, we shouldn't all leave at the same time"

With that, Jarvis and his entire team gathered their weapons and prepared to depart. The skilled snipers descended from their elevated positions, and the group swiftly made their way into the waiting vehicles. As they were leaving, Jarvis turned back and firmly declared, "And let this be a lesson the next time you find yourselves in a dispute, you come directly to me! I will not tolerate any further incidents without my involvement and oversight." The authoritative tone in Jarvis's voice left no room for argument, underscoring his expectation that any future conflicts would be brought to his attention for proper resolution.

Chapter Twenty-One
Lorraine

Lorraine sat patiently in the backseat of the taxi; her eyes fixed on the vehicle's exterior as she waited for the driver to return. She had observed him stepping away briefly, likely to attend to a personal need. As he approached the car, Lorraine noted that he was walking on the wrong side, his hat pulled low over his face, obscuring her view of his features.

This minor detail did not deter Lorraine, however, as she remained calm and composed, ready to resume her journey. The driver opened the car door, and there sat Lorraine, her senses immediately on high alert. Lorraine's instincts were correct to be on high alert, as several red flags emerged.

Anticipating the need for a swift escape, she discreetly unclipped her seatbelt, As the taxi driver leaned in, a potent aroma of alcohol wafted towards her. The driver's apparent intoxication, evident from the strong smell of alcohol, is not only illegal but poses a severe risk to safety. When he finally looks up at her from the open car door, Lorraine was shocked by the dramatic transformation she has witnessed. It's Detective Jackson!

Jackson's devilish appearance and altered state are deeply troubling, suggesting he may be experiencing personal difficulties that have led to this dangerous behaviour. What had led him to this state? Why was he operating a taxi in such a condition? This was a question that left Lorraine feeling deeply unsettled and concerned.

"Jackson?"

"I lost everything today… because of you!"

"I don't understand Jackson…"

"Now you will get what you deserve!"

Detective Jackson's behaviour is utterly reprehensible and deeply concerning as he suddenly, aggressively lunges towards Lorraine in the confined space of the car, a blatant violation of personal boundaries and a clear demonstration of predatory intent.

Lorraine is suddenly feeling vulnerable and trapped! Lorraine recoils in alarm, desperately attempting to create distance between herself and the threatening situation. However, Jackson swiftly seizes her legs and yanks her forcefully towards him, overpowering her efforts to resist. As she slides inexorably closer, Lorraine frantically grasps for any available object that could aid her in pulling away. But Jackson's relentless grip makes her efforts futile.

To Lorraine's horror, she then observes that Jackson has already unzipped his trousers, his aroused state fully exposed, indicating his clear and unwelcome intentions. Faced with this deeply disturbing and non-consensual scenario, Lorraine is filled with a sense of dread and a desperate need to escape Jackson's predatory advances.

As she desperately struggles to free herself, she manages to break one of her legs free from his grasp. Seizing the opportunity, she swings her liberated leg backwards with as much strength and force as she could muster, delivering a powerful kick that sends her assailant reeling backwards.

The sudden, unexpected strike catches him off guard, providing her with a critical chance to potentially escape this dangerous situation.

Chapter Twenty-One Part Two
Team Alpha

The Taxi driver's making his way back to the car, but seems to be approaching from an unexpected angle. It's puzzling to observe him heading towards the rear of the car where Lorraine is seated, rather than the driver's side. The members of Team Alpha, already on high alert, are quickly unfastening their seatbelts, preparing themselves for any potential developments or confrontations that may arise.

The next minute, they see the taxi driver lunge at Lorraine, pulling her towards him.

"Oh, no! here we go…"

With a renewed sense of determination, they jump out of the car and race towards the taxi driver, who had just been forcefully knocked backward, most likely from a powerful kick. As they arrive on the scene, they quickly grab the driver's collar and pull him back, throwing him roughly to the ground. One of them then proceeds to punch the driver, rendering him unconscious.

Wasting no time, they make their way to the trunk of the vehicle, intending to retrieve something to tie up the taxi driver.

However, they discover that someone else has already been tied up and placed in there.

"What the Fuck is going on here?

One of Team Alpha goes for their car, opens the boot, and throws the taxi driver in. The other member checks on Lorraine.

"Are you ok Lorraine?"

"You know my name?"

"Yes, we will explain, First, we need to get you to your destination."

Lorraine was completely taken aback and overwhelmed by the shocking turn of events. She finds herself in a state of bewilderment, utterly unsure of what has just transpired, or why Jackson, the person she thought she knew, would act in such an inexplicable manner.

The sudden appearance of the two strangers who had intervened to rescue her, have only further compounded her confusion and uncertainty about the entire situation.

Lorraine remains silent, her mind racing as she struggles to process everything that is unfolding around her.

Chapter Twenty-One Part Three
Dreams

Lorraine is covertly ushered through the discreet rear entrance of Dreams by the two individuals who had just rescued her from her perilous situation. The question of how they knew to bring her to this specific location begins to weigh heavily on her mind. As the initial shock and disorientation start to subside, Lorraine finds herself becoming increasingly curious and eager for answers.

She knows she needs to understand the circumstances that have led up to her dramatic extraction and subsequent arrival at this seemingly predetermined destination. With a growing sense of unease and uncertainty, Lorraine prepares to voice the many questions that were now surfacing, determined to uncover the truth behind this mysterious turn of events. McMatters strides into the office, a sense of purpose and determination in his steps.

There, on the sofa, sits Lorraine, wrapped in a blanket and clutching a stiff drink. Beside her are two men, whom McMatters instantly recognises as part of Jarvis' alpha team. The scene before him was undoubtedly a significant development, one that demanded his full attention and strategic consideration. McMatters' keen observation and familiarity with the key players involved allows him to quickly assess the situation and prepare to navigate the complexities that lie ahead.

"Lads, come! I need info."

The two members of aloha team follow McMatters outside the door. They don't normally interact with the big boss McMatters; they usually deal with Jarvis.

"What happened?"

"We were on the day shift, monitoring Lorraine's activities. As she typically would on a Friday or Saturday night, Lorraine got ready and hailed a taxi. But the driver immediately headed in the wrong direction, away from the club where she should have been heading.

The driver then pulled over, got out, and walked around to the passenger side, where Lorraine was seated in the back. He proceeded to grab her legs and pull her towards him, clearly intending to assault her. At this point, we had already intervened, and we quickly dragged the driver back, knocking him unconscious before he could continue his attack on Lorraine.

We attempted to restrain the individual and conceal him in the cars trunk, but upon inspection, we discovered that someone else was already bound and incapacitated in the boot. Bringing Lorraine here was our initial objective, but now we are faced with an unexpected and complicated situation involving the taxi driver and the additional person found in the trunk."

"OK, one minute… Let me think…"

McMatters enters the room to see Lorraine, and puts his finger to her lips.

"I know you have questions but I have two important ones I need answers to quickly first. Do you know who the taxi driver is?"

"Yes, I do. It is the same Detective Jackson who helped my mum."

"Do you know who the other person in the boot is?"

"No. But it could be my real taxi driver."

"Thank you. I need to go and deal with this. Please stay here and don't move, drinks are in the decanters, help yourself, but stay here."

"Ok"

McMatters walks out of his office.

"Ok lads! Show me who is in which car."

They exited out of the back door and walk towards the cars parked together.

"The one who attacked Lorraine is in the silver BMW, my run around."

"Take it and burn it. I will square you some money to cover the car."

He gets in his car and drives off.

"OK let's help this man. Open the boot."

They open the boot and staring at them is a man, very frightened shaking and bleeding. McMatters calmly, before unbinding him says.

"Ok so you were attacked earlier on. I now have him and you don't need to worry. I will now help you out of here and we will get this rope off you, ok?"

The man appears disoriented and unsteady, but nods, as they carefully extract him from the car. Upon closer inspection, they notice a concerning gash on his head, which is actively bleeding.

He has sustained a serious blow. Likely from some kind of impact during the incident. Given the severity of the injury, it is evident the man will require immediate medical attention and transport to the hospital, for proper treatment and evaluation by healthcare professionals.

"OK we are going to take you to hospital now as you need checking over. For your inconvenience and distress here is £1,000. We will leave your taxi here until you return. I will get it cleaned for you."

"Thank you I don't know what to say."

"You were lucky my men found you."

"Is the woman, ok? I heard her scream before I passed out again."

"Yes, she will be, we got there in time."

The man nodded, then wobbled.

"Take him to hospital please, see he's, ok?"

"Will do boss."

Chapter Twenty-One Part Four
Javis get the update

As Jarvis sits behind the wheel, he quickly dials his various teams to receive crucial updates on the ongoing operations. When Jarvis connects with the Alpha team, he notices with concern that they have not yet clocked off, even though they were scheduled to have completed their shift by now. Reaching out to the Bravo team next, Jarvis is dismayed to learn that they have no information regarding the current whereabouts of either the Alpha team or Lorraine.

Suddenly, one of the Alpha team members answers Jarvis's calls, prompting him to listen intently as they provide a status update, aware that any delay or discrepancy could jeopardise the mission's success.

"Hi boss, the shit has hit the fan. I Can't explain over the phone. Can you collect me from the hospital? I will tell all en-route to Alpha team part two."

"On our way," Jarvis said, looking at his driver. "I guess the fun isn't over yet."

Jarvis has grown accustomed to hearing unsettling reports, Jarvis wondered what it would be this time.

He was neither shocked nor concerned, for he knew that his trusted associate, McMatters, was more than capable of handling the situation. Jarvis is, however, intrigued and eager to learn the full details of this unfolding scenario.

The investigation led Jarvis and his team to an abandoned car graveyard, one of the two locations where Alpha Team were known to frequently burn things. Jarvis' keen understanding of his men's habits and patterns proves accurate, as he correctly anticipated their arrival at this remote site. At the far end of the junkyard, Jarvis' man was there, listening to the chilling cries emanating from the trunk of the car, his man not showing a single flicker of the screams bothering him.

In the process his man lost his BMW, but Jarvis knew McMatters would have seen him right.

"OK" Jarvis opens the boot of the car they was in and grabs two tops, one for him and one for his man, they changed tops and throw the others on the fire.

"Let's get back to the club I think we deserve a drink."

Chapter Twenty-Two
The Police Station

With it being a busy Saturday night, the police station was abuzz with activity. Sergeant Cole, eager to wrap up his shift and head home, had just finished sorting through the piles of paperwork related to Detective Jackson's latest case.

After a long and demanding day of managing the various incidents and emergencies that had unfolded across the city, Cole couldn't wait to finally leave the station and enjoy some much-needed rest and relaxation. The constant flow of calls, reports, and administrative tasks had kept him and his team on their toes, leaving little time for breaks or personal time.

As the senior officer on duty, Cole had been responsible for overseeing the coordination of resources, the delegation of responsibilities, and the timely resolution of each situation that had arisen. It had been a taxing and relentless shift, but with the last of the paperwork now complete, he could finally look forward to the prospect of returning to the comfort of his own home and unwinding after a challenging day on the job.

Sergeant Cole, a seasoned law enforcement veteran, found himself in a challenging position as he needed to address Detective Jackson's team. With Detective

Jackson currently suspended pending an investigation, there were numerous loose ends that required careful attention and coordination to properly tie up. Sergeant Cole recognised the importance of providing clear direction and maintaining morale within the team during this transitional period, as they worked diligently to ensure all outstanding matters were addressed thoroughly and efficiently.

His experience and leadership skills would be crucial in guiding the team through this delicate situation and ensuring the investigation remained on track despite the absence of their former supervisor. One of the most significant loose ends threatening the success of the overall mission was Operation Dreamy.

Unfortunately, due to the reckless actions taken by Detective Jackson, the integrity and secrecy of this critical operation were severely compromised.

As a result, the decision has now been made to shut down Operation Dreamy entirely, as continuing with the plan would be far too risky given the breach of confidentiality.

This is a major setback that will require careful damage control and the revaluations of alternative strategies to achieve the desired objectives. The team must now work quickly to contain the fallout from Detective Jackson's mistake and determine the best course of action moving forward, as the stakes are incredibly high.

Sergeant Cole was nearing the end of a gruelling day that had pushed him to his limits. The relentless challenges and frustrations he had faced throughout the day had worn him down, leaving him feeling exasperated and longing for a respite from the seemingly unending difficulties. As he reflected on the trials and tribulations he had endured, Sergeant Cole fervently hoped that he would never have to experience another day quite as trying and taxing as the one he was leaving behind.

Tomorrow, he will receive updates on the grisly incident that unfolded at a local pub. However, in the present moment, he is simply too exhausted to dwell on the details of the distressing occurrence.

The events that transpired have likely left him emotionally and mentally drained, making it difficult for him to engage with the harrowing information right now.

Chapter Twenty-Three
Jarvis

Jarvis had carefully assembled his team of trusted associates and had just concluded a vital conversation with the taxi driver who had been the victim of a vicious assault at the hands of the notorious Jackson. The driver expressed a profound sense of gratitude for the unwavering support and assistance that Jarvis and his team had provided during this harrowing ordeal. Recognising the driver's vulnerable position and his pressing need for aid, the driver inquired whether Jarvis and his team could offer him a ride back to the club to retrieve his taxi.

Jarvis, demonstrating his steadfast commitment to helping those affected by the incident and ensuring the driver could safely recover his vehicle and resume his livelihood, readily agreed to provide the man with a lift, underscoring Jarvis' compassionate and proactive approach to addressing the needs of the community he had sworn to protect.

Jarvis felt a genuine sense of compassion and a strong desire to assist the struggling taxi driver he had encountered that evening. However, he also recognised the critical need to firmly impress upon the driver the paramount importance of keeping the events and details of their interaction strictly confidential, even from the driver's own wife. Jarvis understood the highly sensitive and potentially compromising nature of the situation they found themselves in, and he knew he had to stress to the driver the absolute necessity of maintaining complete discretion. While Jarvis empathised with the challenging circumstances the driver was facing, he could not risk the potentially severe consequences that could arise from any disclosure or sharing of the night's happenings.

Jarvis had placed in him by strictly refraining from divulging the specifics to anyone, no matter how close or trusted they may be. The stakes were simply too high, and Jarvis had to make sure the driver comprehended the critical importance of maintaining absolute silence about their encounter.

McMatters took a keen personal interest in the taxi driver when he arrived to collect his car. Eager to maintain the driver's loyalty and cooperation, McMatters extended a generous offer of employment, inviting him to work as a private driver for their exclusive club.

This strategic move indicates that McMatters recognises the value in having the taxi driver on their payroll, as it would grant them greater control and oversight of his actions and allegiances. Observant and perceptive, Jarvis discerned the underlying motivation behind McMatters job offer.

By bringing the taxi driver into their workforce, McMatters could effectively monitor his activities and prevent him from potentially disclosing or acting upon what had transpired earlier that night involving Detective Jackson and Lorraine. This arrangement would safeguard McMatters interests and mitigate risks associated with the taxi driver's independent status. Employing the driver would secure his allegiance and provide McMatters with a valuable measure of security and influence over a potentially influential witness.

"Thank you! thank you, sir! I accept your kind offer."

"Come and see me tomorrow. We will work out the details."

"Thank you again."

"Nicely played, boss," said Jarvis.

McMatters provided Jarvis with a comprehensive update on Lorraine's situation, conveying the gravity the condition and the critical need for immediate intervention, McMatters will get something to help Lorraine sleep from the healthcare professionals.

The details shared by McMatters painted a vivid and unsettling picture, leaving Jarvis deeply concerned for Lorraine's well-being. Jarvis was taken aback by the severity of the attack, they wasn't sure how Lorraine would respond though.

The information imparted by McMatters highlighted the unexpected and alarming turn of events, underscoring the pressing necessity for the doctors to swiftly provide Lorraine with the necessary assistance so she could sleep easy without her mind thinking too much.

"One of my men will collect the prescription straight away," said Jarvis as he turned around to look directly at one of his guys.

"No problem, boss. On it."

"The issue with you-know-who is dealt with. No more hassle on that side."

"Nice to hear, Jarvis. Good job. I need to get back to the club to check on Lorraine."

Chapter Twenty-Three Part Two
McMatters

McMatters returned to his office, where Lorraine had remained. The initial shaking has started to subside, and the tears have ceased as she finished her cocktail. This calm, however, belies the underlying tension and emotional turmoil that has gripped the room. McMatters' arrival back in the office signals a pivotal moment, as he must now navigate the aftermath of the situation and determine the appropriate next steps to address the concerns that have been raised.

The stillness is palpable, and McMatters knows he must tread carefully to defuse the charged atmosphere. McMatters looks at Lorraine with empathy, recognising the immense trauma and suffering she has endured from the assault.

No one should ever have to experience such a horrific violation of their personal safety and bodily autonomy. Lorraine is indeed fortunate that the detective, did not further victimise her through an act of sexual violence. The emotional and psychological scars from such a devastating experience can last a lifetime, and McMatters is acutely aware of the profound impact this must have had on Lorraine's well-being and sense of security.

He feels a deep sense of compassion for her ordeal and is committed to ensuring that she receives the support and justice she deserves.

When McMatters looks at Lorraine, he sees a woman whose natural beauty requires no artificial enhancements. Her skin has a radiant, luminous quality that shines forth without the need for makeup or other cosmetic products.

The dress she wears, though likely a recent acquisition, now bears the signs of a forceful encounter, with a tear visible near the bottom hem where it was presumably grabbed or tugged.

Despite the damage to her attire, Lorraine's inherent loveliness remains undiminished, a testament to the power of her innate, unadorned beauty.

"Jarvis!"

Jarvis enters the room and is immediately struck by the profound impact the situation has had on Lorraine. Surveying the scene. Jarvis takes a moment to appreciate the gravity of what has transpired, knowing that McMatters decisive action has effectively removed this dangerous sexual predator from the situation and provided a profound sense of relief and security.

The knowledge that this threat has been decisively neutralised can offer a profound reassurance and peace of mind.

"Yes, boss?"

"I'm leaving here early tonight. I'll take Lorraine back to my place and make sure she recovers okay."

"I'll look after this place. Not a problem."

"Thank you, Jarvis. Tomorrow, you can update me on your events."

"It will be something you'll enjoy boss, what a night! ."

Jarvis hastily made his exit from the office, swiftly departing the premises and leaving the scene in his wake. Meanwhile, McMatters assumed control of the situation, taking charge and guiding the shaken Lorraine downstairs to the waiting car.

With Jarvis now gone and Lorraine safely ensconced in the car, the stage was set for the next critical phase of their carefully orchestrated plan to commence. McMatters and Lorraine arrived at his luxurious home, and Steve promptly ushered Lorraine into the living room. With a welcoming gesture, he guided Lorraine through the entryway and into the comfortable, well-appointed space that served as the central gathering area of his home.

The transition from the outside world to this private domain signalled a shift in the dynamic between them, as they now found themselves in the more intimate setting of his personal living quarters. McMatters' assistant, Susan, immediately perked up upon hearing the distinct sound of McMatters' arrival home. She hurried to the room, eager to greet and assist her employer. Susan knew from experience that McMatters' return signalled the start of a new set of tasks and responsibilities that required her full attention and diligence.

Anticipating McMatters' needs, Susan quickly made her way to the room, ready to provide a warm welcome and offer her services in whatever capacity they were required.

"Hi Susan this is Lorraine. She had a shock tonight. She was attacked and I think a hot chocolate might help."

"It certainly will help; I'll be right back."

Without hesitation, Susan set off to fulfil her duties. She had been one of McMatters' trusted personal assistants for over five years, having proven her competence and reliability time and time again. While McMatters had another assistant, Jeffery, this evening was Jeffery's night off, leaving Susan as the sole assistant available to handle the tasks at hand.

Susan promptly returned with the requested refreshments. For McMatters, she brought a refreshing beverage, while for Lorraine, she thoughtfully provided a warm and comforting cup of hot chocolate.

To accompany these drinks, Susan also delivered two delectable club sandwiches, ensuring a satisfying and well-rounded meal for the pair. This attentive and efficient service demonstrated Susan's commitment to meeting the needs of her colleagues in a timely and considerate manner.

"Food will also help."

"Thank you, Susan. You can have the rest of the night off. You have been most helpful."

"Oh, thank you Mr McMatters."

Susan retreated to her private quarters, which were located on the property. While the McMatters assistants reside at the main house with the McMatters, they each have their own separate living accommodations in the form of a fully equipped cottage, situated at the bottom of the garden.

This secluded cottage provides the assistants with a comfortable and private living space, complete with two bedrooms, a kitchen, dining area, living room, and its own well-tended garden.

Susan and her husband, Jeffrey, take great pride in maintaining the cottage's beautiful, well-manicured outdoor space, ensuring they have a peaceful and picturesque environment to call their own, within the larger McMatters estate.

McMatters, sat down beside Lorraine and gently encouraged her to partake in some food and drink. As Lorraine complied with this suggestion, the positive effects became evident. By the time she had finished, Lorraine's appearance had noticeably improved.

The colour was returning to her previously pale face, indicating that the nourishment had helped revive her. McMatters' attentive and caring gesture had made a tangible difference to Lorraine's well-being, demonstrating the importance of providing support and attending to the basic needs of those who may be struggling.

Chapter Twenty-Three Part Three
Lorraine

Regaining her composure, Lorraine blinked her eyes repeatedly, momentarily disoriented as she found herself in an unfamiliar, expansive room. The space was furnished with an abundance of plush, luxurious seating, including a three-seater sofa, two two-seater couches, and two cosy armchairs, all upholstered in a rich, creamy leather with a warm, biscuit-coloured tone.

Dominating the room was a massive, wall mounted television positioned above an open fireplace adorned with charming, cottage-style stonework. The walls were painted in a soothing, neutral cream hue, complementing the natural pine flooring beneath her feet. In front of the fireplace, a large, fluffy white rug covered the floor, adding a sense of comfort and elegance to the space. Lorraine's eyes scanned the unfamiliar surroundings, taking in the meticulous attention to detail and the overall air of luxury that permeated the room.

She swiftly turned and realised that the house before her belonged to McMatters. Previously, she had only caught a glimpse of his bedroom, and that had been during the midst of an intimate, passionate encounter. The recollection of that charged, private moment added a layer of weight and significance to her current presence at his residence, heightening the intensity of the situation. As Lorraine reflected on the evening's events, she found herself balancing between recovery and lingering trauma. While a subtle sense of improvement had begun to emerge, the weight of her recent experiences still pressed upon her consciousness. Her gaze fell to her cherished dress, now marred by the night's ordeals.

This sight stirred a complex mixture of emotions, frustration intertwined with a deeper, more poignant reminder of all she had faced.

The ruined garment embodied the stark contrast between her expectations for the evening and the harsh reality she had encountered. In this moment, Lorraine confronted the challenge of reconciling her desire to move forward with the undeniable impact of her recent past, each thread of her damaged dress. Lorraine was angry at Detective Jackson, angry he had pushed the boundaries, she was grateful that when it mattered help was around, she was confused at the whole process though, so many thoughts and feelings was running through her head.

"Lorraine?" said McMatters.

Lorraine turns to face McMatters and smiles warmly. She realises that McMatters has been genuinely concerned for her well-being and has been taking care of her. This realisation brings Lorraine comfort and puts her at ease. McMatters' attentive and caring behaviour reassures Lorraine, causing her to feel relieved and grateful.

The knowledge that McMatters has been vigilantly watching over her during a difficult period provides Lorraine with a sense of security and support. This feeling is both reassuring and comforting to her.

McMatters' consistent care and concern for Lorraine's welfare deepens her trust and appreciation for him, which in turn strengthens their relationship.

"Where am I?"

"This is my home, Lorraine. Welcome."

"I have some questions."

"Let's get you upstairs and out of that ripped dress. Then you can ask me anything."

"Okay."

McMatters gently took hold of Lorraine's hand, his touch soft yet purposeful, and guides her up the grand, sweeping staircase towards his private quarters. The ornate architecture and lavish furnishings of the stairway instil a sense of grandeur, heightening the anticipation of their ascent.

Upon reaching the threshold of his bedroom, McMatters swiftly opens the wardrobe, revealing a selection of neatly folded garments. With a careful and considerate manner, he selects a soft, comfortable t-shirt, ready to provide Lorraine with a change of clothing. The intimate setting, combined with McMatters' deliberate movements, create an air of quiet anticipation and care as he attends to Lorraine's needs. Steve's actions convey a familiarity and understanding between the two individuals, suggesting a level of trust and consideration that had been established through their interactions.

The scene evoked a sense of comfort and security, with McMatters' attentiveness and consideration for Lorraine's wellbeing taking centre stage. Lorraine began methodically peeling away the dress, gradually revealing the enticing satin bustier, garters, and tights concealed beneath.

The delicate fabric bore a subtle rip, adding an alluring edge to the ensemble. Steve, exhibiting his characteristically caring and gentle demeanour, tenderly assisted Lorraine in the process of undressing, delicately helping to unveil the layers and expose the captivating lingerie. This intimate moment highlighted the burgeoning sense of trust and intimacy shared between them as they partook in this private, sensual experience together.

The gradual disrobing, accompanied by the slight imperfection in the fabric, heightened the overall sense of desire and sensuality permeating the scene.

Steve carefully and attentively guided Lorraine through the process of putting on the t-shirt, gently manoeuvring her arms into the sleeves with a practiced, delicate touch.

The seamless, considerate motion demonstrated Steve's experience and concern for Lorraine's comfort and ease. Having securely dressed Lorraine, McMatters then turned his focus to the bed, pulling back the quilt and meticulously smoothing out the linens to create an inviting, comforting oasis.

With a warm, welcoming gesture, Steve then prompts Lorraine to climb into the neatly prepared bed, signalling that it was now time for her to settle in and embrace the promised respite and relaxation of the cosy setting.

"Could I possibly get a drink of water?"

Steve strode across the room with a sense of determination, his steps purposeful and unwavering as he makes his way towards the small side table in the corner. Arriving at his destination, he reaches out and grasps the ceramic water jug resting atop the table's surface.

With a steady hand, Steve carefully tilts the pitcher, allowing the cool, clear water within to pour forth, producing a gentle, soothing sound as it flows into the waiting glass. Pausing for a moment, he brings the refreshing drink to his lips, taking a moment to hydrate himself, his movements poised and composed, betraying a sense of control and focus that permeates his entire demeanour.

"OK, ask your questions. I have some too," said McMatters.

"Why did that detective attack me?"

"I'm afraid I don't have a definitive answer for you, Lorraine," McMatters responds, his tone laced with a sense of unease.

"However, I can say with certainty that the detective was closely monitoring your actions, closely observing and tracking your every move." McMatters words carried a palpable weight, conveying the gravity of the situation and the unsettling reality that Lorraine was under close surveillance."

"That's wrong! He must be very sick."

"When the detective attacked me, two men rushed to my aid. Who were they?"

"There were a couple of my men," Steve explained, his tone conveying genuine concern for Lorraine. "I had noticed the detective following and observing you, which left me uneasy, so I asked those two men to keep an eye on him."

Steve's words were deliberate and measured as he sought to provide a comprehensive and persuasive account of the situation. By offering additional context and clarifying his reasoning, Steve wanted to convey his commitment to ensuring Lorraine's safety and well-being, underscoring the rationale behind his precautionary measures.

Through this detailed and explanatory approach, McMatters hoped to foster a deeper understanding and acceptance of his decisions, ultimately strengthening the credibility of his account.

"So that's why they knew my name."

"Yes."

It was abundantly clear to Lorraine that the two men had known her destination because of this. This realisation struck her with a sense of ease. The unsettling implication was that the detective had been closely monitoring or tracking her activities. Lorraine felt a growing sense of vulnerability, knowing that her privacy and security had been compromised in a way that left her at a distinct disadvantage.

"What do you know about what the detective was doing?"

"Lorraine, the detective had been seen by our men at various junctures during the course of his surveillance. While tasked with monitoring your movements, he evidently developed a powerful and inappropriate attraction towards you. Detective

Jackson's desire for you grew so intense that he was caught indulging in self-gratification on multiple occasions while on duty. Tonight's assault on you was the culmination of this disturbing obsession. I am relieved that I listened my intuition and instructed my men to closely observe him, as their vigilance has allowed us to safeguard you, Lorraine."

"Thank you, Steve. I am most grateful. Could you also thank your two men for stopping the detective?"

"I will, of course."

"So, what happened to the detective? I hope he rots in jail."

"You could say he will rot, but not in jail. He doesn't deserve something so kind."

Lorraine was struck with a sense of puzzlement and uncertainty as she contemplated the implications of McMatters' words. The ambiguity of his statement left her wondering whether it could possibly mean that Detective Jackson had met his maker. She paused, her brow furrowed, as she carefully considered the potential meaning behind his cryptic remark.

"Is he dead?"

"I hope so," replied McMatters, with a hint of trepidation in his voice.

"The detective in question had indeed been a deeply troubled and disturbed person, one who had attempted to violently attack you Lorraine in a reckless and unwarranted manner. His actions had been a blatant attempt to unlawfully take, a brazen disregard for your personal autonomy and property." McMatters shuddered at the thought of someone touching his Lorraine, recognising the gravity of the situation and the need to remain vigilant against such predatory and unethical behaviour in the future.

"Who am I to you?"

"I'm sorry, Lorraine, I know we haven't known each other for long, but I truly believe there is something special between us. I've felt a deep connection with you from the moment we first met, and I would be honoured if you would allow our relationship to grow into something more.

I care for you deeply and I'm ready to take this next step, if you are willing. I know it may seem too fast, but I feel a strong pull towards you, and I don't want to miss the opportunity to explore the potential we have together. What do you say, Lorraine? Will you give us a chance to see where this could lead?"

Lorraine was overjoyed when McMatters expressed his interest in her. She had never encountered anyone quite like him before, and this newfound connection filled her with excitement and a strong desire to learn more about him. The mutual intrigue they shared was palpable, and Lorraine eagerly looked forward to the opportunity to get to know McMatters on a deeper level.

This budding relationship held the promise of something truly special, and Lorraine was determined to nurture and explore it further.

"Yes, I'd like to get to know you more, Steve."

Chapter Twenty-Three Part Four
McMatter's Place

McMatters carefully guided Lorraine onto the bed, ensuring she felt safe and at ease in his company. He then proceeded to disrobe, joining her beneath the sheets as they sat up together, engaging in an intimate, unhurried conversation.

His gentle guidance and attentiveness created a safe, comforting environment that allowed Lorraine to feel at ease during a challenging time. The unhurried, intimate conversation they shared brings a deeper understanding of each other, this interaction provides Lorraine with much-needed solace and relief from her recent troubles. McMatters' patience and understanding shine through as he carefully navigates their conversation, showing great respect for Lorraine's personal boundaries and allowing her to share at her own pace.

McMatters was carefully and tactfully probing into the details of Lorraine's life, driven by a genuine desire to understand her better. Steve recognised that there were certain personal matters and questions that only Lorraine herself could provide insight into, as they were inherently tied to her own unique experiences, perspectives, and innermost thoughts.

McMatters understood the need to tread lightly and allow Lorraine the space to share information at her own pace, recognising the sensitive nature of delving into an individual's private life.

His approach reflected a patient, empathetic, and respectful attitude, aimed at gradually building a more comprehensive understanding of Lorraine, through her own words and willingness to open the communication.

The depth of McMatters' empathy and his genuine desire to understand Lorraine better is truly admirable. His tactful approach to learning about her life demonstrates a remarkable level of emotional intelligence and compassion.

"So, Lorraine, how did you come to know Detective Jackson?"

"He immediately stepped in to assist my mother, after she had been violently assaulted by her now former partner. It was his dedicated team of professionals who worked diligently to build a case and press charges on my mother's behalf. They ensured that justice would be served for the abhorrent act of domestic violence she had endured."

"I see, and your mum is where?"

"She's currently residing at my place, and I'm uncertain how long she plans to stay. However, this arrangement does have a positive aspect. By having her here, I can ensure her well-being and monitor her progress in abstaining from alcohol consumption. Additionally, I can help protect her from associating with any more undesirable romantic partners who may take advantage of her or treat her poorly."

"Does your mum not have her own place?"

"No, not in years. She abandoned her own home to live with whichever man wanted her at the time. Then she gets battered, drained of money, drinks heavily to forget, and ends up homeless again. This time I'm putting a stop to it. She's living with me where I can keep an eye on her and stop the drinking."

"Have you always had a good relationship with your mum?" asked McMatters

"No not really. Over the years, I've been let down a lot by my mum, and that's only if she was around at the time. But she's my mum, and I can't bear the thought of seeing her out on the streets again. She's had it rough lately, and despite the disappointments, I still feel a sense of obligation and care for her wellbeing. While the relationship has been strained, she is my mother, and I can't simply turn my back on her, especially when she's facing difficult times. There's a complex emotional bond that keeps me tethered to her, even if the trust has been broken numerous times in the past.

I want to be there for her, even if it means risking further heartbreak, because at the end of the day, she is family, and family is important, no matter how complicated the history may be."

"I see… Well, tonight you can stay with me. I insist on it. I need to make sure you are alright after the traumatic events you've experienced. It's crucial that you get the rest and care you need during this difficult time. I won't take no for an answer. Your wellbeing is my top priority, and I won't feel at ease unless I can provide you a safe, comfortable place to recuperate and process everything that's happened. Please, stay with me tonight so I can look after you and ensure you get the support you deserve. I'm here for you, and I'm not going to let you face this alone." Said McMatter's

"OK, thank you." Said Lorraine

Lorraine is luxuriating in the expansive, oversized bed, cocooned in the most sumptuous, high-quality sheets and quilt.

She is being meticulously attended to and pampered, with every need anticipated and catered to by her dedicated staff. The sheer size and lavishness of the bed envelops her, allowing Lorraine to sink into a state of unparalleled comfort and relaxation, free from the demands of the outside world. This indulgent setting provides Lorraine with a sense of opulence and exclusivity, as she revels in the personalised service and exceptional attention she is receiving.

Before Lorraine even realised what was happening, she found herself completely overwhelmed and disoriented.

One moment she was wide awake, and the next, she had drifted off into a deep, dreamless sleep almost instantaneously. The transition was so sudden and unexpected that Lorraine scarcely had time to register what was occurring before she had already succumbed to the overwhelming fatigue that had overcome her.

The speed and unexpectedness with which she lost consciousness caught her entirely off guard, leaving her with no opportunity to resist or prepare for the abrupt onset of sleep.

The following morning, Lorraine awoke feeling slightly disoriented, momentarily uncertain of her surroundings.

However, her confusion quickly subsided as she recognised the familiar setting of his bedroom. Just then, McMatters, entered the room carrying a tray laden with a delightful breakfast spread. The tray held two fluffy pancakes generously smothered in rich, creamy butter, a steaming cup of freshly brewed black coffee, and a single, delicate flower nestled in a small vase, adding a touch of natural beauty to the scene. At the sight of this, Lorraine sat up in bed, her gaze fixed intently on the stack of fluffy pancakes before her. As she took a bite, her eyes drifted towards her own attire a comfortable McMatters t-shirt that clung gently to her frame.

Across the room, Lorraine couldn't help but notice McMatters, was dressed in nothing more than a simple apron, his toned physique on full display, and what a body he had. The contrast between their states of dress, with Lorraine fully clothed and McMatters nearly nude, created a tantalising and undeniably alluring visual.

Lorraine felt a surge of attraction and desire coursing through her as she admired McMatters' confident, unabashed state of undress, finding the entire scene utterly captivating and irresistibly sexy.

"It's like that is it?" said McMatters catching Lorraine's glances.

"M..m…ayb...e." Lorraine said teasingly

"You need to eat all your food misses."

McMatters wearing nothing but his trusty apron and a whole lot of confidence, decides to leave the room his grand exit. Down the stairs he goes, Lorraine imagined his big sausage playing jump rope with every step. Lorraine pictured his sausage swinging side to side as he went downstairs, it made Lorraine laugh as she pictured it.

Every time Steve came back upstairs Lorraine started laughing hysterically. Steve was utterly perplexed by Lorraine's uncontrollable laughter, as he could not for the life of him figure out what had prompted such a fit of giggles. Each time Lorraine attempted to explain the source of her amusement, she would become consumed by another bout of hysterical laughter, leaving McMatters even more bewildered than before.

Despite his best efforts to discern the cause of Lorraine's hilarity, the more he inquired, the more she dissolved into a fit of unrestrained, infectious laughter, leaving him completely in the dark as to what had triggered such a reaction. Steve was just glad she was laughing considering recent events.

Lorraine was eager to get home as quickly as possible, as the night had been quite eventful, and her mother was still unaware of the happenings. She contemplated giving her mother a heads-up regarding her return, but then realised that doing so might prompt her mum, Maxine, to conceal her recent activities.

Lorraine concluded that it would be better to catch Maxine in the act, particularly since Lorraine had given strict instructions. No men and no drinking allowed. Lorraine had made her expectations crystal clear, and Lorraine felt a sense of responsibility to ensure that Maxine adhered to those rules, while she was recovering.

"Steve, any chance I could get a lift home?"

"I will take you myself."

"Thank you for last night."

"Don't mention it, glad I was able to help."

Lorraine tenderly leaned in and pressed her soft, warm lips against McMatters' in a passionate, lingering kiss. After savouring the intimate moment, she reluctantly pulled away and began preparing to depart, eager to return to the comforts of her own home.

Chapter Twenty-Three Part Five
Lorraine's Place

Steve drove Lorraine home in his gleaming, silver Mercedes sedan, expertly navigating the winding streets until they arrived at her residence. With the utmost care, he pulled the luxurious car up to the curb and brought it to a smooth, controlled stop, ensuring a safe and comfortable arrival for his Lorraine.

Steve had not yet had the opportunity to see where Lorraine lived, and he was quite pleasantly surprised by the well-maintained state of her property. While he was intrigued by the prospect of one day seeing the interior, Steve knew it was best to take things at a measured pace. He was not in any rush, understanding the importance of allowing their relationship to develop naturally and at a comfortable tempo for both.

"Do you want to come in?"

"Rain check? I've a meeting to get to."

"No problem at all, next time it is."

"How about a meal though, later?"

"That would be lovely."

"I will come pick you up at… say… 6pm?"

Lorraine leaned over and gently placed a tender kiss on his waiting lips, savouring the warmth and familiarity of the gesture. With a slight smile, she then gracefully exited the car, her movements fluid and purposeful as she made her way up the driveway leading to her home.

The brief but meaningful exchange between Lorraine and Steve served as a poignant punctuation to their time together, a subtle yet convincing display of the affection and connection shared between them. Lorraine opened the door to find her mother standing before her, her hands firmly planted on her hips in a posture that immediately conveyed a sense of determination and authority.

The sudden appearance of her mum, positioned in this assertive stance, created an unmistakable impression of disapproval or displeasure, setting the stage for a potentially tense encounter between the two of them. Lorraine braced herself, knowing she would need to tread carefully and be prepared to engage in a persuasive dialogue to address whatever concerns or grievances her mother had brought to the doorstep.

"And what time do you call this? What happened to your lovely dress?"

"Let me get in and grab a brew, then I'll tell you all about my eventful experience."

Lorraine expertly crafted a rich and decadent latte, meticulously adding the perfect amount of velvety smooth chocolate powder and a delightful dusting of salted caramel sprinkles to create a truly indulgent beverage. Carrying the tempting drink, she confidently made her way to the front room where her mother, Maxine, was patiently waiting. The aroma of the freshly prepared latte must have been tantalising.

"OK, so where do I start?"

"The beginning. That is normally where most people start."

"Ha ha! OK, so I got in the taxi and halfway to the club, the driver turned off and parked up. He went for a pee, then when he returned, he attacked me, pulled my legs, and tried to force them open, hence the ripped new dress that's now ruined.

I kicked at him, and as it forced him back, someone grabbed him, battered him, and went to put him in the boot of the taxi, only to find the actual taxi driver, already tied up in the boot."

"Oh no, he didn't touch you, did he?"

"No... But there's more. Detective Jackson was the one who attacked me."

Maxine's eyes went wide, and she drew in a sharp breath upon hearing this unexpected and startling news. She was utterly taken aback, her expression reflecting the sheer surprise and disbelief she felt in that moment.

The revelation had caught Maxine completely off guard, eliciting an immediate visceral reaction as the implications of this news sank in. Maxine's gasp conveyed the depth of her shock and the intensity of her emotional response to the surprising information that had just been presented to her.

"Why?"

"There's more. The guys who rescued me from Jackson work for Mr McMatters. They had been following Jackson because they noticed that he'd been watching me. He'd been caught pleasuring himself while observing me," said Lorraine.

"How could he? Why?"

"I know I had lots of questions too. McMatters' men took me to the club, but the shock of it all had set in by then and I couldn't talk or move.

McMatters has dealt with Detective Jackson, Mum; he's never going to bother us again. McMatters helped me a lot with all of this. I stayed at his place last night. Don't worry, nothing happened, he just hugged me. I slept a lot."

Maxine, a typically confident and self-assured mother, found herself uncharacteristically worried for her daughter's wellbeing. This marked a significant shift, as Maxine had rarely experienced such profound concerns about her child's situation before. Maxine had heard stories about Mr McMatters and it wasn't good either. The gravity of the circumstances she now faced compelled her to confront emotions and anxieties that were foreign to her typical parenting approach.

Maxine's unwavering faith in her daughter's resilience and capabilities had, for the first time, given way to a palpable sense of apprehension and a heightened need to ensure her child's safety and well-being.

Lorraine perceptively recognised and acknowledged the worries and anxieties that her mother was experiencing. She demonstrated a keen sensitivity and atonement to her mother's emotional state, picking up on the underlying concerns that her mother may have been hesitant to express directly.

Lorraine's ability to empathise with her mother's perspective and provide a supportive, understanding presence likely helped to create an open and validating dialogue between the two of them.

"So, what does it mean?"

"In what way?"

"Does that mean we're off the hook, no more hassle from the cops?"

"I hadn't thought about it, but yes. With the detective dead, I guess there's no more pressure to do anything."

"Oh, I'm relieved."

"But Mum, I like Steve a lot, and it's mutual. He's a nice guy. Yes, he can never be crossed, and yes, he could be dangerous, but Mum, he's so good and nice to me."

"Please be careful, Lorraine."

"I will, but you must never say anything about Detective Jackson. All Steve knows is that he helped you when you were attacked. That's it. Never say anything else."

"I won't, I promise, I notice your on first name terms though, are you in a relationship with him?"

"yes, I believe I am, I mean we'll I will see where it goes. Now what did you get up to while I wasn't here?"

"After a long day, I decided to unwind. I turned on the television and lost myself in captivating programming for a while. Then, I took a warm, soothing bubble bath to rest my sores, which are getting better. Even the bruises are reducing. My rib is still bad, but it will mend."

"I'm glad you relaxed a bit."

Lorraine then recognised that what she needed most at that moment was to indulge in a soothing, restorative bubble bath. The idea of submerging herself in warm, fragrant water and allowing the gentle bubbles to envelop her body and soothe her mind filled her with a sense of eager anticipation.

Lorraine knew that taking the time to pamper herself in this way would provide her with the tranquillity and rejuvenation she craved after a long, stressful day. The prospect of slipping into a tub overflowing with plush, aromatic bubbles filled her with a growing conviction that this was precisely the self-care ritual she required to unwind and recharge.

Chapter Twenty-Four
Jarvis

Jarvis, the efficient right-hand man, had just brewed a fresh pot of aromatic coffee when his boss, McMatters, entered the office. The aroma of the freshly brewed coffee filled the air, creating a welcoming and inviting atmosphere as McMatters arrived for the workday.

Jarvis, anticipating the needs of his boss, had the coffee ready and waiting, ensuring a smooth and productive start to the day for both.

"Morning boss."

"Morning Jarvis."

"Is Lorraine home now?"

"Yes, just dropped her off, maybe now we can have a full catch up."

"Sounds good to me. Okay, so you know I had the meeting with the Bennetts and the Santos. Well, I arrived and set up early as I normally do, as you know. Once both families had arrived, I quizzed them on the previous events. It turns out that the Santos family member was not selling dope at all.

He had simply been on holiday and had brought it back with him for his own personal use. I had already known what went down so I was able to determine that the Santos family member was not engaged in adding to their empire, as initially suspected. Instead, he had innocently brought back a personal stash of marijuana from his vacation"

"So, the Bennetts had trashed a pub for no reason?"

"Yes, and that annoyed me immensely. The lesson was delivered with a sharp, pointed reminder of who holds the power and authority, reinforcing the established rules and expectations."

"Sounds like you had fun. What was the punishment? Each time you are very creative in your lessons!"

"The Bennetts are currently undergoing a significant restructuring of their family dynamics. The expression on their faces conveyed a striking visual, as the head of the family, head rolled across the floor, while the body remained firmly seated, almost resembling the movement of tumbleweeds in the wind, I had to refrain from laughing.

When I instructed them to tidy up the mess, they seemed to be on the verge of protesting, but didn't want to lose their heads as well. A shift in the Bennetts' family structure is underway, they were told to clean up and clean up they did."

This notion of the head rolling caused McMatters to burst out laughing. Jarvis was well known for his creative and unorthodox methods of punishing anyone who dared to defy him or his directives.

McMatters felt a sense of relief and reassurance knowing that he had Jarvis on his side. Jarvis's ruthless yet effective approach to dealing with those who went against him or his orders provided McMatters with a strong deterrent and protection against potential adversaries. The mere thought of Jarvis's retribution was enough to make McMatters feel secure in his position and confident in Jarvis's ability to swiftly and decisively handle any threats or challenges as they arose.

McMatters, the influential figure behind the Jarvis organisation, is known to possess a particularly dark and unforgiving side that is often kept well hidden from the public eye.

Those familiar with the inner workings of this powerful empire understand that McMatters, the true mastermind orchestrating Jarvis's operations, is a force to be reckoned with. The retribution and consequences meted out by Jarvis himself are often perceived as severe, but they pale in comparison to the ruthless actions and punishments that McMatters can deliver personally to those who cross him or the organisation he controls.

The mere mention of McMatters' name strikes fear into the hearts of those who are aware of his formidable reputation and unwavering determination to protect his interests and maintain his dominance.

Jarvis is the public-facing figure, the one who handles the negotiations, interacts directly with the families, and metes out his own brand of retribution. However, Jarvis is not a lone operator. Behind the scenes, McMatters serves as a reliable backup, ready to provide support and resources whenever they are needed. While Jarvis maintains a visible presence and carries out the day-to-day operations, McMatters lurks in the shadows, ready to unleash carnage on a grand scale should the situation call for it. This symbiotic relationship between the two ensures that their organisation maintains a formidable presence. With Jarvis as the public face and McMatters as the ominous, powerful force that can be summoned to deal with any serious threats or challenges that arise.

"Tonight, I'm taking Lorraine for a meal."

"I will get your favourite place booked, 7pm?"

"Yes! Thank you, Jarvis."

McMatters was a frequent patron of Demetrio's, a charming Italian restaurant situated on the outskirts of town. What drew McMatters to this establishment was the inviting ambiance it offered, particularly the cosy booths that provided a sense of privacy and intimacy. The quieter setting of the restaurant, away from the bustling city centre, created a calming and relaxing dining experience that McMatters thoroughly enjoyed.

The combination of the restaurant's authentic Italian cuisine and the comfortable, secluded seating arrangements made Demetrio's a favourite dining destination for McMatters. The owners of this establishment have a long standing, close personal relationship with McMatters, as they have been almost lifelong friends who grew up together in the same community., Demetrio who is older looked out for McMatters in his younger days. This close-knit dynamic allows them to cultivate a warm, welcoming atmosphere and consistently deliver exceptional meals that keep customers coming back. In return, McMatters provides a valuable layer of protection and security for the business, ensuring its smooth and successful operation. The mutually beneficial partnership between the owners and McMatters is a key factor in the establishment's ability to thrive and maintain its reputation for excellence.

Over the years, various individuals have attempted to extort protection money from Demetrio's. Those who dared to pursue this ill-advised course of action soon learned the error of their ways, as McMatters has a reputation for being a formidable and unyielding figure.

His ability to instil fear and break the resolve of even the most hardened individuals is well documented, with many having been reduced to tears, pleading, and even calling out for their mothers in a desperate attempt to appease him.

McMatters' sheer presence and unwavering determination have made him a force to be reckoned with, and those who have crossed him have invariably lived to regret their decision.

Chapter Twenty-Five
McMatters

Steve arrived at Lorraine's place a little earlier than their scheduled meeting time at five pm. Despite typically exhibiting a confident and self-assured demeanour, he finds himself feeling unusually nervous on this occasion.

Steve is eager to see Lorraine and her home environment, and he is particularly interested at the prospect of meeting Lorraine's mother. This nervousness is somewhat out of character for him, as he generally maintains a poised and unflustered composure.

However, the importance Steve places on this encounter and his desire to make a positive impression on Lorraine and her mother has triggered a rare moment of uncharacteristic anxiety within Steve normally assured disposition, maybe it was due to them now being in a relationship.

As Steve strolls up the neatly paved driveway, he can't help but feel a sense of admiration for the vibrant and well-manicured front garden that greets him. The lush greenery, the colourful blooms, and the carefully tended landscaping all contribute to a visually appealing and inviting atmosphere. Reaching the front door, Steve confidently rings the bell, eager to engage with Lorraine, and perhaps learn the secrets behind such an impressive display of horticultural prowess. Lorraine's mum answers the door.

"Hello?"

"Hello! You must be Maxine? I am Steve."

"Oh, I see."

"LORRAINE!" Maxine shouts very loudly up the stairs, "LOVER BOY IS HERE!"

Steve chuckles with amusement at Lorraine's mother's futile attempt to embarrass her daughter. Lorraine's mother's actions, clearly intended to humiliate or mortify Lorraine, instead have the opposite effect, providing a source of entertainment and levity for Steve.

Steve finds Lorraine's mother's misguided efforts to be an amusing and light-hearted moment, one that underscores the dynamics at play within this family dynamic. Rather than feeling uncomfortable or offended, McMatters was entertained by the theatrical nature of Lorraine's mother's antics, which failed to achieve the desired reaction from her target and eased his nerves.

"Shit! You're early," said Lorraine.

"Sorry!" shouted Steve.

"Come in then, find a spot, park your bum. I'll be down in a minute," said Lorraine to Steve.

"Mother, make Steve a drink please?"

As Steve crossed that threshold, his world exploded into a kaleidoscope of breath-taking beauty! The sheer magnificence of the style and decor that enveloped him was beyond anything he could have imagined. Steve's jaw dropped, his eyes widened, and his heart raced as he tried to take in the awe-inspiring spectacle before him.

Never in his wildest dreams had Steve encountered such an extraordinary display of interior design mastery. It was as if he'd stepped into a realm of pure aesthetic perfection! Words failed him completely as Steve stood there, utterly spellbound by Lorraine's incredible talents. The mind-blowing elegance and harmony of the home's ambiance left Steve thunderstruck.

Steve realised, with a jolt of humbling amazement, that he had grossly underestimated Lorraine's phenomenal eye for detail and her supernatural ability to craft a living space of such unparalleled beauty and sophistication. Every corner, every surface, every carefully curated element sang with an otherworldly charm that left McMatters weak in the knees, struggling to comprehend the sheer artistry surrounding him.

It was a moment of pure, unadulterated wonder that would be forever etched in his memory. Steve's senses must have been in complete overdrive as he stepped into this otherworldly realm of design brilliance. The seamless fusion of digital and physical elements is nothing short of miraculous.

How on earth did Lorraine achieve such perfection? It's as if the very fabric of reality has been rewoven into this breath-taking tapestry of innovation and artistry. Every step, every turn was an adventure into the unknown, a journey through a wonderland of technological marvels.

This house isn't just a structure; it's a testament to human ingenuity, a beacon of what's possible when imagination and technology collide in the most spectacular way. It's not just impressive; it's a revolution in design that leaves one utterly speechless and completely awestruck!

Steve never would have guessed that behind the door to an old house was this amazing decor Steve thought he just might have to get Lorraine to decorate some of his house.

"I had the same reaction you know," said Maxine.

Steve's mind raced as he surveyed the whirlwind of activity around him. He caught a glimpse of Maxine watching him amused then another decorative section would take him on a journey, like being on a dizzying carnival ride with no idea what surprises awaited him around the next bend.

The constantly shifting scenery and frantic pace left him feeling disoriented, yet also intrigued by the unpredictable nature of his surroundings. Steve couldn't quite grasp the full scope of what was unfolding, but the thrill of the unknown spurred him onward, eager to discover what other wonders and mysteries this peculiar setting had in store.

As Steve returned from the living area to the kitchen, he noticed Maxine and Lorraine engaged in laughter, clearly amused by the questions circulating in McMatters' mind.

The sight of the two women giggling suggested that they were privy to some information or inside joke that had eluded Steve, piquing his curiosity and leaving him wondering what exactly had prompted their amusement. Their light-hearted reaction stood in contrast to the serious contemplation occupying Steve's thoughts, creating a noticeable tension in the atmosphere as he re-joined them in the kitchen.

"This place is …. "

Steve found himself utterly at a loss for words, unable to articulate the frustration and sense of helplessness he was experiencing. The words he desperately sought to express his internal turmoil simply would not come to him, leaving him trapped in a cyclical pattern of mental anguish as he struggled to verbalize his thoughts.

Despite his best efforts, he could not seem to break free from this debilitating inability to find the right words, which only compounded his feelings of inadequacy and despair. Stuck in this linguistic quagmire, Steve was left feeling powerless to effectively communicate the turmoil consuming his mind.

"I know! Isn't it fantastic?" said Lorraine.

"Oh yes! I love it! You designed all of it?" Asked Steve.

"Yes, I had to get someone in to bring it to life, but yes I designed it."

"We have a reservation so we need to go, but I'd love to see the rest of the house sometime."

"I bet you would," said Maxine.

"Mum gets your mind out of the gutter."

"Nice meeting you Maxine."

Lorraine swiftly and decisively ushered him towards the exit, simultaneously casting a pointed, disapproving glare in the direction of her mother. The combination of her forceful physical motion and her piercing, accusatory gaze creates an unmistakable air of tension and confrontation as she shepherds him out of the room.

Lorraine's actions and body language convey a sense of urgency and determination, as if she is intent on removing him from the situation as quickly as possible, while also making a clear statement to her mother through the intensity of her resentful, challenging stare.

Upon arriving at the renowned Demetrio's restaurant at six forty-five pm, Lorraine and McMatters were warmly welcomed as if they were long lost friends. The staff treated them with the utmost courtesy and respect, making them feel like royalty.

Although this was Lorraine's first visit to Demetrio's, she had heard countless praises about the establishment, and her high expectations were more than exceeded. The ambiance of the restaurant truly captured the essence of Italy, transporting Lorraine to a charming Mediterranean setting. From the authentic decor to the inviting atmosphere, every aspect of Demetrio's conveyed a genuine Italian flair that Lorraine found captivating.

As a passionate admirer of Italian cuisine, Lorraine was thrilled to indulge in the restaurant's delectable offerings, knowing that she was in for a culinary experience that would delight her senses and satisfy her cravings for the flavours of Italy.

Lorraine, desiring a hearty and flavourful meal, selected the chicken pasta carbonara as her entree. The carbonara, a classic Italian dish, features a creamy sauce made with eggs, cheese, and cured pork, which perfectly complements the tender chicken and pasta.

In contrast, Steve was craving a more traditional Italian staple, chose the spaghetti Bolognese. The Bolognese sauce, a rich and savoury blend of ground meat, tomatoes, and aromatic herbs, is a beloved comfort food that pairs excellently with the al dente spaghetti noodles.

The attentive waiter brought over two expertly crafted drinks, demonstrating an impressive knowledge of Steve's personal preferences. Despite not explicitly stating her order, the waiter was able to accurately deduce that her favourite cocktail was a blue ocean. This level of personalised service and anticipation of the customer's needs reflects the waiter's keen observational skills and deep familiarity with the establishment's clientele. Steve was brought single malt whisky on rocks, which added an extra touch of customised hospitality to the dining experience. Lorraine was taken aback when the waiter arrived with the oversized portions at her table.

The sheer size of the dishes placed before her was quite alarming, and she momentarily felt overwhelmed at the prospect of consuming such an inordinate amount of food. The towering plates presented a daunting challenge, causing Lorraine to momentarily doubt whether she would be physically capable of finishing the meal. The disproportionate servings threatened to push the limits of her appetite, leaving her to wonder how she would possibly make her way through the entire contents of the supersized dishes placed in front of her.

Lorraine's eyes widened in astonishment as she glanced upwards, taking in the sheer magnitude of the meal that had been placed before her. Steve observed her with amusement, closely studying the myriads of emotions playing across Lorraine's features as she processed the unexpected scale and portion size of the dish. The substantial nature of the meal had clearly caught Lorraine off guard, eliciting a range of captivating reactions that did not escape Steve's discerning gaze.

Lorraine's facial expressions betrayed her surprise and wonderment at confronting such an unexpectedly large and hearty serving, which clearly amused and entertained her dining companion Steve.

"So, Lorraine! What do you think of my favourite restaurant?"

"I love it here; I haven't been before."

They exchanged casual, friendly banter and conversed light-heartedly in the intervals between taking bites of their meal. The lively, relaxed dialogue interspersed throughout their dining experience helped create a convivial atmosphere. It fostered a sense of comfortable camaraderie between them as they enjoyed each other's company over the course of the meal.

"So, I do have some questions as I am sure you have some too. All I ask is your truthful with your answers."

Lorraine nodded in acknowledgment, her mouth currently occupied and preventing her from providing a verbal response. The action of a subtle nod communicated her understanding and agreement, despite the temporary inability to speak due to her mouth being full at that moment.

"What do you do Lorraine? Like work, income etc.?"

"Well, from a young age, as you know, I didn't have the upbringing I should have had, but I did learn to take what wasn't mine. It took many years to perfect my skills; now, most don't realise something is missing until hours later. I have rules, though: only shiny things, only from those who have insurance, etc."

Lorraine found herself in a difficult position, torn between her desire to withhold certain information and her unwillingness to be dishonest. On one hand, she was deeply concerned about the potential consequences of sharing certain details, fearing how the recipient might react or use that knowledge.

This apprehension made her hesitant to disclose everything. On the other hand, Lorraine's strong aversion to lying prevented her from simply fabricating a response or concealing the truth entirely.

Lorraine found herself grappling with this internal conflict, uncertain of the best course of action that would balance her need for discretion with her commitment to ethical communication, so Lorraine continued

"I don't need to work as such. I was left a considerable amount when the shop owners died. They had helped me for years, taking me in, feeding me, and putting a roof over my head. They taught me rules and respect."

"So, they gave you the tools to use but set boundaries for how they can be used?" asked Steve

"Yes. When they died, I sold the shop, bought an apartment which I did up, sold it, and bought the house where I am now."

"Thank you for being honest with me, Lorraine. It means a lot."

"So, you're not scared off?"

"Not at all." said Lorraine

"My turn. So, Steve, I know the club is the legal side of you, but I want to know the other side of you."

"I was always switched on and headstrong. I'm willing to do what others won't. I don't mind getting my hands dirty."

"So, you can give as good as you get, play rough when needed, be forceful, direct, and stubborn. You watch everything to protect everything, and nothing is off the table?"

"Damn, Lorraine, that is a flipside indeed."

"As you're not being very direct, let's try this another way. Yes or no only."

"Robbery?" quizzed Lorraine

"Yes, I dabbled." Said McMatter's hesitantly replied

"Assault?"

"Yes, oh yes you could say that."

"Laundering?"

"Yes, but not for me."

"Drugs?"

"Yes, comes with the territory."

"Arson?"

"Yes, I prefer not to."

"Murder?"

"...Not sure you want to know."

"I knew there was more to you, a dark horse, smooth talker."

"So, have I scared you off?" asked Steve he was now worried she wouldn't be interested in a relationship with him.

"If you had, I'd already be out the door." Explained Lorraine

"I feel there is much more to you than meets the eye"

The idea of being with someone who possessed vast knowledge and was unafraid, thrilled and aroused Steve. The prospect of such an intimate encounter, with a partner who exuded such confidence and expertise, ignited a sense of excitement and anticipation within him.

Steve found the thought intensely alluring, as it promised a level of connection and understanding that was both stimulating and reassuring. The knowledge that his Lorraine would navigate the experience with skill and poise only served to heighten Steve's feelings of arousal and desire.

Steve abruptly rose from the table, hastily paid the bill, and grasped Lorraine's hand. He desperately needed her companionship, as his overwhelming desire to take her right then and there, was becoming increasingly difficult to suppress.

The mere thought of being intimate with her was already starting to physically arouse him, intensifying his sense of urgency and anticipation. Steve felt a primal, almost uncontrollable urge to act on his romantic impulses without delay, the strength of his attraction to Lorraine proving to be truly overpowering in that moment.

Once comfortably situated in the car on their way to Steve's house, Lorraine astutely picked up on the subtle physical cues indicating her companion's growing arousal. Instinctively, Lorraine reached over and began lightly tracing her fingers along the fabric of Steve's pants, teasing and tantalising him with her delicate touch. Lorraine was acutely aware of how desperately he craved her attention and affection in that moment, as her own emotions had reached a fevered pitch, consumed by a primal need for his intimate presence.

The increasing tension and building desire between them were palpable, fuelling an irrepressible longing that demanded to be satiated.

Chapter Twenty-Five Part Two
McMatters' Place

Once McMatters and Lorraine arrived at Steve's secluded residence, the palpable sexual tension between them had reached fever pitch. Bypassing the main house, Steve guided Lorraine through a series of well-trimmed hedges, leading them down a winding path that evoked the feeling of navigating a carefully curated maze.

Turning left and right, they eventually reached a clearing - a meticulously maintained open space adorned with a whimsical statue of Cupid, the mythical god of love, poised with his iconic bow and heart shaped arrow.

Lorraine couldn't help but chuckle at the romantic tableau before them. In that moment, the atmosphere was charged with anticipation, and Steve seized the opportunity, pulling Lorraine close and initiating a passionate kiss.

The couple's embrace conveyed a sense of urgency, fuelled by the allure of their secluded, intimate setting and the promise of the mind-blowing intimacy that lay ahead. Steve slowly and deliberately began removing Lorraine's top and jacket, gradually exposing her lacy, delicate bra.

The deliberate, sensual motions heightened the tension and anticipation in the maze as Lorraine's upper body was gradually revealed. Steve's skilled hands deftly unfastened each button and zipper, taking care to maintain eye contact with Lorraine as the layers of clothing were peeled away, heightening the intimate, seductive atmosphere.

The gradual disrobing built a palpable sense of desire and excitement, as Lorraine's shapely figure was gradually unveiled before his hungry gaze. Lorraine then swiftly removed her Steve's shirt, her lips eagerly pressing against his bare chest as she methodically popped open the buttons one by one. The sensual act was charged with palpable desire, as Lorraine's caresses and kisses trailed across his exposed skin, eliciting a heightened emotional and physical response.

This intimate moment was filled with a palpable sense of passion and growing anticipation between the two individuals. Slowly Without hesitation, Steve swiftly unbuttoned and removed his pants, allowing them to fall freely to the floor.

With a firm yet gentle motion, he then lifted Lorraine's skirt, exposing her legs and revealing her figure. This bold and deliberate action set the stage for the passionate encounter that was about to unfold between the two individuals. moving her underwear aside, gently caressing her intimate area.

Lorraine teased his arousal. The situation was rife with potential, poised and ready for decisive action. The conditions had been carefully cultivated, creating an environment primed and optimised for immediate, impactful intervention.

All the necessary elements were in place, aligned and synchronised, awaiting the spark that would catalyse meaningful progress and change. Steve firmly grasped Lorraine, lifting her up and positioning her body so that her legs were straddling either side of him. This intimate, provocative pose allowed for maximum physical closeness and contact between the two individuals.

The strategic placement of Lorraine's limbs suggested an escalating sexual tension and a growing sense of passion and desire. Steve's actions demonstrated a confident, assertive approach as he, maneuverer Lorraine into this compromising yet alluring position, then he gently teased Lorraine, playfully toying with her emotions and pushing her right to the very brink of her sensations.

Steve knew exactly how to captivate her, skilfully dancing along the delicate line between excitement and apprehension, leaving her teetering on the precipice of ecstasy. With a masterful touch, Steve expertly manipulated Lorraine's desires, heightening the tension until she could barely contain her anticipation, her body trembling with unbridled yearning for his next move.

Steve, a prominent figure, skilfully and persuasively conveyed to Lorraine a range of powerful sensations and emotions that she found increasingly difficult to contain. As Steve's words and actions elicited a profound sense of sexual arousal within Lorraine, she found herself unable to suppress the resulting outbursts and cries that betrayed her heightened state of excitement and desire.

Steve reclined on the floor, his body relaxed and receptive, as Lorraine straddled him. She moved with a practiced grace, skilfully stimulating his senses and eliciting pleasurable sensations. The intimate encounter unfolded with a fluid rhythm, Lorraine's deft touch and undulating motions orchestrating a captivating dance that left Steve thoroughly enthralled.

Lorraine's encounter with Steve reached a dramatic and intense climax, marked by a powerful, explosive, and highly emotional exchange between the two individuals. The intensity of the situation was palpable, as Lorraine and Steve experienced a profound and overwhelming convergence of feelings and reactions that unfolded in a loud and captivating manner. The sheer force and rawness of the experience left a lasting impression, underscoring the depth and complexity of the dynamic between Lorraine and Steve.

Steve and Lorraine reclined together on the soft, verdant grass, with Steve still intimately joined with Lorraine. This passionate, sensual moment allowed them to bask in the afterglow of their lovemaking, savouring the deep physical and emotional connection they shared.

Surrounded by the tranquil natural setting, they revelled in the feeling of being completely entwined, their bodies melded as one. This private, tender encounter spoke of the intense desire and affection that burned between the two lovers.

"I hope no one heard us!" said Lorraine giggling.

Steve gazed at Lorraine with a warm smile, acknowledging the profound effects she had on him. "The impact you've had on my life... You've come into my world like a powerful whirlwind, shaking up my senses and emotions in a truly magical way. The connection and feelings we share are extraordinary, transcending the mundane and elevating our relationship to a realm of enchantment and wonder."

Steve rolled Lorraine over on the grass and gradually and deliberately moved within her, Steve's actions reflecting the tender, affectionate desire he felt for her. Lorraine could palpably feel the electricity, the charged energy building between them, and she yearned for him to continue his sensual, rhythmic motions, savouring the intimate connection they shared.

For a second time, Steve and Lorraine experienced a gradual yet intense build-up of physical and emotional tension, culminating in a shared moment of profound release and satisfaction. Their bodies moved in a synchronised rhythm, waves of pleasure washing over them as they reached the pinnacle of their intimate encounter. This powerful, experience left them both feeling deeply connected and fulfilled as they climaxed together.

McMatters and Lorraine hastily began redressing themselves, hurriedly collecting their scattered clothing that lay strewn about the secluded garden hidden within the dense maze of towering conifers. The intimate encounter they had shared now required a swift and discreet return to a state of propriety, as they worked to conceal any evidence of their recent passionate tryst from prying eyes. With a heightened sense of urgency, they quickly adorned themselves, ensuring their appearance was restored to a presentable state before venturing out from the private, verdant enclosure in which their ardent escapade had unfolded.

"I'm famished. Let's go and get some food," said Steve.

"I wonder why we are so hungry?" Lorraine giggled.

Steve and Lorraine entered the kitchen, which bore a striking resemblance to Lorraine's own kitchen in terms of its overall design and layout. The primary distinguishing factor was that the island in this kitchen served as the cooktop, rather than a standalone appliance as was the case in Lorraine's kitchen. This subtle yet significant difference in the kitchen's configuration immediately caught their attention, inviting them to further explore the nuances that set this space apart from the familiar comforts of Lorraine's own culinary domain.

"We'll eat outside while the sun sets. How about a filled omelette?"

"Perfect." Said Lorraine

Lorraine sat patiently outside, eagerly anticipating the arrival of Steve and the delectable omelette he was preparing. In the meantime, Lorraine had taken the initiative to pour them each a refreshing glass of chardonnay and artfully arranged a selection of freshly sliced strawberries as an accompaniment to their meal.

The combination of the aromatic wine, the fluffy omelette, and the sweet, juicy berries promised to create a truly indulgent and satisfying dining experience for the two of them to share and savour together. They stood side by side, captivated as the vibrant hues of the setting sun painted the sky in a breath-taking display. The warm glow cast a tranquil ambiance over the scene, marking the end of a truly spectacular evening they had shared together.

Watching the sun dip below the horizon, they felt a sense of contentment and appreciation for the special moments they had experienced. The sunset served as a poignant bookend to an evening filled with shared laughter, engaging conversation, and the deepening of their connection. As the last traces of daylight faded, they knew this memory would forever be etched in their minds as a cherished reminder of the magic they had created.

Chapter Twenty-Five Part Three
Go Secure

Jarvis was poised to urgently contact McMatters, as the situation at hand demanded immediate attention and required a secure line of communication. The matter was of the utmost importance, necessitating prompt action and the establishment of a confidential channel to convey the critical information.

Jarvis recognised the gravity of the circumstances and the need to reach McMatters without delay, aware that any delay could have serious consequences. With a sense of urgency and purpose, Jarvis prepared to initiate the crucial call, knowing that secure and timely communication was paramount in addressing the pressing issue at hand.

"Hello Jarvis."

"Go secure."

McMatters immediate reaction was to swiftly put down the original phone and instead reach for a separate, specialised device that they kept on hand for situations when they needed to ensure complete privacy and prevent any unwanted eavesdropping. This alternate phone was a precautionary measure McMatters had taken, anticipating the potential need for making sensitive calls without the risk of being overheard by unintended parties. The swift transition to this secure communication device demonstrates McMatters foresight and commitment to maintaining confidentiality, even in the face of a potentially compromising scenario. McMatters phones Jarvis back.

"Jarvis what's the score?"

"A rival family has encroached upon our established territory, and we have suffered two casualties as a result. One of our men was struck by a crossbow bolt, while another was stabbed in the back with a blade. These intruders clearly recognised our associates and were aware of their affiliation with our organisation. This brazen attack represents a significant escalation in the ongoing territorial dispute, and we must respond swiftly and decisively to defend our interests and avenge the harm done to our people.

Our dominance in this area will not be challenged without consequences, and we will take the necessary actions to ensure that our position of power remains firmly intact."

"What's the family name?"

"Blythe."

"Do we know yet what they deal in?

"Heroin, LSD and something else I'm waiting on more information."

"OK, do no overlap with current families, we need a meeting with all bosses like last time. This time I will be in the shadows."

"Will do boss, hide n seek?"

"Yes, just in case I need to pick them off one by one."

It's one reason no one liked it if McMatters got directly involved. Bodies dropped at a fast rate, but no one ever sees him. On each body, a card is left with no prints or handwriting just a printed black card with the letter M.

Over the years, gossip between families pointed out that the M stood for McMatters.

McMatters, a notorious man, has managed to instil a pervasive sense of fear and unease within the community. His aggressive tactics and ruthless control over the area has left many families living in a constant state of apprehension.

However, a new family has recently moved into the neighbourhood, seemingly unaware of the established power dynamics and the consequences of defying McMatters' authority. It has become clear that this newcomer family requires a stern lesson on how things operate within this territory. The existing power structures and the unwritten rules that govern the community must be made abundantly clear to them.

Failure to conform and submit to the established order will likely result in swift and decisive action from McMatters, sending a message that challenges to their dominance will not be tolerated. The new family must understand that resistance is futile, and the only way to ensure their safety and well-being is to fall in line with the expectations set forth by the powerful McMatters syndicate.

"Get all men suited and booted. Let's use the Kevlar for this. Only main men in power suits; the rest can wear anything they feel most comfortable attacking in, but all wear Kevlar under normal clothing. You too, Jarvis."

"Will do, boss."

"Let me know what time, and I will be there."

McMatters exited the call, his mind swirling with the weight of the conversation.

As he turned around, he noticed Lorraine standing silently behind him, her presence palpable.

A sense of unease crept up his spine as he pondered just how much of the discussion she had overheard. The uncertainty left him feeling uneasy, unsure of how to proceed or what her reaction might be. Steve knew he would need to tread carefully, as Lorraine's knowledge of the situation could potentially complicate matters moving forward.

"It's fine, don't worry. I know your history. I know how you work."

"Lorraine, this could be dangerous. We don't know who they are."

"Don't worry. Just make sure you are safe. Be careful."

"All I ask is that you never lie and never cheat, because they are deal breakers for me."

"Deal! Sit. I will explain the situation."

Lorraine carefully listened and considered the details that Jarvis had provided. While the information did give Lorraine some cause for concern, she possessed a strong understanding of how the process works. Lorraine's natural strengths in organisation, planning, and preparation would serve her well in ensuring the successful execution of the tasks at hand. Despite any initial apprehension, Lorraine felt confident in her ability to meticulously coordinate and carry out the necessary work, drawing upon her proven skills in these critical areas.

"Can you cover the club with a team for protection and keep it running smoothly while I help Jarvis? At least then I wouldn't need to worry about the club."

"I will, yes."

Steve faced a critical decision regarding the leadership of the club, as he was tasked with helping Jarvis. While Steve had some reservations about Lorraine's specific capabilities to effectively manage the club's operations, he ultimately recognised that finding a trustworthy and reliable individual was of paramount importance.

Despite any potential skill gaps, Steve determined that Lorraine's proven integrity and dependability outweighed the concerns about her technical proficiency. In the end, Steve concluded that Lorraine's strong character and unwavering loyalty were the decisive factors that made her the right choice to oversee the club, even if her managerial experience was not as extensive as other candidates.

Steve prioritised finding someone he could genuinely trust to uphold the club's values and objectives, and he believed Lorraine was that person, despite any lingering doubts about her full range of operational expertise. Interestingly, Steve had also developed deep, unwavering feelings for Lorraine. He was completely smitten and yearned for her presence in his life, eager to share all their activities and experiences.

The powerful emotions he was grappling with led him to believe that he was falling irrevocably in love with Lorraine.

Driven by this profound connection, Steve felt a strong need to ensure Lorraine's safety and well-being, wanting nothing more than to provide her with a sense of protection and security. Steve felt a sense of relief and reassurance knowing that Lorraine would be taking over the management and oversight of the club in his absence. With Lorraine's capable leadership, Steve could feel confident that the club's operations would continue smoothly, allowing him to focus on facilitating a positive and productive transition.

Steve was known for his meticulous approach whenever sensitive matters arose. Rather than succumbing to anxiety or undue concern, he exhibited a calm, self-assured demeanour, confident in his

ability to navigate any challenging situations.
However, Steve also recognised that his role extended
beyond just safeguarding his own interests.
Maintaining control and providing leadership for two
additional influential families was also of paramount
importance to him too.

This heightened responsibility drove Steve to be
exceptionally cautious and deliberate in his decision-
making, as the well-being of multiple powerful
entities depended on his prudent handling of the
circumstances at hand.

Lorraine observed that Steve was visibly preoccupied,
though not in a distressed or concerning manner. She
could discern a palpable sense of contemplation and
strategizing unfolding within his mind, as if he was
deeply engaged in a process of active plotting and
meticulous planning. His demeanour suggested a
thoughtful, focused state rather than one of anxiety or
unease.

Chapter Twenty-Six
Jarvis

Jarvis was pacing back and forth in the middle of the office when a knock suddenly came at the open doorway. Team Charlie and Team Delta then entered the room, their footsteps echoing against the walls as they made their way inside.

Jarvis immediately ceased his restless movements, straightening his posture and turning to face the two teams that had just arrived. The interruption had clearly caught his attention, and he waited expectantly for them to approach.

"Hi boss."

"Hi guys. Okay, now that Detective Jackson is no longer in the picture, your new assignment is keeping tabs on the new family on the block. Be vigilant! We lost two of our guys today. Charlie, you two take day, and Delta, take night. Report anything and everything we need to know."

"On it boss."

Jarvis left the room, drink in hand, and began pacing as he often did when contemplating his next moves. Pacing was his preferred method of processing and refining his plans, allowing him to think through the details and potential outcomes while physically working through his thoughts.

The rhythmic motion of walking back and forth helped Jarvis focus his mind, enabling him to meticulously consider every angle and contingency as he plotted his course of action. This ritualistic behaviour was Jarvis's way of ensuring he was fully prepared and his plans were airtight before putting them into motion. The steady pace of his steps mirrored the careful, deliberate nature of his strategic thinking, demonstrating his unwavering commitment to achieving his objectives through thoughtful, calculated measures.

Jarvis now had the critical task of contacting the other two families who will be involved in the situation. This step was essential to facilitate open communication, gather more details, and work towards a constructive resolution. Reaching out to the families directly would allow Jarvis to better understand their perspectives, concerns, and desired outcomes. By engaging with the families in a personalised and empathetic manner, Jarvis could build trust, explore potential compromises, and guide the process in a way that addresses the needs of all parties involved.

"Santos, how's it going?"

"Good Jarvis, However, I've been hearing concerning whispers that we may be facing some formidable new competition that has recently entered the market. I'm confident that with your exceptional capabilities, you have a solid plan in place to address this challenge and firmly establish our dominance. I have the utmost faith in your ability to straighten out this situation and cement our position as the premier provider in this space."

"Indeed, Santos. Speaking of the very same place where I am currently awaiting a scheduled meeting, we must demonstrate a substantial forceful presence to make a strong impression for this upcoming event. The display of a sizeable and commanding force will be crucial in conveying our authority and resolve on this matter.

Only through projecting an undeniable show of force can we effectively negotiate from a position of strength and secure the outcome we seek during this critical juncture."

"You say when, and we will be there without fail. We cannot allow this new family to get the impression that they can simply do as they please... without regard for established protocols and expectations. It is crucial that we maintain a firm and consistent stance, ensuring they understand the importance of adhering to the rules and norms that govern our community. Our presence alongside yourself and the Bennetts will make it abundantly clear that we are prepared to intervene and assert our authority whenever necessary, leaving no room for them to disregard the boundaries we have set."

"Exactly, Santos! OK, I need to speak to the Bennetts. I will let you know the details."

Jarvis is quite pleased with the progress and development of the current leader of the Santos organisation. The leader has come a long way, and

Jarvis feels they have learned a great deal under his guidance.

Now, Jarvis' next step is to reach out and connect with the feisty and spirited Bennetts, another key group within the larger network. Jarvis believes establishing a productive working relationship with the Bennetts will be crucial in furthering the collective goals and objectives of the Santos.

With the current leader's mentorship and the potential to collaborate with the Bennetts, Jarvis is optimistic about the future direction and impact of the organisation.

"Bennett! How's it going?"

"I'm fuming, Jarvis! This new... bloody family. Who do they think they are?"

"I know! Tell me about it."

"Tell me you have a plan?"

"You know I do. Ok, so... we first need to show a sign of force and strength, so I will need everyone at the farm, I will confirm the time as soon as I have the info."

"Will they be there? Will they get a lesson?"

"You know they will."

"Good, are the Santos joining us?"

"Yes, they will be there."

"Good. Speak soon, Jarvis! I look forward to a time."

Jarvis placed the phone back in its cradle, satisfied with the assessment of the new Bennett's leader. This individual was described as feisty yet logical in their approach, a combination that pleased Jarvis immensely. The previous Bennett's leader had been a significant obstacle, and Jarvis had made the difficult but necessary decision to remove him from power, demonstrating that Jarvis would make heads roll. Now, with a more pragmatic and reasonable figure at the helm, Jarvis felt confident that his choice to remove the former leader had been prudent and justifiable.

This shift in leadership promised to be a positive development that would align with Jarvis's broader strategic objectives. Jarvis's attention was drawn back by a knock at the open door.

"Evening boss."

The elite Team Alpha and Bravo, highly trained and disciplined, swiftly and confidently entered the office, their movements coordinated and purposeful. The two specialised units, renowned for their exceptional skills and unwavering dedication, had been asked to pop in for update on mission.

"Hi guys, I'll get straight to it. How's Lorraine?"

"She's with the boss, boss."

"I see. Any issues?"

"No, she's good."

"OK, I need you to continue watching over Lorraine for now. We have some trouble brewing, and McMatters will want her covered. She'll be here at the club helping to take a load off. By all means, switch day and night if needed, lads."

"I could do with helping the wife with our new baby, boss. So… If I could switch with someone from days, I can help the wife get some sleep. She's a ratty bitch without her sleep."

"Day team?"

"I'll swap, no problem."

"Thanks, guys."

Jarvis, the right-hand man, has summoned his entire staff to gather for an important announcement. While some employees have been explicitly requested to attend in person, others have received subtle indications that something significant is unfolding. The specifics of what is transpiring and when it will be officially confirmed have yet to be disclosed, leaving an air of anticipation and curiosity throughout the organisation.

The experienced and attentive bar staff promptly arrive at the office after Jarvis had discreetly signalled for them to enter the premises.

Jarvis, with a subtle yet decisive motion of his hand, invited the bartenders to come inside, indicating that their services were required for the current occasion taking place within the office setting.

"Evening" Jarvis began.

"I've implemented updates and changes. First, Lorraine will take over the day-to-day running of the club for a while as we have trouble brewing, so we'll have our hands full. Teams Alpha and Bravo will be on Lorraine protection duty. Keep your eyes peeled for anything amiss, guys."

"Will do, boss. I'll get the decanters refilled now as well, boss, while I'm in here," said Paulie.

"Thanks, Paulie."

The bar staff exited the office with the precision and efficiency of a well-oiled machine. In their wake, the doormen and security personnel swiftly and decisively entered, taking their positions to ensure the establishment's safety and security as the evening's activities commenced.

"Hi guys."

"Hey boss, how's it going?"

"Manic, but you know I like it that way. OK, so here's the score: a new family is hustling in, and we need to go to school. I need extra vigilance and bag checks at the door. The boss won't be around as much, but when he's not here, Lorraine will be running the place. Teams Alpha and Bravo are on Lorraine's security team."

"If your goner do it, do it in style boss."

"Exactly my thinking too, two extras for the security team as well."

"Take care boss."

Jarvis strolled over to the ornate decanters, filled with a selection of premium spirits, and poured himself a glass, curious about the latest concoction his friend Paulie had procured for him. As he brought the glass to his lips, the familiar aroma of Tiki Rum wafted up, a refreshing and subtly flavoured libation that provided a pleasant contrast to his usual drinks. Sipping the lightly sweetened rum, Jarvis felt a sense of contentment wash over him, and he resumed his pacing, the change of pace in him as the beverage invigorated both his palate and his mind.

Chapter Twenty-Seven
Sergeant Cole

Sergeant Cole had been stretched very thin ever since Detective Jackson's suspension, which had left him saddled with the additional responsibilities of Jackson's duties. Now, Sergeant Cole faced a challenging decision in appointing a replacement for the now suspended detective.

He had two potential candidates to consider: PC Mayan and PC Winters. As Sergeant Cole evaluated the two different officers, he found himself increasingly inclined to select PC Winters for the position. This inclination may have been influenced by a variety of factors, such as Winters' demonstrated capabilities, relevant experience, or a personal connection that Sergeant Cole felt with the officer.

Regardless of the specific reasons, Sergeant Cole's instincts were guiding him towards PC Winters as the preferred choice to fill the vacant detective role and assist him in managing the increased workload.

"Wendy, could you ask PC Winters to come to my office when free, please?"

"Will do."

Next on the investigator's agenda was a report of a burnt-out vehicle located at the local scrapyard. Intrigued by the unusual circumstances, the investigator promptly conducted a thorough on-site examination. To add to the investigator's grim discovery, a human body was found concealed within the car's trunk. The remains have been transported to the medical examiner's office, where an autopsy is currently underway to determine the individual's identity and the cause of death.

Based on the initial assessment, the damaged vehicle appears to be a BMW model, though its precise make, year, and other identifying details will be confirmed once the investigation progresses and more information becomes available.

The discovery of a body inside the charred car has undoubtedly raised several concerning questions that the authorities are now working diligently to address and resolve through a thorough and comprehensive inquiry.

Sergeant Cole sighed as he picked up the second report on his desk, detailing a disturbing incident that had occurred at a local pub. The grim account painted a concerning picture of how the local situation had deteriorated in recent times.

According to the report, a group of men had forcibly stormed into the pub, armed with an array of dangerous weapons, including knives, machetes, and swords. These individuals proceeded to indiscriminately slash at the unsuspecting patrons, creating a chaotic and violent scene.

In response, the local gang known to control the establishment retaliated by opening fire, spraying bullets haphazardly throughout the pub.

Unfortunately, recently this type of retaliatory violence had become all too common, with the report noting that, as usual, no one was willing to come forward and provide information about the incident. Sergeant Cole couldn't help but feel a sense of unease and concern as he reflected on how the situation had deteriorated, with incidents of this nature seemingly becoming more prevalent in the community.

The grim details of the report only served to underscore the challenges faced by law enforcement in addressing the escalating tensions and violence plaguing the local area. The latest report from the local authorities detailed the grim discovery of two men found deceased under highly unusual circumstances. One of the victims was discovered with a crossbow bolt embedded in his chest, a highly uncommon and perplexing detail.

The individuals were in the middle of the street, though at separate locations that were near one another. This peculiar set of facts has raised concerns for Sergeant Cole, who now worries the situation may potentially involve an escalating conflict between rival gangs.

The unexpected nature of the crossbow-related fatality, combined with the proximity of the two crime scenes, has led the sergeant to suspect the possibility of a gang-related altercation or broader turf war unfolding within the community. Was the torched car and the pub incident directly connected to the two bodies discovered on the street?

This series of events suggests a potential link or underlying relationship between the various incidents. The torched car and the disturbance at the local pub may have been precursor events or part of the same larger sequence of occurrences that ultimately resulted in the two bodies being found on the street.

Further investigation would be needed to determine if these incidents were indeed related and part of a broader chain of connected events. The discovery of the two bodies on the street raises questions about what transpired earlier and whether the prior incidents played a role in or contributed to the tragic outcome.

"Sergeant Cole, I have PC Winters here for you."

"Thank you, Wendy. Please send PC Winters in."

PC Winters, the local police constable, entered the room with her characteristic poise and professionalism. She was impeccably dressed, as always, with her uniform crisp and her shoes polished to a high shine. In fact, the reflective surface of her footwear was so glossy that it seemed to mirror the details of her surroundings, creating the impression that the environment itself was being captured in the gleaming leather.

"Please take a seat, PC Winters." Said Sergeant Cole

"I'd like to talk to you about the detective position that has now opened up. I know you took and passed the exam a few months ago but haven't pursued the role. Would you be interested in taking over from Jackson?"

"Yes, Sarge! I have thought about it but wasn't sure you would consider me for the role."

"You're a very good officer, Winters, so yes, I think you would do well in the role."

"Thank you, Sarge."

"I will speak with HR and get the ball rolling. In the meantime, I have three open cases I need you to take over. I will also assign another PC to the team."

"Thanks again, Sarge."

Detective Winters, promptly gathered the three open case files and exited Sergeant Cole's office. The sense of urgency in Winters' actions suggested the importance and time-sensitive nature of the matters contained within the case files. By swiftly collecting the relevant documents, Winters demonstrated a proactive approach to addressing the issues at hand, indicating a need to review the cases and take appropriate next steps without delay. Sergeant Cole phoned HR.

"Hi Karen! I was wondering if you could please complete the necessary paperwork to formalise PC Winters' recent promotion to the position of Detective. This will involve drafting a new contract that outlines the details of her updated role, including her revised compensation, holiday leave entitlements, and any other relevant terms and conditions.

As you know, PC Winters will be taking over the responsibilities previously held by Detective Jackson. I'd greatly appreciate your help in ensuring this transition is handled properly and all the required documentation is in order. Please let me know if you need any additional information from me to facilitate this process."

"Will do Sergeant Cole."

"Thanks Karen."

Chapter Twenty-Eight
Lorraine

Lorraine couldn't help but ponder what sassy, sarcastic commentary her mum, Maxine, might unleash upon her after learning that Lorraine had volunteered to temporarily take the reins of the club, while Steve was off dealing with the pesky, new rival gang that had blown into town.

As Maxine sauntered into the kitchen, Lorraine braced herself, knowing a delightfully biting remark was likely imminent. Lorraine's brain went into full-on "brace for impact" mode as her mum sashayed into the kitchen, probably sensing the impending doom of her daughter's life choices. You could almost hear the drumroll as Lorraine waited for Maxine's razor-sharp wit to slice through the air like a hot knife through butter.

"Temporary club boss, eh?" Lorraine imagined her mum saying, "Well, aren't you just the little Al Capone in training! I suppose next you'll be asking me to knit you a bulletproof cardigan?"

Lorraine's mind raced with the endless possibilities of her mother's biting remarks. Would it be a zinger about her sudden career change from law-abiding citizen to wannabe mob boss? Or perhaps a sarcastic suggestion to trade her sensible shoes for cement boots? Either way, Lorraine knew she was in for a comedy roast that would make even the toughest gangster's cry... with laughter, of course!

"Morning, Lorraine. Is there any coffee left in the pot?"

Lorraine eagerly snatched up the ceramic jug, its weathered exterior betraying its age and the countless times it had been used to serve refreshment to thirsty souls over the years. With a flourish, she tilted the vessel, allowing the cool, amber liquid within to cascade gracefully into the waiting glasses before them.

The satisfying glug-glug-glug of the pour provided a melodic backdrop as she carefully measured out the perfect portions, ensuring an equitable distribution of the cherished beverage. Lorraine beamed with pride, knowing that this simple act of hospitality would soon deliver the gift of hydration and contentment to both herself, and her mum.

"Mum, I'll be at the club more than usual. I'm helping McMatters out for a bit, running the place."

"I'm practically a nightclub expert - I've mastered dancing, mixing cocktails, and charming crowds. While I lack experience running one, my natural skills and enthusiasm would make me a hit. Just put me in charge, and I'll have the place hopping in no time!"

"Not your scene mum, but thanks."

"You and McMatters are getting close."

Lorraine shoots her mother a familiar, exasperated look, one that conveys a silent resignation, as if to say, "Here we go again with the third-degree lecture." The exchange suggests a recurring dynamic between the two, where Lorraine anticipates another lengthy, probing discussion from her mother, a conversation she has likely weathered many times before. The terse, almost theatrical stage direction paints a vivid picture of the unspoken tension and eye-rolling frustration bubbling beneath the surface of this mother-daughter interaction.

"Lorraine, I mean no harm. It's just nice to see."

"I need to get ready, Mum, but we'll talk more soon."

"Ok."

Lorraine simply didn't have the time or patience to recount the long-winded tales of yesteryear, where youngsters would faithfully divulge their every thought and experience to their mothers. Those were the good old days, when communication flowed freely between generations and nothing was held back.

Alas, Lorraine found herself firmly planted in the modern era, where attention spans are shorter, schedules are packed, and some things are simply best left unsaid to one's dear old mother. Lorraine was filled with eager anticipation for the club and her new position as manager.

Overcome with excitement, she simply couldn't resist the temptation to get a sneak peek at the establishment a bit sooner. Donning her best power suit attire, Lorraine boldly marched through the front doors, determined to scope out the scene and introduce herself to the staff or really, anyone who happened to be there.

With a bubbly smile and boundless enthusiasm, Lorraine was ready to make her presence known, even if the place wasn't technically open until tomorrow.

Chapter Twenty-Nine
Detective Winters

Detective Winters' journey into her new leadership role presents a complex tapestry of personal growth and professional challenges. The transition, while difficult, offers a profound opportunity for self-reflection and development. Her experience highlights the multifaceted nature of leadership, where technical expertise must be balanced with interpersonal skills and emotional intelligence.

The support of her capable team is a testament to the positive work environment she has likely fostered. Yet, her internal struggle with self-doubt reveals the often-overlooked emotional toll of career advancement.

However, it also underscores the pressure Winters may feel as she tries to live up to their expectations and maintain the high standards of the department. Her diligence in navigating her new responsibilities demonstrates a commendable work ethic and commitment to her role. The weight of increased accountability and decision-making authority she feels reflects a deep sense of duty and conscientiousness.

The removal of Detective Jackson's office walls is an intriguing symbolic gesture. It could represent Winters' desire for transparency, open communication, and a more collaborative approach to leadership.

This physical change might also signify her intention to break down hierarchical barriers and foster a more inclusive team dynamic. As the team gathers around her desk, one can't help but ponder the potential for this new arrangement to facilitate closer working relationships and more efficient problem-solving. It's a thoughtful approach that may help Winters bridge the gap between her previous role and her new position of authority, potentially easing her transition and building stronger connections with her team.

"Hi guys! Ok so, Sergeant Cole has passed down three files. The first is the burnt-out BMW where a body was found in the boot. I need someone to go down to autopsy and find out everything they can about the body."

"I can grab that," said PC Jones.

"Thanks Jones."

"Next I need someone to go to forensics to see if they managed to find anything on the car."

"I will grab that boss," said PC Maylan.

"The second file from Sergeant Cole was the pub incident. I need someone to go and see if they can get anyone to talk about what happened in the pub."

"I will take that," said PC Steele.

"Who wants to go put pressure on the pub landlord?"

"I can" said the new to team member PC Martins.

"The last file was two dead bodies found out in the street, one who had a crossbow bolt in his chest. I need two members on this case. How about you two, PC Maitland and PC Barlow?"

"No problem, we will do that."

As Detective Winters watched her team disperse, she found herself immersed in a sea of introspection. The title "Detective Stephanie Winters" echoed in her mind, a phrase both familiar and foreign. This new designation, while undoubtedly a mark of achievement, brought with it a complex tapestry of emotions.

She pondered the journey that had led her to this moment, reflecting on the countless hours of dedication and perseverance that had paved her path. Yet, despite her hard-earned success, a subtle undercurrent of uncertainty lingered.

The weight of responsibility that accompanied her new role was palpable, prompting her to question her readiness for the challenges that lay ahead. Winters contemplation deepened as she perused the paperwork from HR. The generous compensation package before her sparked a mixture of surprise and unease.

The substantial salary increases and the remarkably favourable holiday allowance seemed almost too good to be true. She found herself carefully examining each detail, her analytical mind probing for potential discrepancies or hidden implications. This unexpected windfall prompted a broader reflection on the nature of value and worth in her profession. Was this generous offer a true reflection of the responsibilities she was about to undertake? Or did it perhaps signify something more, an acknowledgment of the often-underappreciated complexities of law enforcement work? As she weighed the decision before her, Winters recognised that this moment represented more than just a career advancement.

It was a crossroads that would shape not only her professional trajectory, but also her sense of self and purpose. The prospect of embracing this new identity and fully stepping into the role of Detective Stephanie Winters was both exhilarating and daunting.

In this moment of quiet reflection, Winters realised that her journey of growth and self-discovery was far from over. Instead, it was entering a new, more profound phase, one that would challenge her to reconcile her past experiences with her future aspirations, and to find her authentic voice amidst the evolving landscape of her career.

Chapter Thirty
Jarvis

Jarvis sat at his desk in the dimly lit club office, his brow furrowed in concentration as he carefully penned the final words of the scathing note he had composed for the new rival crime family. With a steely gaze and unwavering determination, he meticulously crafted each sentence, choosing his words with calculated precision.

This missive would serve as a clear warning, a bold declaration of his organisation's power and unwillingness to cede any ground to the upstart group daring to encroach on their territory.

Jarvis knew this message would leave no room for misinterpretation - it was a direct challenge, a line in the sand that the new family would be wise not to cross.

FAO: BLYTHES

You are required to attend a 9pm meeting at the old steelwork's facility on the town's outskirts. Your presence is mandatory. Failure to comply may result in consequences, so you are advised to make the necessary arrangements to be present at the specified time and location.

Jarvis passes it to the messenger. "Deliver to the Blythe's, please."

"On it," the messenger replies.

Jarvis is feeling particularly assertive and confident now. He is eager and ready to impart his knowledge and expertise, eager for the opportunity to teach a lesson or two. Jarvis believes he is in the optimal mind-set to provide valuable instruction and guidance to those around him, and he hopes the chance to do so will present itself soon.

With a sense of authority and self-assurance, Jarvis is prepared to demonstrate his skills and share his insights, determined to leave a lasting impression through his teachings.

Chapter Thirty-One
Autopsy

As PC Jones approached the autopsy suite, his heart filled with empathy for the difficult task ahead. The challenging environment, with its unsettling scents and clinical atmosphere, weighed heavily on his sensitive spirit.

Yet, beneath his reluctance lay a deep understanding of the importance of his role in seeking justice for those who could no longer speak for themselves. With a gentle resolve, PC Jones reminded himself of the greater purpose behind this uncomfortable duty. He acknowledged his own vulnerability while drawing strength from his commitment to serve and protect.

As he entered the room where the autopsy had just concluded, he carried with him a profound respect for the life that had been lost and a sincere desire to bring closure to those left behind. In this moment of inner struggle, PC Jones embodied the compassionate heart of law enforcement facing the harsh realities of his profession with courage, while never losing touch with his humanity and the ability to care deeply for others, even in the most challenging circumstances.

"Hi, I've come for an update on the body in the boot."

"You have arrived just in time."

"So, do we know who this is?" PC Jones asked, pointing to the body on the slab.

"While we are still awaiting the final dental records, we do have other details about the victim. This individual, a male estimated to be in his early forties, was found gagged and with his hands and feet bound before being set on fire inside the trunk of a car.

The severity of these brutal injuries and the disturbing nature of the crime scene require an immediate and thorough investigation to uncover the perpetrator and bring them to justice as quickly as possible."

"Was he dead before being set alight?"

"Based on the position of the victim's mouth and neck as well as the damage to the airway, it appears they were likely screaming in anguish while the vehicle was alight. This grim detail suggests the individual may have been subjected to a horrific fate, of being burnt alive."

"Oh, shit!" said PC Jones

"Can you check if the dental records are back yet, please?"

"Certainly, one second…"

PC Jones found himself in an incredibly challenging situation, one that would test even the strongest of individuals. As he stood in the autopsy room, he was confronted with an overwhelming sensory experience that deeply affected him.

The distressing scents and sights surrounding him were undoubtedly difficult to bear, and it's completely understandable that he felt a strong urge to leave. PC

Jones's reaction was a natural, human response to a profoundly difficult circumstance. He knew it was okay to acknowledge when something became too much to handle, and there's no shame in needing to step away and take time to reflect. While the burnt body was bad, the thought that he was burnt alive was horrid and sickening.

"OK, so the dental records have returned, and the findings are deeply troubling. It pains me to inform you that the individual lying on this table is none other than the former Detective, Andrew Jackson. The evidence is conclusive. These are the remains of our former colleague, and the circumstances surrounding his demise are most grave and disturbing."

Discovering the lifeless body of someone he knew, especially a former boss, must be an overwhelming and traumatic experience. It's completely understandable that he was feeling shocked, confused, and even panicked. The flood of questions racing through his mind is a natural response to such a distressing discovery. How did this happen? Who? Why?

In this challenging moment, it's important to acknowledge the emotional toll this is taking on PC Jones. He needs time to process his feelings and come to terms with what he's witnessed. While solving the mystery is crucial, it's equally important for him to take care of his own mental well-being.

As he gathers his strength to face this difficult task, PC Jones takes a deep breath as now he needs to inform his new boss Detective Winters but also the rest of the team.

Chapter Thirty-Two
Blythe's

The head of the notorious Blythe crime family has just received an ominous message that has sent waves of fury coursing through his veins. This note, which has been passed down through the intricate web of his criminal organisation, now rests firmly in his grasp, its contents igniting a firestorm of rage within him. The family leader is absolutely seething with anger, incensed that he has been summoned, almost demanded, by some insignificant, faceless individual to appear at the steelwork's facility at precisely nine in the evening.

This brazen act of defiance and disrespect towards his power and authority has left the hardened crime boss fuming, determined to teach this presumptuous upstart a lesson they will never forget. The Blythe's have built a thriving criminal empire through their ruthless and relentless pursuit of illicit profit. Capitalising on the growing demand for heroin and the longstanding popularity of LSD, the Blythe's have amassed a substantial portion of their wealth through these lucrative drug trafficking operations.

However, the core of their criminal enterprise lay in their skilful execution of daring bank and building society robberies, which have provided them with a reliable and substantial stream of ill-gotten gains. Leading this top-tier criminal crew was Hevran, a hardened and uncompromising figure who commanded respect and instilled fear in all those who crossed his path. His crew operated with a level of precision and efficiency that left their victims little chance of escape or retaliation, solidifying the Blythe's' reputation as a formidable and unstoppable force within the criminal underworld.

The patriarch of the Blythe's family has researched the situation and determined that the individual who summoned him works at the local nightclub called Dreams.

Resolved to confront this impertinent person, whom he believes is named Jarvis, the head of the Blythe's household firmly decides that the nightclub is where he will go to strike fear into the heart of this rude offender. With a bold and unwavering stance, the Blythe's family leader is prepared to assert his authority and teach this insolent individual a lesson for their disrespectful actions.

Chapter Thirty-Two Part Two
Charlie & Delta

The Blythe family has become the subject of intense scrutiny by Charlie and Delta, two individual teams engaged in a systematic intelligence-gathering operation. This surveillance effort involves carefully observing and documenting the family's activities, behaviours, and routines.

The meticulous nature of their observation suggests a strategic approach to collecting information about the new crime family. Charlie and Delta have implemented a rotation system for monitoring the Blythe's, ensuring continuous surveillance while maintaining discretion. Their methods indicate a professional and organised approach to intelligence gathering, likely driven by specific objectives or concerns regarding the new family.

During this operation, Charlie team uncovered a piece of information that they deemed highly significant. The nature of this discovery prompted them to quickly return to the Delta outpost, indicating the potential importance of the intelligence to their overall mission.

The urgency of Charlie's actions suggests that the information could have substantial implications for their organisation's activities or security. This situation highlights the complex nature of intelligence operations and the potential impact that new crime family can have on existing community dynamics.

"I don't think it went down too well with the Blythe's."

"What intel did you get?"

"When they got the summons, apparently the head of the Blythe's was fuming and has ordered a hit tomorrow night on the nightclub Dreams."

"Fuck! Looks like we get to have some fun."

Delta team have informed Jarvis of a potential security threat targeting the club, with an attack planned for the following night. This intelligence highlights a significant risk that requires immediate action. The situation demands prompt evaluation and response to ensure the safety of the club and its patrons. Key points to consider include:

Charlie and Delta understood several strategic initiatives would need to be put into place, such as security enhancements designed to bolster the club's defensive capabilities.

"Boss news on the grape vine, tomorrow night they plan to hit us." Charlie tells Jarvis

"Where?" Asks Jarvis

"The club!"

"Nice work guys on getting this Intel. Make your way over to the club."

"Will do boss."

Charlie and Delta teams eyed each other with a mixture of anticipation and trepidation, uncertain of what magical feats their mischievous boss Jarvis had in store for the Blythe's. The pair knew all too well that Jarvis' penchant for elaborate illusions and sleight of hand could sometimes lead to unexpected, and not always welcome, consequences. As they waited anxiously for Jarvis to reveal his latest trick, Charlie and Delta teams braced themselves, unsure whether to expect a delightful surprise or a potentially disastrous outcome from their unpredictable leader's magical machinations. They headed over to the club.

Chapter Thirty-Two Part Three
Jarvis

Jarvis found himself immersed in deep contemplation as he carefully examined the latest intelligence on the Blythe crime syndicate. The impending assault on the local nightclub weighed heavily on his mind, prompting him to reflect on the broader implications of such an act. He pondered the intricate web of circumstances that had led the Blythe's to this point, considering the societal factors that might have contributed to their rise in the criminal underworld.

As he meticulously analysed the details, Jarvis grappled with the ethical dimensions of the situation. He recognised the need for swift action to protect the community, yet he also questioned the most effective and just approach to address the root causes of such criminal activities.

The potential consequences of the Blythe's' actions stirred in him a profound sense of responsibility, not just to prevent the immediate threat, but to consider long-term solutions that might deter future criminal enterprises. Jarvis's furrowed brow betrayed the complexity of his thoughts as he carefully weighed the delicate balance between decisive action and cautious strategy.

Jarvis understood that each decision carried with it a ripple effect, potentially impacting countless lives. This realisation fuelled his determination to approach the situation with wisdom and foresight, seeking a resolution that would not only thwart the Blythe's' plot but also contribute to a safer, more just society. As the urgency of the situation settled upon him, Jarvis found himself reflecting on the nature of justice and the role he played in upholding it.

He recognised that true protection of the innocent extended beyond mere law enforcement, encompassing a broader commitment to addressing the underlying issues that give rise to criminal behaviour.

With this holistic perspective in mind, Jarvis steeled himself for the challenges ahead, resolved to act with both courage and compassion in his pursuit of a satisfactory solution.

McMatters' unexpected arrival at the office proved to be fortuitous timing, as Jarvis had not yet gotten around to reaching out to him. This serendipitous visit, allowed McMatters' quick arrival to present an opportunity, but he was mindful of the potential risks involved.

It's crucial that he addresses the pending issues promptly, but not at the expense of thorough planning and a proper warm welcome for the uninvited guests.

Planning it with McMatters is key. The threat to McMatters' club is indeed concerning and requires their immediate attention.

"Hi, boss. Good timing."

"Afternoon, Jarvis. What's wrong?"

"Well, I just had some intel come in from Charlie and Delta teams. Apparently, we're expecting an attack on the nightclub Dreams tomorrow night."

"Interesting. They're feeling brave."

However, McMatters must resist the urge to rush into action without a well-thought-out strategy. Hasty decisions could lead to oversights or mistakes that may exacerbate the situation.

Jarvis erupted into a fit of uncontrolled laughter, his whole body shaking with mirth, in response to the biting, sarcastic remark that had just been uttered by McMatters. The wry, sardonic nature of McMatters' comment struck Jarvis as incredibly humorous, causing him to lose all composure and give in fully to his amusement. Jarvis found the clever, witty jibe so genuinely amusing that he simply could not restrain his laughter, allowing it to pour forth without inhibition.

"I have all the crew coming in. They should all start arriving shortly."

"So, what are you thinking this time?"

"I'll need you to do your thing. I feel we'll have to be bold on this. The Bennetts and the Santos will be joining us in this operation as it will affect them as well."

"Well, at least tomorrow night isn't a club night. We'll get free rein to have some fun. Is the clean-up crew ready?"

"Yes, they've been on speed dial lately."

"Drink?"

"I won't say no."

As McMatters gently poured the refreshing beverages, a serene atmosphere enveloped them. In the ensuing quiet, they found themselves immersed in a moment of peaceful reflection, each lost in their own thoughts as they savoured their drinks.

Their minds wandered to the upcoming evening, carefully exploring the myriads of possibilities that lay before them. With thoughtful consideration, they weighed their options, allowing their imaginations to paint vivid pictures of potential scenarios.

They pondered not just what they might do, but how each choice could shape their experience and create lasting memories. In this moment of quiet contemplation, they recognised the importance of mindful planning, understanding that their decisions now could greatly influence the quality of their time together.

As they continued to sip their drinks, they silently acknowledged the value of this shared moment of reflection, appreciating how it allowed them to approach their plans with intention and care. Their deliberation was not rushed, but rather a careful exploration of ideas, each possibility examined with the goal of crafting an evening that would be both enjoyable and meaningful.

"I'm thinking we set a trap. Let them think no one is here and one by one bodies drop. If we can lurk in the shadows, I think we could take most out before they even get to think of reacting."

"So, everyone becomes me?"

"In a nutshell… Yes!"

McMatters chuckled at the absurd mental image of a body disposal club. The notion struck him as highly improbable and darkly comical.

"Do you really think we could all carry out such a macabre feat without anyone witnessing it?" he asked, his tone tinged with scepticism and morbid fascination.

"Yes, and the Bennetts can come in from behind them. They'll need to hide until the Blythe's are in the club, though, and the Santos will cover the back of the club and move in slowly."

"Yes, I think I like the plan."

"So do I," said Lorraine.

"Where did you come from?" asked McMatters.

"Hiding in plain sight."

Lorraine's laughter suddenly bubbled up, a contagious expression of mirth that quickly spread to her companions. McMatters and Jarvis, unable to resist the jovial atmosphere, soon joined in, their chuckles and giggles filling the air as the trio shared a light-hearted moment together. The infectious nature of Lorraine's initial laughter had a ripple effect, drawing the others into a shared experience of genuine amusement and camaraderie.

Chapter Thirty-Three
Lorraine

Lorraine's gentle exploration of the office space, particularly her decision to sit at Steve's desk, speaks volumes about her dedication and eagerness to understand her new workplace. It's truly admirable how she's taking the time to absorb the atmosphere and connect with her surroundings.

By metaphorically stepping into her boyfriend's shoes, Lorraine is demonstrating an exceptional level of empathy and commitment to her new role. This insightful act will undoubtedly enrich her understanding of the professional dynamics and help her thrive in her new setting. It's heartening to see such a considerate and perceptive approach to starting a new chapter in one's career.

Up until this point, Lorraine had not actively contemplated the nature of her relationship with Steve in much detail.

She had simply knew they were in a committed relationship and had behaved accordingly, without giving it much conscious thought. It was rather peculiar that Lorraine felt so at ease and content in the relationship so quickly, almost as if it had developed organically and naturally without her having to overthink or analyse it.

The seamless transition into this newfound intimacy and understanding with Steve was quite unexpected, yet Lorraine found herself feeling remarkably comfortable and secure in their connection from the very beginning.

Not only that but the event with Detective Jackson re-awakened something that Lorraine put to bed many years ago and she missed the action, Lorraine's life for many years had been dull and lifeless but now it seemed to be enjoyable once again. Lorraine knew Steve didn't know some areas of her life an issues she had no choice but to conquer, maybe one day she will tell him about it, Lorraine was not new to this lifestyle.

"OK, Lorraine. Now that you're seated, are you sure we can't scare you off?" asked Steve.

"Nope, I'm good," Lorraine replied.

"The taxi driver will be here shortly. Are you okay dealing with him?"

"Don't worry, I can sort it out."

"On the hook, there are a set of keys for his new car. He's your personal driver for work."

"You are very good. You know that my car is here. Can we get him to follow one of the lads so they can take it back to mine?"

"Good idea."

"Come, Jarvis. We've got a trap to set up and run through."

As the office emptied, Lorraine found herself in a moment of introspection. The departure of Steve and Jarvis, left her in a cocoon of silence, a rare interlude in the usually bustling workspace.

This unexpected solitude offered her a chance to reflect on the day's events and gather her thoughts before heading home. The quiet office seemed to amplify the passage of time as Lorraine waited for her taxi driver. She pondered on the nature of transitions how quickly a space can transform from a hive of activity to a haven of tranquillity.

As the minutes ticked by, Lorraine found herself appreciating this brief respite.

It was a reminder of the importance of pausing amidst life's constant motion, a chance to breathe and centre oneself before moving on to the next task. The sudden knock at the door, precisely ten minutes later, jolted Lorraine from her reverie. Paulie's arrival marked the end of this contemplative interlude, seamlessly bridging the gap between solitude and companionship.

"Miss Lorraine, I have the driver here. Also, would you like a drink?"

"Thanks Paulie, that would be lovely! Could I have a lighter drink today please? Let's go with schnapps, Russian vodka and lemonade."

"Coming right up."

Paulie exited the room and stood hesitantly in the doorway. There, he encountered the driver, whose expression conveyed a sense of profound worry, disorientation, and bewilderment.

The driver's demeanour suggested a state of profound uncertainty and unease, as if grappling with a challenging or unfamiliar situation that had left him feeling lost and unsure of how to proceed.

Lorraine called to him.

"Please come in and take a seat."

"Firstly, I'd like to thank you. I hadn't seen you since that night we were attacked, and I am sorry for what happened to you."

"It wasn't you who attacked me; you have no need to apologise, is it Lorraine?."

"Yes, Call me Lorraine now, I know that night you were shaken and hurt. We made you a promise that you could work for us. Are you interested in doing so?"

"Oh yes! You've all been very kind to me and my family."

"That settles it then. From now on, you will be my personal driver, and you will be well looked after."

"Thank you, thank you!"

"These are the keys to your car. Mr McMatters runs a luxury business, and with that, I have some outfits for you and a mobile phone so I can get hold of you anytime needed."

"That's very generous of you."

"I need you to follow one of the lads who will be driving my car. He will drop the car off at my house, he will need bringing back, then I will need picking up from here later on."

"Yes, I will do that. Thank you again!"

Lorraine's journey to her current position is a fascinating study in personal growth and unexpected turns of fate. Her newfound role as a nightclub manager represents a significant departure from her previous path, yet she has embraced it with remarkable enthusiasm and aptitude.

The sense of pride and satisfaction Lorraine derives from her leadership role is understandable, given the challenges and responsibilities that come with managing a thriving establishment. Her ability to adapt to this position speaks of her resilience and perhaps untapped leadership qualities.

Lorraine's past inclinations towards illicit activities, particularly her penchant for acquiring luxury items through dubious means, add a layer of complexity to her character.

This aspect of her personality raises questions about the nature of morality and how our past experiences shape our present circumstances. Her seamless transition into a world associated with organised crime is particularly thought-provoking, suggesting a certain flexibility in her moral compass that allows her to navigate these ethically ambiguous waters with apparent ease.

The juxtaposition of Lorraine's professional success with her involvement in criminal activities presents an interesting moral dilemma. Her story also prompts reflection on the nature of adaptation and the human capacity to thrive in diverse, even morally ambiguous environments.

Chapter Thirty-Four
Detective Winters

Detective Winters has assembled her team to receive updates on the three active cases under her supervision. As a newly promoted Detective, she is still acclimatising to her title and the associated responsibilities. Her extensive experience as an officer provides a solid foundation, but the transition to a leadership role presents new challenges.

In her current position, Detective Winters is responsible for overseeing complex investigations. This responsibility carries significant weight, as the outcomes of these cases will directly reflect her leadership and decision-making capabilities.

The recently promoted detective is keenly aware of this fact, which contributes to a sense of apprehension about her new role. By convening her team to discuss the latest developments in these cases, Detective Winters is taking a proactive approach to her leadership duties. She recognises the need to leverage her investigative expertise and past experiences to effectively guide her unit.

Her goal is to lead her team towards successful resolutions of these important cases, demonstrating her competence in her new position of authority.

It also underscores the importance of effective communication and leadership skills in managing complex criminal investigations.

"Hi everyone, please gather around for a quick update. PC Maitland and Barlow, how's the investigation going regarding the two bodies found dead in the street?"

"No one is willing to come forward, it seems. Both men worked for Jarvis, although no one will confirm this. Both men died instantly, and it looks like it might have been at the hands of a new crime family that has recently come to the area. I don't have a name yet, though," said PC Barlow.

"Good work. Keep pressing."

"OK, let's see. PC Martins, how are you doing with the pub landlord?"

"Not very good, to be honest. Basically, he refuses to say what happened or who did it. Apparently, he was in the cellar at the time that it all went down."

"Don't worry, PC Martins. PC Steele, did you manage to find any witnesses?"

"No, everyone is too scared to talk, boss."

"Keep going. Check for any CCTV in the area."

"Will do, boss."

"PC Maylan, how was it in forensics?"

"So far, half the car is processed. They are working on the interior today. Fingers crossed we will find something to help us."

"PC Jones, I hope autopsy wasn't too bad."

"The smell is sickening, but I've news on the body. It's not good either and quite distressing. Dental came back on the burnt body from the boot. It is our old boss, Detective Jackson, he was alive at the time he was set alight and possibly bound."

Detective Winters observes and reflects as the room was filled with gasps, and everyone looked so scared and upset when they heard it was Jackson's burnt body. It's just awful, and she's so worried about how everyone's going to cope with this she thought to herself: The whole situation feels so unsettling and frightening.

What if something like this happens again? How can we possibly feel safe now? This is such a tragedy, and she's really concerned about the impact it's going to have on all of us. She kept thinking about poor Jackson and his family it's just too horrible to imagine what they must be going through.

This is going to haunt us for a long time, she was sure of it. Detective winters was feeling anxious about what might come next and how they were going to get through this. Detective Winters picked up the phone with a sense of unease, knowing that the matter at hand required a sensitive, in-person approach.

She placed an internal call to Wendy, the department's administrative assistant, to inquire about the availability of Sergeant Cole. Detective Winters understood that this issue would need to be addressed face to face, rather than through a distant, impersonal phone conversation.

The gravity of the situation weighed heavily on her mind as she waited for Wendy's response, hoping that Sergeant Cole would be free to discuss the pressing concerns that had arisen.

"Hi Wendy, is Sergeant Cole free?"

"Yes, for the next thirty minutes."

"Can you book me in please? I'm on my way up."

Detective Winters addresses her team. "I understand this is a deeply personal and sensitive matter for everyone involved, as he was our former boss. It's understandable to feel worried or distressed by this situation. Please know that I have arranged for a therapist to be available if anyone needs someone to talk to. I strongly encourage you to utilise this resource if you are struggling with this news or need additional support, I need to go and brief Sergeant Cole. I'm confident that by working together, we can get through this. Your well-being is my top priority, so please don't hesitate to reach out if you require anything."

Detective Winters arrived outside Sergeant Cole's office. Wendy waved her to go in.

"Hi, Sergeant Cole, I have an update."

"Come in, please sit down."

"So far, we have only one piece of disturbing information. I have the autopsy result: the burnt body is Detective Jackson."

"Oh, Jesus Christ! Do we know if he was already dead before he was burned?"

"He was alive before being burned. It looks like he was bound hand and foot."

"Oh my. Have you offered counselling to the team?"

"Yes."

"Thank you, Detective Winters."

Chapter Thirty-Four Part Two
Sergeant Cole

Sergeant Cole was deeply troubled and profoundly disturbed by the recent news regarding Detective Jackson's tragic demise. The discovery of the detective's burnt and lifeless body, found stuffed inside the trunk of a car, left Sergeant Cole with a growing sense of unease and a multitude of unanswered questions. How had Detective Jackson met such a grisly end? Who was responsible for this heinous act, and what was the motive behind it? The agonising thought of the detective enduring such a horrific fate, potentially suffering and screaming in the throes of a fiery death, sent chills down Sergeant Cole's spine.

The sheer brutality of the crime weighed heavily on his mind, leaving him consumed by the need to uncover the truth and ensure that justice is served for his fallen colleague. Sergeant Cole deeply empathised with the members of Detective Jackson's former team. Having to process and confront the harrowing, graphic details surrounding Detective Jackson's tragic demise would have undoubtedly taken an immense emotional toll on his colleagues.

Sergeant Cole recognised the profound impact this news would have had, as they grappled with the profound loss of their fellow officer under such sombre circumstances. He understood the profound sense of grief, shock, and anguish his former team members were likely feeling in the wake of this devastating development. Sergeant Cole was dreading the sombre task that now lay before him.

He knew he would soon have to deliver the devastating news of Detective Jackson's death to the officer's family, and the thought filled him with a profound sense of dread and unease.

Sergeant Cole was acutely aware that he would need to convey the grim and harrowing details surrounding the tragedy, which only compounded the difficulty and emotional weight of the situation. Facing the grieving relatives and loved ones was a responsibility he wished he did not have to shoulder, as he anticipated the heartbreak and anguish his words would inevitably cause.

Chapter Thirty-Five
The club

McMatters and Jarvis, found themselves in a race against time as they prepared for the looming threat of an impending attack. With only an hour to spare before the expected assault, they knew they had to act swiftly and decisively to protect their nightclub and family. Joined by the steadfast Bennetts and Santos, who were strategically positioned in case the attackers arrived earlier than anticipated.

Jarvis' men stood ready, their eyes fixed on the security cameras, poised to spring into action the moment the Blythe's were spotted. McMatters and Jarvis, embodying the unwavering spirit of leadership, were resolute in their determination to safeguard the club and its members.

As the seconds ticked by, they steeled themselves, knowing that when the moment of truth arrived, they would be there, standing firm in the face of adversity, ready to defend their community with every fibre of their being.

The teams at McMatters and Jarvis' control were dressed for the occasion, united in their tactical attire and accessories. This carefully curated ensemble was designed to enhance their mobility and preparedness, with knife and gun belts loaded and at the ready. Jarvis had outfitted himself with an upper body kit, complete with swords strategically positioned down his back, within easy reach should the situation demand their use.

Dressed in a sombre uniform of black clothing, their faces obscured by dark body paint for concealment, McMatters, Jarvis, and the entire covert team assembled in the shadowed confines of the club in darkness, hidden from sight, only the whites of their eyes visible.

They waited in silent, unwavering vigilance, their anticipation and sense of purpose palpable in the stifling atmosphere. The enveloping darkness of their surroundings mirrored the gravity and high stakes of the situation they were about to confront.

Chapter Thirty-Five Part Two
The Blythe's

The Blythe's were meticulously planning their attack on the club where they knew Jarvis was employed. Fuelled by the insulting slight they had previously endured, the Blythe's were determined to deliver a lesson to Jarvis that would leave a lasting, indelible impact. Their preparations were thorough and calculated, as they sought to ensure Jarvis would never forget the consequences of his actions against them.

The Blythe's were poised to strike, driven by a sense of vengeance and a desire to settle the score, no matter the cost. The Blythe's had just finished collecting the knives and swords, preparing for an imminent attack on the nearby club. With a sense of urgency, they knew they only had approximately five minutes before they would make their way over to carry out their planned assault.

The head of the Blythe's, a seasoned military commander, would be spearheading the impending attack at the forefront of a group of twenty hand-picked men. The prospect of leading this critical operation filled him with a sense of eager anticipation, yet also an underlying trepidation.

While the thrill of battle coursed through his veins, he could not ignore the gravity of the situation and the potential consequences that lay ahead. As the moment of engagement drew nearer, the weight of his responsibility weighed heavily upon him, tempering his excitement with a sober awareness of the risks and sacrifices that such a mission entailed. The Blythe's team departed their base, prepared and determined to carry out their mission.

However, their men were given instructions that raised concerns. They were told to essentially operate with minimal oversight, free to inflict as much damage as possible during the operation.

This unsupervised, unchecked approach carried significant risks of escalating the situation and causing unintended, potentially excessive harm which only excited the Blythe's leader.

323

Chapter Thirty-Six
Lorraine

Lorraine was wisely choosing to avoid the brewing storm and keep a low profile as the imminent attack on the club loomed. Recognising that her dear mother Maxine had been cooped up at home ever since the traumatic incident, Lorraine decided it was high time to get her out of the house for a change of scenery. Lorraine knew Maxine hadn't ventured out since the brutal attack, so she figured a trip to Steve's favourite restaurant Demetrio's, would do her mother a world of good. Lorraine had been sitting around twiddling her thumbs for a solid three hours, eagerly awaiting the grand entrance of her dear old mum, Maxine.

Finally, after what felt like an eternity, Maxine emerged from the upstairs lair, making her grand descent down the staircase. And low and behold, she was looking quite fetching, if Lorraine did say so herself. The nasty bruises that had once marred Maxine's delicate features had thankfully faded, which certainly helped to enhance her overall aesthetic appeal.

However, Lorraine couldn't help but notice that Maxine seemed a tad on edge, understandably so given the unpleasant incident that had recently befallen her. Her poor mum was clearly a bit apprehensive about venturing out into the world again after her harrowing ordeal.

But Lorraine was determined to be the supportive, caring daughter and ensure that this outing would be nothing short of a rip-roaring good time, or at least, as good a time as one could have while constantly looking over one's shoulder.

"I promise you Mum, you'll love Demetrio's, and he's single." Lorraine hinting at her mum she should get back on the horse.

"I think I've had my fill of bad men."

"Oh no, he's not like that. He actually seems rather sweet and caring."

"We'll see."

"I know you're worried about going out, but you're with me, and we're going to have a wonderful meal."

"Is it expensive? I can't afford to go out splashing the cash."

"It's on me, Mum. Don't worry. Now, let's get moving."

Lorraine got her driver to take them to the esteemed Demetrio's restaurant, her anticipation palpable. Upon arriving, she and her mother Maxine, strolled through the entryway, and Maxine's eyes immediately widened in sheer wonderment.

The establishment was an absolute visual feast, its decor exuding an air of sophistication and elegance that left the Maxine utterly captivated. Maxine could scarcely believe her eyes as she took in the breath-taking ambiance, her mind racing to process the sheer beauty that surrounded them.

"Lorraine, this looks too expensive!" said Maxine.

"Don't worry…" replied Lorraine.

"Welcome! Lorraine, is that you?" said Demetrio.

"Yes, it is, and this place looks so good!"

"It's nice to see you again. Is Mr. McMatters not dining today?"

"Not today."

"So, who is this wonderful woman?" Demetrio gestured to Maxine.

"This is my mother, Maxine Spencer."

"Welcome, welcome! I'm so pleased to meet you."

Demetrio, with a flourish of exaggerated chivalry, gently grasped Maxine's delicate hand and proceeded to plant three dramatic, lip-puckering kisses upon her knuckles.

His moustache, meticulously waxed to a fine, upturned point, tickled her skin as he showered her with this over-the-top display of affection, no doubt intended to elicit a swooning reaction from the unsuspecting Maxine.

"Come, you can sit at the best table in the house."

Lorraine couldn't help but chuckle as she watched Demetrio dote on her mother Maxine, gently pushing in her chair as she sat down. The subtle display of chivalry seemed to fluster Maxine, whose cheeks flushed with a bashful blush. Who said chivalry was dead!

Lorraine found the entire scene rather endearing, amused her mother reaction to Demetrio's flattering attention. It was a heart-warming moment, a glimpse into a potential budding romance between the two and a reminder that even in their golden years, a little old-fashioned charm could still make someone's heart flutter.

Lorraine couldn't have asked for a more delightful man than Demetrio for her mum. He was a truly wonderful, kind, and considerate man the kind of person that any woman would be lucky to have by her side.

For Maxine, the prospect of being with someone as thoughtful and caring as Demetrio would be an absolute dream come true. He was the total package, he was charming, attentive, and the kind of guy who would go the extra mile to make his significant other feel valued and adored. Lorraine was undoubtedly counting her blessings to have landed such a gem of a man in Demetrio, plus he could cook.

Lorraine and Maxine thoroughly enjoyed a delightful and delectable dining experience together. Every time the captivating Maxine caught a glimpse of the charming Demetrio; an irresistible rosy glow would spread across her cheeks. After the meal had concluded, the ever-observant Lorraine made her way over to the establishment's counter to handle the financial responsibilities.

"Lorraine, may I ask if it would be okay if I call your mum sometime? It would be nice; I don't have many friends my age."

"Of course you can. Here, let me write down her number for you."

"Thank you, Lorraine. Thank you very much."

"The meal was fantastic, as always."

Lorraine sauntered over to the table, where Maxine was engaged in what appeared to be a captivating conversation with a potted plant. Clearing her throat, Lorraine gently nudged her mother's elbow, suggesting it might be time to call it a night and head for the exits before the table tried to convince Maxine to move in.

Chapter Thirty-Six Part Two
Maxine

Maxine felt like she was finally experiencing the joys of being a true human being once more, light as a feather and filled with endless possibilities for her future. Just a short while ago, she had been highly sceptical when her daughter Lorraine raved about the wonders of this mysterious figure named Demetrio. But now, Maxine couldn't help but wonder if she might get to see Demetrio again, her heart fluttering with a sense of excitement and anticipation she hadn't felt in ages.

It was as if she had been reawakened from a long, dreary slumber, ready to embrace whatever delightful surprises might lie in store. Maxine gazed down at her hand, still tingling from where Demetrio had placed his lips so tenderly. She reverently stroked the spot he had kissed, savouring the sensation. It had been an eternity since any man had doted on her in such a chivalrous and affectionate manner. In fact, Maxine couldn't ever remember a man doting on her in such a manner before today.

Maxine couldn't help but feel a bit giddy, like a swooning schoolgirl, at Demetrio's gentlemanly display of affection. She mentally pinched herself, hardly believing her luck that such a charming and attentive suitor had graced her with his amorous attentions.

Maxine couldn't help but chuckle to herself as she reflected on the long line of culinary catastrophes that had been her dating history. It seemed the men she encountered were either completely hopeless in the kitchen or downright allergic to any domestic task that didn't involve a microwave and a bag of chips. She had grown accustomed to lowering her expectations when it came to a potential partner's ability to craft a decent meal, resigning herself to a life of lukewarm leftovers and frozen dinners, with the added drunk in the mix.

But deep down, Maxine couldn't help but long for that elusive unicorn, a man who could cook a proper, edible meal without burning the house down in the process. Alas, such a specimen remained firmly in the realm of fantasy, leaving Maxine to once again contemplate takeout menus and dream of a day when her significant other might be able to boil water without supervision.

Chapter Thirty-Seven
The Blythe's arrive at the Club

The Blythe's cautiously approached the club, pushing open the door to a conspicuous silence. Noting the unsettling lack of activity, they immediately readied their weapons, their senses on high alert. The head of the Blythe's family quickly motioned for the others to spread out and explore the premises, their every step filled with a growing sense of trepidation as they navigated the eerie stillness that had enveloped the once-lively establishment.

The situation had taken an ominous turn, and the Blythe's knew they needed to proceed with the utmost caution, for they were now venturing into the unknown, their safety far from assured.

The eerie, muffled thud, akin to the sound of a person being struck forcefully in the abdomen, followed by an unsettling silence, immediately put the leader, Hevran Blythe, on high alert. He knew he could not afford to let their presence be known, as that would alert the enemy to their arrival. Blythe's dilemma was compounded by the fact that he could no longer communicate with his team, as doing so would inevitably give away their position and compromise the element of surprise they had been banking on. The situation had become increasingly precarious, and

Blythe had to tread carefully to ensure their mission remained undetected by the watchful adversary.

As McMatters and Jarvis caught sight of the Blythe's arriving, they quickly surveyed the scene and estimated around twenty men, all equipped and prepared for a confrontation.

The signal of their impending presence quickly spread throughout the club, and an eerie silence fell over the crew, the tension palpable. The arrival of the Blythe's, a formidable group, had clearly put the entire club on high alert. The men, armed and ready for a fight, stood their ground, their resolute expressions and tense postures conveying a sense of unwavering determination. Another two thuds took place in different areas of the room.

The silence that ensued was deafening, as everyone in the club held their breath, anticipating the impending clash. This moment of calm before the storm was charged with an electrical energy, a palpable sense of foreboding that hung in the air. The scene was a testament to the high stakes and deep-rooted rivalries that often characterised the world these men inhabited, where alliances and loyalties were constantly tested, and the threat of violence was never far from the surface, another thud followed by silence.

Blythe's continued to move into the club, their eyes scanning the area as they made their way towards the far end. To their right, the well-stocked bar beckoned, while the expansive dance floor lay ahead, turning their gaze to the left, they spotted the set back stairs leading up to a dimly lit mezzanine level.

As the Blythe's moved through the club they were unaware that the Bennett's had discreetly followed them into the club. The Bennett's, drawn by the allure of the evening's festivities, had quietly trailed the Blythe's. Two more thuds took place, Blythe turned to the sound but couldn't see a thing.

In the darkness of the silent nightclub, the home teams meticulously executed their mission, taking out the enemy Blythe's one by one with precision and stealth. Amidst the small, muffled sound effects, that repeated around the room McMatters found himself positioned against the wall, patiently waiting for the opportune moment to strike more of the enemy.

Suddenly, another Blythe came within reach, and with a quick, decisive motion, McMatters lunged forward, driving the sharp blade of his knife deep into the unsuspecting target from behind, two more soon followed a pile of bodies quickly building up at his feet.

A brief, muffled cry echoed through the shadows, gargling noises of someone choking on their own blood, followed by the eerie silence, A Blythe crumpled to the floor, his life extinguished in his service to the greater cause.

The team's unwavering determination and expert execution, even in the face of the seemingly insurmountable darkness, served as a testament to their dedication and the unwavering spirit that fuelled their mission. This triumph, though bittersweet, would inspire them to push forward, undaunted by the challenges that lay ahead, as they continued their fight for a brighter future.

Jarvis stood at the entrance to the exclusive VIP area upstairs, McMatters would soon head upstairs, his eyes the only visible feature in the pitch-black environment. As Jarvis surveyed the scene from above, Jarvis couldn't help but notice that the head of the prestigious Blythe family was the sole remaining individual standing, surrounded by the lifeless forms of the twenty men he had brought with him. The tragic fate that befell the Blythe's family was truly heart breaking.

All twenty members of this once vibrant clan now lay lifeless, their bodies scattered throughout the club's premises. The scene blood splattered, pools of blood formed around the bodies. Yet, amidst the overwhelming loss, one figure stood tall and resolute, the leader of the Blythe's, a testament to the resilience of the human spirit.

This solitary survivor, having endured the unimaginable, now faced the daunting task of rebuilding and honouring the memories of those who had been taken from this world too soon if he gets out alive.

Five lifeless bodies lay scattered around McMatters feet, amidst the crimson carnage, a harrowing testament to the ferocity of the confrontation.

Undaunted, McMatters unwavering focus settled upon the lone figure near the foot of the stairs Hevran Blythe, the notorious leader of the now dead men.

Sensing the implacable determination in this mistaken approach, Hevran began to backpedal, the realisation dawning that he was the sole survivor of his once formidable crew. With blades drawn and nerves steeled. McMatters knew this was no time for hesitation or mercy the stakes had been raised, and only one man would emerge victorious from this fateful showdown.

The Bennetts pushed further into the club and waited as Hevran Blythe stood in the dimly lit club, he was confronted with a daunting sight. A group of eyes, all steadily making their way towards him. Faced with this overwhelming and potentially life-threatening situation, Hevran knew he had to act quickly and decisively.

His options were stark and unforgiving. Either he could attempt to flee by climbing the nearby stairs, or he would be forced to confront the approaching men, risking his very life.

In that moment, Hevran's heart raced with a mix of fear and adrenaline, as he weighed the perilous choices before him. The sheer number of adversaries closing in left him with little room for error or hesitation.

Yet, even in the face of such adversity, Hevran summoned his inner strength and resolve, understanding that his only hope for survival lay in making a bold and courageous move. With a deep breath, Hevran steeled his nerves and made the critical decision to ascend the stairs, knowing full well that the path ahead was fraught with danger and uncertainty.

But in that pivotal moment, he refused to surrender to the overwhelming odds, driven by an unwavering determination to overcome the threats that loomed before him.

Surveying the scene with growing horror, Hevran's eyes darted around the room, taking in the grim sight before him.

His men, his trusted companions, lay motionless on the floor all of them dead. Some were scattered haphazardly, while others were piled together in a macabre display. Hevran felt a chill run down his spine as the gravity of the situation sank in, leaving him overwhelmed with a sense of profound fear and dread. Hevran quickly realised that he had severely underestimated the formidable power and capabilities of his adversary.

In comparison to Jarvis's well-organised and experienced crew, Hevran felt like a mere insignificant minnow completely outmatched and outclassed by the sheer scale and prowess of his opponent's forces. This stark realisation sent a chill down Hevran's spine, as he now understood the grave mistake he had made in his assessment of the situation.

Facing such an overwhelming challenge, Hevran knew he would need to re-evaluate his strategy and tactics if he hoped to have any chance of emerging victorious against Jarvis and his seasoned team.

Hevran found himself in a precarious situation, surrounded by men approaching from all sides of the dimly lit room. Feeling outnumbered and adversary he moved quickly now up the stairs hoping to find an alternative escape route that would allow him to avoid the encroaching individuals and the perilous circumstances he now faced. Unsure of what lay ahead, but determined to find a way out of this increasingly threatening scenario.

As Hevran approached the top of the walkway, he encountered a lone door. Beside the entrance, a solitary figure stood, presenting a potential one on one confrontation. Suddenly, the room was illuminated as Jarvis hit the switch, eliciting a panicked response from Hevran Blythe.

Hevran's confidence grew, as he was skilled with his weapons and believed he could handle this individual adversary.

"Hevran, you have made many mistakes tonight...," said Jarvis.

"Who are you?"

"You have lost all your men because you were careless and lacked power."

"Who are you?"

"You refused a hand, Hevran, when it was offered to you. You had an opportunity, and instead of accepting it, you chose to attack."

Blythe was now trembling with apprehension, acutely aware of the perilous situation he found himself in. He knew all too well the identity of the individual standing before him, and a sense of dread and uncertainty gripped him.

At this moment, Blythe was at a complete loss, unsure of how to proceed. Escape seemed impossible, as the bottom of the stairway was swarming with too many men for him to contend with. And here, directly in front of him, was Jarvis… a formidable presence that only heightened Blythe's feelings of vulnerability and impending danger.

Blythe now deeply regretted his impulsive decision to attack Jarvis without first gathering critical intelligence and information about his adversary. Had he taken the time to thoroughly research and understand Jarvis' capabilities, resources, and potential vulnerabilities, Blythe may have been able to devise a more strategic and effective plan of action. Rushing into a confrontation without proper preparation and foresight often leads to unforeseen complications and unfavourable outcomes.

This lapse in judgment has left Blythe in a precarious position, wishing he had been more diligent in his reconnaissance efforts before engaging this formidable opponent.

"I … I… didn't know, I should have checked I…"

"Yes, you should have, and now you have lost all your men. Well… all apart from the small handful who are currently in the pub waiting for your return. If you return, that is."

"I'm sorry. I have learned my lesson. It won't happen again."

"I know it won't, because here in this club are three families whom you have angered. All dealings are done through me, and I have a boss who is not happy at all, but he's a fair man."

"Mr Blythe!" said McMatters, stepping out from the shadows from behind Blythe startling him.

Blythe whirled around in a panic, his heart racing, only to find the imposing figure of the big boss of Jarvis, and Blythe, standing directly before him.

Overcome with sheer terror, Blythe involuntarily lost control of his bladder, the stain of urine visibly rolling down his leg as he stood there, paralysed with fear in the presence of the intimidating authority figure.

The sudden and overwhelming sense of dread had caused Blythe to completely lose his composure, leaving him humiliated and vulnerable in the face of his superior's commanding presence.

"You will be taken and dropped off at home Mr Blythe. Tomorrow, you will return here in the day where yourself, the Bennetts, the Santos, Jarvis and I will have a meeting. You will be on time Mr Blythe, one 'o'clock sharp."

"O.K....ok."

McMatters solemnly nodded to Jarvis, and with that subtle gesture, Jarvis immediately signalled the group downstairs.

The scene that unfolded was reminiscent of the biblical parting of the Red Sea, as the crowd of people swiftly and obediently cleared a path from the stairs all the way to the exit, allowing the two men to traverse the space unimpeded. This orchestrated display of deference and control served as a stark reminder of the power dynamics and hierarchical structures at play within the environment.

Blythe cautiously made his way downstairs, weaving through the crowded group of men. With Blythe's embracement and sadness at the loss, feeling uneasy walking pass all the men, he quickened his pace.

He hastily pushed open the heavy door, eager to exit the claustrophobic atmosphere of the club he now wished he never entered. As he stepped outside, Blythe couldn't help but feel a sense of relief to be free of the oppressive environment he had just navigated.

Jarvis followed Blythe outside with his eyes being the only thing that was white and gestured for Blythe to get in Jarvis' car.

The End

Dreaming

"Dreams" expertly continues in book two Dreaming, taking readers on a rollercoaster ride filled with unexpected twists and turns. As the narrative unfolds, themes of dominance and power struggles interweave with profound expressions of love, flickers of hope, and soaring aspirations. This captivating journey not only entertains but also elicits a rich tapestry of emotions preparing you to laugh at the absurdities, cringe at the uncomfortable truths, and ponder deeply about the unpredictable nature of life. The pressing questions linger: How will dreams evolve as circumstances shift? And what seismic changes might occur when an ex-lover unexpectedly re-enters the scene? These elements promise to keep readers on edge as they anticipate how relationships will be tested and transformed forever in this enthralling tale.

Joanne Keele

Printed in Great Britain
by Amazon